The Promise Keeper
Copyright © 2021 by L. Marie Wood
Cover art copyright © 2021 by Lynne Hansen
Second Edition

Library of Congress Catalog Card Number 2021930567
ISBN 13: 9781941958889/eBook ISBN: 9781941958858/
Kindle: 978-1-941958865

For more information, contact queries@cedargrovebooks.com

www.cedargrovebooks.com

L. MARIE WOOD

THE PROMISE KEEPER

Acknowledgements

First, as always, I want to thank God for giving me this gift.

I want to thank Laura Fasching, Chuck Jenkins and Jasmine Torres for letting me bounce ideas around. Thanks to Cyriaque Kotomale and Maurille DeSouza at the Benin Embassy and Chris Starace for providing Fon translations. Chris's informative website started my interest in Fon. If you are interested in the language, visit www.geocities.com/fon_is_fun/. Thanks also to Laura Fasching and Michael Wood—my reading committee—for hitting my "odd" timelines.

Special thanks to Michael Wood for putting up with my late nights and long hours. Your support is invaluable.

For Michael

Of life I know nothing. Of death I am sure.

PROLOGUE

The smell of blood wafting up to her nose was exquisite. It penetrated the musty air with its pungency. The aroma was all encompassing, full-bodied and complete in a way that nothing else was. The earthy, metallic smell of it was electric, invigorating; the touch of it was like satin against her skin. She loved it – everything about it. The look, the feel, the smell, the taste. She breathed deeply of it as it flowed from his body in a crimson deluge, allowing the scent to tantalize her nostrils and mix with the stagnant air in her lungs. She dipped her hands in it and collected some to rub on her face and neck, her forearms and calves, covering herself with its warmth. She even touched herself with the blood on her hands, sharing it with her most intimate place. She knew it wasn't normal, that what she was doing wasn't right, but that didn't matter to her then. The concept of right and wrong hadn't mattered to her in a long time.

She looked at him again, at the man who had given her immortality through his seed, the man who had given his blood to her. He was young, only 22 years old, with the most beautiful eyes she had ever seen—a rich hazelnut brown with emerald green flecks in them that sparkled like jewels. The man she had loved lay before her on bloody sheets. He was handsome, virile, and dead.

In the moonlight, his body was flawless, shadowed here and there where his muscles rounded, where his curves crested. His body was perfect. It was tight, firm. She had the chance to experience the pleasures his body could give many times before that day. Before his last day. She had, in fact, sampled him one last time before taking his life. His face was masculine, sporting high cheekbones and full lips. His shoulders were broad, his chest wide, supporting a strong, shapely neck. His waist was slender and his stomach was flat, rippled with fine-tuned abdominal muscles. His body affected a V shape that was every much as tempting to the touch as it was to the eye. His pubic hair was coarse, more so than the hair on his head.

In the past, she had taken pleasure in running her fingers through it as he lay on the bed next to her, spent from effort, with his mind teetering on the edge of sleep. But not that night. To look at him, to touch his skin, to taste of the perspiration that coated his body after he made love to her, had been a fantasy until the day she realized she had looked too long.

At 6'3", he was well proportioned, sleek. His legs were firm, muscular, and shapely. She couldn't help but stare at them, blood splattered and rigid, as they went up, up, up, coming together behind the round of his testicles. She raised a bloody finger to her lips and tasted what was left of him. His blood had begun to cool on her hands and the texture was thick like the skin over luke warm gravy. She rolled her tongue to the roof of her mouth, pressing the blood there, savoring it like fine wine. Then she let her saliva carry it down her throat, deep inside of her. Her heart throbbed at the taste of him, at the thought of him coursing through her body, becoming part of her. It never ceased to surprise her, the way her body reacted to the taste of human blood. The mere sight of it sparked arousal, the sight of it made her come close to losing control. Even in the early days, when to taste of blood was akin to drinking poison in her mind, her body acted out of some primal lust for it, some unquenchable desire. For many years she tried to suppress it. She used to force herself away from its luring aroma, choosing starvation instead. But that was short lived. Now, instead of fighting the feeling, the desire, the need, she allowed the pleasure to take over, to wash her in warmth that penetrated her mind, body, and soul, if, in fact, she still had one. Her desire for blood was unstoppable, insatiable. She was powerless against it. But none of the warmth that usually came when she drank of it filled her that day. Not when she allowed herself to look into the eyes of the man that lay slaughtered in his bed, the man that she loved as she had no other.

Jonathan.

Why did it have to be this way? she thought bitterly, her body and mind suffering more than they had in years. She had promised herself that she would never use him the way she used the others: For food. For blood. She stayed away from him during the times when her hunger was so great she couldn't be trusted to be rational. She hid the truth of what she had called life for more years than she cared to remember. She had been so careful not to include him in that aspect of her existence, as difficult as that had been. So why, then? Why was she forced to murder the only man she had ever loved?

The answer was as clear to her then as it had been when they started, when she knew the risks of falling in love, she just didn't want to face it.

He had come to her in a dream, as he was fond of doing. Before she drifted to sleep, lying in the arms of her beloved, she knew he was near. She was used to him being around, milling, watching, waiting. She was able to ignore him most times; her only acknowledgement of his presence was the glance she cast reflecting her anger, anger she had harbored since the day he made her what she was. Her anger had never ceased, had never lessened nor dimmed. It was always forefront in her mind, making her bitter and ruthless to her victims. She showed no mercy when she took them. In fact, she took pleasure in watching them squirm within her grasp, like bugs caught in a spider's web. She liked to hear them whimper their pleas. How she enjoyed the sound of their tortured voices, the look of death in their eyes. It was an inherent pleasure, one that seemed to come from somewhere deep inside her, a dark room locked away in the caverns of her mind. It frightened her, the depths of her sadism. Maybe, she sometimes thought, she would have been damned in life as she was in death.

On this night she had been falling into a blissful sleep following a most satisfying evening with Jonathan. As she drifted off, she fancied that she could still feel his touch on her skin, warm and firm, as it had been when he grabbed her buttocks and pulled her closer with every thrust. He had commanded her body that night, putting her in the positions of his liking, slapping her upturned bottom until blush sprang upon the skin, licking, sucking, biting her anywhere and everywhere until he was satisfied. Then he lay still beside her, his pants of pleasure evening out to regular drawn breaths, his body settling in for the night.

She laid awake until the sweat that had coated his body dried into his

3

brown skin and his breathing became deep and steady. Those were the times she adored, those minutes between being awake and falling to sleep. When life seemed like a dream, airily light, when the surreal haze of uncertainty hovers over what can be seen and touched. That was when she most felt like a woman, a living being, like she had been so many years before.

Letting the sound of Jonathan's breathing lull her to sleep, she drifted to a place where she was the girl she remembered herself to be long ago. She walked aimlessly in the tall grass as she once had, her bare feet sinking into the cool dirt under the shade of the mango trees that rimmed the pathway. In her in-between state, she could almost smell the air, sweet from ripening fruit on the vine, crisp and fresh in the light of the morning sun. The sensations were breathtaking. And painful. Her memory had become so sharp, so photogenic, that the images she called up were more than just vague memories of times past. Instead, they were tangible and meaty; she felt like she was reliving them when they pressed into her consciousness, hearing every sound, feeling every touch. Her memories tortured her with their palpability, smothered her in their truth. She would never again feel the warmth of her mother's embrace, would never feel the coolness of the stream that ran nearby the house she shared with her family coursing over her toes. She understood that. But her memory gave those things back to her to experience all over again. The sensations tore at her like a knife in her heart.

She drifted away into a sleep that was surface and light, yet all consuming. In the distance she heard a sound. A whisper that sounded distorted and far away, as though coming from another apartment. The sound was so faint, she wondered if she heard anything at all.

Keep your promise.

The voice didn't stir her, didn't make her open her eyes to see who was speaking. Some part of her mind knew to whom the voice belonged. It screamed for her to wake up, telling her that he was there, in the room with them—in the room with Jonathan—but she didn't listen to it. The part of her mind that had enfolded itself in the warmth of Jonathan's body, into the life of a living mortal woman, turned a deaf ear to the intrusive warning, to the intruder itself.

But still she heard him whisper softly, like a parent to a napping child. *Keep your promise.*

If Jonathan heard the words he didn't show it. His body lay next to hers, deep in sleep and seemingly unaware of the presence. The part of her mind that heard the voice, deep in the recesses of her psyche, thought it was just as well Jonathan slept. It was better that he sleep, keeping his eyes shut, and his mind oblivious to the horror he was about to face than to wake to witness his mortality.

She kept dreaming, ignoring the hollow warning to wake up that sounded in the folds of mind. Her mind fed her associations, both physical and mental. It showed her the sun and she felt its warmth on her skin. It sent a breeze to flow through her hair and her skin sprung goose bumps in kind. It was starting again and she was helpless to prevent it. This was her memory at play and it was always the same. She shifted in bed as her body twirled in the land of the past, dirt shifting under her feet, leaves rattling in the wind. She filled her lungs with the sweet scent of the air, breathing of it in deep gulps, enjoying the memory for what it was worth; living life again as she had many lifetimes ago.

The trees moved in the wind, whistling their song as each leaf rose and fell, undulating at the whim of the wind. She kept spinning, her eyes shut in the world of her dreams, preferring to feel rather than see, for she knew what lay in the distance. She knew he was there as he always was. Waiting.

He stood beside a gnarled tree, misplaced among the luscious limbs of the mango trees that surrounded it. She stopped spinning and dropped her hands to her sides as she had when they first met. She opened her eyes to the bright summer day and saw him standing beside the tree looking at her with eyes that had seen the four corners of the earth in a casual blink, with eyes that told everything yet revealed nothing. She didn't feel fear, didn't feel the shyness that she might have felt had a boy from her village crept upon her and stared while she twirled unaware, caught up in the beauty of the day. Instead, she felt comfortable, relaxed. As he approached her she regarded him with soft eyes, the way a lover would regard her mate as he returned to their bed. She didn't see the evil etched upon his face, the malice that twisted his mouth, the triumphant glee that danced in his eyes. She saw only him to whom she had given herself. To whom she would soon belong.

Her mind begged her to wake up, to spare her the memory masked in a dream, but she didn't stir. Part of her enjoyed the memories as much as she hated them. Returning to a time when nothing mattered except the love of a mysterious stranger. The innocence, the inhibition she felt then; she cherished the memory of those feelings as much as she did those of her family. That was something she would never admit aloud. Not to anyone.

He approached her, his face a cloud of mystery, the way it always was in her memory. She held her ground as he drew closer, the voice inside that told her to run away wrestled into submission by the part of her that embraced the fantasy. She stood silent, waiting for him to speak.

"My dear Zaji, at last."

He spoke in a voice that was a thousand voices, in tongues that caressed many languages. To some he might have spoken the purest of French, to others Mandarin, but to her he spoke the language of her people in a velvet voice, rolling the words in his mouth, savoring them the way one might a delicacy. He hypnotized her with every inflection, every word.

He came to her as he always did when this memory resurfaced, the memory itself was a primer for him, the main attraction. He appeared as he had when they met in the grove that would witness her metamorphosis. Running the softest of hands along her cheek, he touched her, caressing her skin as if it were pure silk. He spoke in hushed tones, keeping his words between them, burning them into her heart, her very soul. His touch, the feeling of air swirling about them, the surreal texture of the world, seemed as it had then, identical to the day her life changed. But his words were different. She strained to hear him, to truly hear the words he spoke and break through the sensually hypnotic melody his voice carried. His smooth tenor filled her, strummed her senses, making her melt in his arms. She fought against it, somehow knowing that they had transitioned from a memory that replayed itself over and over, torturing her with each beginning, to a new environment, one not quite a dream, but far from waking lucidity. Through the veil of her own desires she could see him smiling coyly, using his lips and eyes to seduce her, knowing she couldn't resist. The part of her that wanted to succumb lurched toward him, pressing her body closer to his. How he toyed with her, making her want him with only a look.

She shut her eyes to break his spell, cutting off their connection so that she could regain her composure. In the recesses of her mind, she heard a voice call to her. The voice was light and airy, juvenile in its innocence, pure in its timbre. It was the voice she possessed years before, when she was still a girl of the world and not the monster she had become.

"Yéyé." One word was all the little voice that flitted around inside her head uttered, but it cleared the fog surrounding her consciousness. The voice was urgent, firm, solid in the midst of the surrealism of her dream. She knew then what he was planning to do. She knew then, for the first time, that she would never let it happen, no matter what the consequences were. *Baby.*

She awoke with a knowledge that both empowered and devastated her. She stared at the space in front of the bed she and Jonathan shared, at the place where he would surely show himself, and cried tears full of sorrow and anguish. She turned to look at Jonathan once more before allowing herself to step into the reality that would change her life, and instantly wished she hadn't. In age he was no more than a boy, but in spirit, he was a wise elder. His face, so peaceful in sleep, would soon be no more than a memory to her. She would never see Jonathan smile again, feel his touch, or taste his kisses. Her mourning of him would be lifelong, eternal.

Zaji. The name given to her at birth by her mother. The name whose meaning she would never be able to realize. Womanhood in the truest sense—physical and mental maturity combined—she would never see in her mortal life. She chuckled at the sentiment as she rose from the bed, preparing for the work ahead. That she had died a child seemed like a cruel joke to a body that felt aged and worn.

Zaji. The name echoed in her head, spoken by a voice she couldn't place. She hadn't used that name since she took the great sleep in her homeland. The night she died, she returned to her grave after a visit to a place she would never again call home. She made herself lay inert for decades, trying to still her heart and stop her breathing. But still she rose, weak and weary from lack of sustenance after years of hiding, years of denying her nature, such as it had become. But not dead, no. On the contrary, she was very much alive. Her senses were heightened; even the minutest of sounds rang loudly in her ears. The cool air that met her when she arose from her grave felt harsh against her skin, like needles penetrating flesh that had been rubbed raw. The air she inhaled seemed to burn the delicate lining of her nostrils. Her discomfort was insufferable, yet she had never felt so full of life. She had never felt so alert, so vibrant, so consumed with hunger. It was then, when her hunger could no longer be contained, that she took her first prey: A pretty girl whose beautiful upturned eyes and trusting smile would never escape Zaji's memory. She knew, as she drank ravenously the blood of an innocent, its metallic tang like sweet nectar caressing her tongue and throat, that she was no longer Zaji, the oldest daughter of Hiji and Mariama of Dahomey. Nothing about her present state resembled the person she had been in the past.

Before.

She was forever changed. Tainted. Holding on to that girl, the sweet Zaji who thrived on life and the quest for knowledge, would be impious. Zaji was dead. So she let her go and became someone else. She became Angelique.

The name served her well through the centuries, proving to be as versatile as it was timeless. In recent years she'd opted for the shorter Angie, loosening it up, making it blend in more with the casual nature of the times. She had learned to be a chameleon over the years, changing as the situation dictated, fading into the shadows when necessary. She rarely formed ties with people because she didn't want to let anyone get close. She couldn't. Only those whose deaths were written on the wall knew her true being.

Except Jonathan.

He had known her heart if no other part of her. The Angie that he knew was pure to him, she was everything Zaji had not been allowed to become: A sexual being, a compassionate, worldly woman with needs and desires that stretched beyond those of the flesh. She felt free with Jonathan. Free to love, free to live, free to be real. She hid the truth from him to protect him, not to deceive or lull him into a sense of security and take his life when the time suited her. She genuinely loved Jonathan as she had loved no other. Spilling his blood would be the hardest thing Angie would ever have to do.

Angie laid garbage bags along the floor before she killed him. They were cut open along their seams and made to lay flat to catch the blood that might fall to the floor. Angie anticipated her steps before beginning. She was used to it—the process, the detail. She'd done it many times before. The disposal used to be easier. In times past and in different lands, one didn't have to be so diligent. Covering tracks was not as much of a concern. A body could be left to rot wherever it fell, as long as it wasn't within the confines of a house. The animals would have cleaned and scattered the bones long before the authorities found the body, compromising the evidence they might have been able to gather. The authorities never salvaged enough evidence to be able to charge anyone when that happened, and more often than not, the case remained unsolved. Forgotten. Even the families of the deceased let go of their vendettas after a while. Everything was easier then, but times changed. The police in the United States were far more precise than those in the West Indies. They were employing fingerprinting techniques that Europe had yet to consider. Angie had learned to be careful.

Jonathan slept silently as she worked, oblivious to what lay ahead. After all of the preparations were made, Angie stood over him one last time. She let her mind wander, thinking of what the last minutes of his life would be like. She would begin to suck his neck, caressing it with her tongue, enticing the jugular vein to show itself. She would bite lightly at first, just enough to make his pulse quicken, to make the blood flow through his veins in torrents. He would rouse then, would reach up to hold her as he enjoyed what he would perceive as an invitation to love making. He would caress her sides, run his hands through her hair, cup her behind as she worked. He would moan as he always did when she kissed his body, his mind floating away with every flick of her tongue. Jonathan would do all of this without opening his eyes. He wouldn't see the determination on her face nor the sadness in her eyes. He wouldn't know terror until the final moment, when it was too late.

Angie's eyes filled with tears again as Jonathan's breathing kept its smooth, steady pace. The fantasy she had entertained of a life with him was fading before her eyes. The fanciful existence of her daydreams was nothing more than a kiss carried on a breeze. She realized then that they would never have been able to be together. It would never have worked. There were too many questions that would have gone unanswered, too many secrets she would have had to keep. Inevitably, he would have asked how she kept her youthful looks while he continued to age—those same looks that beguiled him when he was in his twenties, that would have, undoubtedly, beguiled him then. Would she be able to stand by and watch as his body failed, or would she force him to drink her blood, tricking him, perhaps, in a moment like this one? Could she, every day for years, avoid being detected while she fed? If Jonathan caught her, would he be able to accept her as she was? Nonsense. No one could be expected to accept such monstrosities. Angie would lose him, one way or the other, if they stayed together. It would have to end at some point, before suspicions were raised, before something was done that couldn't be undone. It had to end while it was still beautiful.

Angie leaned in to begin her work when a voice rose from behind her. Startled, she pulled back from Jonathan and turned to face its owner. Him. The names for him that she held in her mind were a jumble; no one word came through clearly enough to be spoken. She was sure that he did that to her, confusing her thoughts when he appeared so that she would be unable to resist him. She had been teaching herself to ward against him when his mind probed into hers like hot tongs against flesh. She had gotten stronger, better at keeping her thoughts from him, denying him a view of the world she saw through her eyes. She started the moment she awoke from the great sleep when her only desire was to become invisible, to disappear among the masses, and had been practicing ever since. Still, he was able to find her wherever she went, no matter how far. Still, he tightened his reins around her neck.

He stood motionless, as though he were a statue. His chest neither rose nor fell, for no air entered his lungs.

"Angelique," he said, rolling the name off his tongue like fine wine. "I like that name. It's not nearly as nice as Zaji, but it suits you just the same."

Angie was silent, watching him as he stood in the doorway. The need to protect Jonathan from him overshadowed her anger, her fear.

"But what's this 'Angie' business?" He continued, sucking his teeth. "So trendy. Common. That will never do."

Angie watched him, her body trembling.

"What's the matter, Angelique? Not a kind word for me? That isn't the least bit hospitable."

"What do you want?" Angie hissed.

He smiled. He had taken on the countenance of an attractive man, African American features in brown sugar skin. He was tall and slender with a muscular build and the most endearing eyes she had ever seen. Any woman seeing him stride on the Harlem sidewalk below would do a double take. Of all the forms he visited her in, this one was the most irresistible to her and he knew it. He played on her weaknesses, unchanged in all her years. He knew how to get what he wanted from her and he wanted something now. And she knew exactly what it was.

"This century certainly suits you, my dear. You're as brash as the mortals running around in the streets. What happened to my mild-mannered, timid little Zaji?"

He was in front of her, crossing the space between the doorway and the place where she stood in an instant. He extended his hand to caress her cheek. Angie turned away and moved closer to the bed upon which Jonathan lay.

"Why are you here?" She spoke softly, trying not to wake Jonathan.
He eyed her suspiciously, dropping his hands to his sides and pacing the
floor. He unzipped the black jacket he wore and revealed a slim figure
clad in a white Oxford shirt and black slacks. The clothes fit him well.
She couldn't help but look at the place where the bottom of his shirt met
his belt at the top of his pants, imagining the beauty of his pelvic muscle
through the material. He was trying to distract her with his movements, so
deliberately sensual—a masculine projection of his hips as he took a step,
pressing his abdominal muscles against the cloth of his shirt so she might
see the outline of his muscles. He wanted her to see him, to desire him
so he could break the wall surrounding her thoughts. And she did desire
him; she did want to see more of what his body had to offer. But she was
resilient.

He walked toward the window to look out at the people below, aimless
souls wandering the streets, heading to their next destination, going about
their meaningless lives in oblivion. Their very auras called to him, desperate
in their naiveté, always looking, always searching for more—bigger, fancier,
prettier. The wealth of unattached souls beyond the window enticed him,
seduced him like a woman might a man, but he had business to attend
to. Angie sensed the conflict raging within him and silently prayed he'd
acquiesce to the delicacies outside, but she knew he wouldn't.

She snickered under her breath as she watched him watching her out of
the corner of his eye. His brow furrowed in concentration as he attempted
to penetrate her mind. But he couldn't break through. He couldn't see the
things she had hidden, compartmentalized and stored away. He couldn't see
the answer to his question, couldn't sense that she had something to hide.
He could only see what she wanted him to see. All of her work had paid
off. She suppressed the urge to gloat as he stood by the window.

"I asked why you are here," Angie pressed, feeling stronger, more
confident.

"Just a visit," he said after a long silence. He strolled toward Angie again,
stopping right in front of her, standing so close that he could have kissed
her had he wanted to. "Can't I drop in on you from time to time?"

Prologue

Angie stood silent for a moment, taking time to choose her words before she opened her mouth. She knew why he was standing so close to her. He wanted to smell her breath, her sweat, to see if he could detect fear on it. She swallowed before speaking.

"I'd rather you not." Her voice betrayed her, allowing the slightest quiver at the end of her sentence. She hoped he hadn't noticed, knowing he had.

He stood still, motionless as he stared in her eyes, through them, into her very soul, to find the secret she was keeping from him. His eyes were urgent as he stared at her, inside her, looking. His probing was like a cold, wet finger along her spine. Angie forced herself to keep her breathing even. Jonathan's heavy breathing resounded loudly in the room.

"I'm sure you would," he said, confidence lacing his voice. "We haven't yet gotten to the point where we can enjoy each other's company, have we Angelique?" His finger traced the line of his jaw seductively. "We haven't yet begun to share things with one another. And we should, my dear. We are a family. No?" Angie could feel his fingers along her own chin, fondling it absently, though he hadn't raised a hand to touch her. With a smile that depicted both the sensual and the ravenous, he moved his eyes to where Jonathan lay on the bed. He spoke with such certainty, Angie felt her legs shake. "I'm sure you'd like to keep him all to yourself."

With a flick of his wrist, he pulled the cover from Jonathan's body, revealing his nakedness.

"They are so beautiful, aren't they?"

Angie went to Jonathan quickly, covering his body to shield it from view. In her haste, she almost woke him. Her breathing hitched as he changed positions, shifting from his side to his back. His breathing remained steady. He never opened his eyes.

"Is that all you wanted?" Angie spat. "You've seen him. Now go!" The tone of her voice both surprised and frightened her.

He walked toward the door slowly, seeming to mull her question over. She could feel him probing her once more for good measure, finding nothing, and retreating from her mind as quickly as he had come. At the door he sighed and said,

"Things should be different between us, Zaji. I so enjoyed our times together. We could be that way again." His voice was filled with poisonous sincerity, rife with trickery and coercion. Angie felt ill in his presence.

"Never," she said fiercely, the anger within her welling up and flushing her cheeks. "You preyed upon the mind of a child. I will never be that person again, thanks to you. That, I can never forgive."

A smile spread across his face as he felt her anger. In it, he could see the things she tried desperately to conceal. She was as open to him then as an infatuated lover. Satisfied, he said, "I still see you, Zaji. Every part of you. You are mine. Forever."

Angie sucked her teeth and turned away from him. He laughed, the richness of it filling every corner of the room, every crevice of her mind. She heard him utter, "I see you," though his lips had not moved. A chill spread quickly over her skin.

"Until we meet again, dear Zaji. Beautiful Angelique," he said, the glee in his voice sounding somehow obscene. And then he was gone.

Angie trembled in his wake. She cast her eyes over every crevice of the room, searching for him. It couldn't have been that easy. Though she wanted to believe she had hidden the truth from him, his abrupt departure made her think otherwise. He knew something. Somehow she had let him in and he saw it, at least some portion of what she was trying to hide. He didn't know everything. If he did, he surely would have killed Jonathan and taken her away. He was suspicious of something. She was sure of it.

In a whirlwind, Angie descended upon Jonathan. She could still feel his presence in the room, hanging in the air like smoke. He was watching her. And Jonathan. She needed to work fast before he caught her at her most vulnerable, before he read the grief-filled thoughts that stood on the other side of the wall.

Angie bit into the smooth flesh of Jonathan's neck brutally, abandoning the slow approach she had envisioned. The visit changed everything, took away the time she wanted to spend with Jonathan, removed the luxury of doubt. Jonathan's body bucked against hers as she split his flesh, the spasm controlled only by his muscles. His will had already left him; it had been

14

carried out of his body in the blood that spilled from his wound. Angie cried as she felt Jonathan's body fall limp and still beneath her. His blood tasted bitter to her as no one else's had, but she had to drink it. All of it. Or else he would be ruined, damaged like she was. Or worse. Angie couldn't let that happen, not to Jonathan. The flow of blood from his neck wound slowed, lessening to a stream, and then finally a trickle. In the end, she had to suck deeply, pulling his life's blood from his neck instead of accepting it into her mouth without effort.

Finally, Angie stood and looked down at Jonathan, at the bloody mess she made of him. Blood had spurted out of his neck and run down his chest, had spilled onto the sheet beneath him, saturating it, before dripping onto the bags lining the floor. She smeared it on his supple skin, like a child finger painting on a canvas, her hands moving of their own volition. Jonathan's lifeless eyes looked back at her, seeing but not seeing, judging in the finality of the ever after, accusatory even in death. She always hated their eyes. The way they stared at her when she stood over them, their dying pleas still reflected in their rigidity. She hated the way their gaze felt on her skin, like a cold, dead hand caressing her neck from the grave, engulfing her in the darkness that was their nightmare.

The sight of his eyes was far worse than any others she had seen. Jonathan was beautiful in death, more so than he had been in life. There was an innocence in him as he lay lifeless on the bed, drained of his blood with his body temperature cooling, that hadn't been present in his living countenance. She thought it obscene that she would see him as attractive in such a state, but she did. He was her love in life and more so in death. She had killed him out of love and drained him out of protection.

Keep your promise.

Angie might have been able to hide the truth from the visitor that time, but she wasn't savvy enough to thwart his suspicion. If she had let Jonathan live, it wouldn't have been long before he tapped into his mind to learn the truth. Jonathan had his own suspicions about her disappearance. She left for seven months without telling him where she was going or where she had been. He almost didn't take Angie back when she returned to Harlem, her bags in hand and a sheepish grin on her face. She had hurt Jonathan and she knew it, but she had to do it. For everyone's sake.

Jonathan's suspicions and disjointed thoughts would have been enough to pique her visitor's interest. He would have probed deeper, farther into Jonathan until his sanity, his entire being, was lost. Angie knew what the visitor wanted. She knew why he had come.

He was the Promise Keeper, there to make sure she kept her promise to him.

Angie's tears warmed her face and neck as they flowed freely from her. She leaned over Jonathan to smell his scent one last time. Her nipples grazed his cooling flesh as she hovered over his still body. Angie's sobs were deep, emanating from her diaphragm, from the depths of her soul. They were the sounds of sadness, the sounds of loss, the sounds of despair.

"Démon!" she screamed as they closed in on her. She chose to revert back to the language she had used long ago in another place and time, to call out the name of her accuser. They burst into the room, thrusting the door open with such force it banged against the wall behind it and bent the doorstop against the molding. They were so loud, so arrogant, catching her with Jonathan's blood on her hands. So triumphant.

"De a lo towe csi ouhe!" she said, her tongue curling around the words she spoke in her native tongue, a language she hadn't spoken since she was a girl. Her intonation was guttural and her eyes were fierce as she growled her command. *Get your hands off me!*

But it wasn't the policemen who stood cautiously in the doorway, timid even with their guns waving, confused by the mixture of fear and adrenaline that coursed through their veins, that made her call out with such hatred. It was the one who stood behind them, silent and unseen, as though he were an apparition. He might very well have been invisible to the men in the room, their sweat rich with trepidation as they rushed towards her, yanking her arms behind her back and forcing her away from that which used to be Jonathan Clay. Her only love. Her precious prey. But to Angie, he stood out like a light in the dead of night. The Promise Keeper was there with her as surely as he had been when she came to be, as surely as he would be when she ceased to exist.

To the Promise Keeper, she offered a malevolent smile. How spiteful he was! The arrogance that dwelled within him licked out like fire to caress her face in its heat, yet she refused to turn her head. She glared at him, defied his eyes that commanded her to shy away, to cower, to give in. She would not reveal her secret. She would not succumb to him, no matter what the price. *Maybe*, she thought with a resignation she had never known, *the price will be my salvation.*

How it was. How it won't ever be again.

That's what Angie said when Marcel asked what she did to end up in that shit hole we called home. She said that she had murdered him for his blood. Any kind of admission of guilt was uncommon in The Death House, so hearing Angie confess was a shocker to us. Most of the girls claimed their innocence until the very end. Shit, even I did, or I changed the subject when it came up so I didn't have to talk about it at all. Lying is easier than owning up to the truth any day. Nobody inside knew the truth about anybody. The lie *became* the truth after a while, for most of us. And we were the lucky ones. It was the poor slob who couldn't get what really happened out of their mind that was the worse for it, the girl whose remorse eats her up inside.

Some people just stop talking about it all together. They clam up and change the subject, like I did. It usually happened when they were getting close to check out time, when talking about it was like talking about some horrible curse. I did the same thing everybody else did. I wasn't any different, not really. Hell is Hell. We just react to it a little differently, but that doesn't change the fact that we're all in Hell together.

Hearing Angie say what she said—that she wanted his *blood*—scared the shit out of me and everybody else that heard it. But when you think about it, when you allow your mind to get around it all, you realize that truer words had never been said. In some way or another, all of us killed the person we were about to die over for their blood. That was the real reason behind the excuse—'He stole my money', 'She called me out of my name', I just hated the motherfucker'. We wanted their blood. We wanted to see it, smell it, in some cases taste it, rub it all over our bodies, whatever tickled our fancies at the time. But it wasn't something that we said aloud for the world to hear. It was private. Call it a fetish, call it freaky, evil, sick, call it whatever you like, but it was ours.

Some of the girls couldn't even admit the truth of it—the need for the blood—to themselves. It frightened them, made them sick to think that somewhere inside them, they liked it. They couldn't accept that a desire within them made them do what they did, crave what they craved. Those were the ones that I felt sorry for. They couldn't deal with what they had done, with who they were. They were the ones who bit the skin off their wrists in the middle of the night rather than face the demons lurking in the shadows again.

But Angie was different.

The Death House at Raskin Correctional Facility. Our final home before we were sent on to meet our maker. Most of the girls I knew died there, sad to say. I only knew one other girl who was in the Death House that got out. She didn't live long afterward—that almost makes you wonder if there is a God. She got out of prison, bought a bus ticket to Tennessee where she planned to start over, and got killed in a train crash on the way. Shit like that makes me wonder if God, that entity we credit with creation and salvation, likes to play games with us here on earth, like we're pieces on a chessboard. How else can you explain the suffering, the irony that is life? This girl escaped the chair only to die in a ball of flames weeks later. I should have gone to the chair, as God is my witness, but here I stand, alive and obscenely well considering the path that brought me to this point. I'm sure there are things in your life that will make you understand what I'm saying. It could be something you've always known, something that has always been there but you never paid attention to. But it's there. The things I'll say in this journal will sound ridiculous at first, but their truths will be clear by the time you finish reading. The horrors spelled out on these pages will make sense to the most basic of your emotions. That fact used to scare me when I thought about it, but I can't keep it from you. You deserve to know why.

I beg you Brian, read this to the end. Your life depends upon it.

My name is Lucerne, but people took to calling me Lucky when I was a kid. Even when I was sentenced to die in that bitch of an electric chair up at Sing Sing, my family—the ones that still talked to me by that time—addressed their letters to Lucky Green. Hmph. That makes me laugh, even now.

Lucky. I've been anything but lucky in my life with my temper, my men, my skin. Nothing went the way I thought it would have when I was young. None of those childhood dreams were ever worth the time I spent on them in my sleep. I changed from being a cute little schoolgirl interested only in mathematics and afternoon sweets to a punk kid who dropped out of school and intimidated my neighborhood. I robbed, battered, and scared the hell out of everyone I could on my block, and that was saying something, considering the people who hung around my way. Hell, I spent the better part of 1952 terrorizing the old ladies and cussing at the old men that lived on my block. I had gotten so big one summer, and my temper came into me so good, I decided I would take all the things I wanted instead of working for them like everyone else did. I became the girl everybody was afraid of, not because I was 5'10" and 200 pounds of muscle, not because the look on my face made them afraid to make eye contact with me, but because I didn't care about anything. And I liked it. I spent a couple of years stealing from my neighbors, people that had known me for as long as I'd lived up north. But it got old after a while. I needed a change. I moved out of my mother's house and got a place on Manhattan Avenue. Even though I was making a pretty good living for myself from pawning the stuff I lifted, I picked up a gig at a liquor store a couple of blocks from my house. I wanted to be sure I had money coming in every month. Life was good until I met the man who would be the love of my life and the cause of everything that happened after the spring of 1954, the good and the bad. Truthfully, there isn't much good to speak of.

Tommy Kettering came into the liquor store around 6:00 p.m. that night. I was just about to get off work and seeing another customer come in the door before I had counted my till pissed me off. But I didn't stay angry for long. He walked his long legs up to the counter and looked me in the eye, smiling with them like I had never seen a man do before. I melted right then and there, before he ever uttered a sound.

"Gimmie a bottle of Thunderbird and don't forget to write your number on the bag," Tommy said, his voice thick and confident.

The line was corny, I knew that much, but the lips that had formed the words were luscious, hypnotic. They were full and brown, pinkish in the middle, where the bottom met the top. His teeth were white, brighter than any of the men who lived around my way. They almost looked like they had been polished. He had a mustache crowning his upper lip, that wasn't too thick or too thin. It had a little slit in the center, splitting the hair in half. God, how I loved to look at his mouth. I wonder sometimes now if it really looked the way I remember it. I lost the only picture I had of him years ago, right after I got out of Raskin Correctional, so I don't have anything to judge my memory against. Could his lips really have been that beautiful? Could they really have been that smooth, that creamy, that silky when they touched my face, or is my memory building him up to be more than he was? The mind has a way of doing that, making more out of people and things than they really were. Was that man really as fine as I remember him being, or has absence made the heart grow fonder? Since I've changed, things that I experience now seem more intense. The sun seems so bright some mornings that I can't come out of the house until it subsides for fear that it will burn my retina. The air is so crisp sometimes I fear it will tear my skin clean off. Even the sound of my favorite song, the mere melody, the lyrics crooned by King Pleasure's enraptured voice—*Oh baby, you make me feel so good*—has changed to my ear. It has become abject, pitiful. So my memory of him, the way his mouth looked when it formed the words he spoke with a voice as smooth as velvet, the way his body looked reflected in the mirror across from my bed when he made love to me, all those things about him that I cherish in my mind might be skewed because of who I have become. Because of what I am. So I write these words now to remember him before my memory of him changes even more with the passing of time.

Tommy leaned on the counter and looked at me like he could see deep into my soul. I had been with men before and I knew how to satisfy myself, but no one had ever filled me up the way he had with just a simple look. (Thank God my mother has left this life and can't read what I've written here. Maybe she has met the maker she believed in her whole life and can't see me in my current state. Maybe she's nothing more than fertilizer for the weeds growing in the cemetery my brother buried her in. Either way she's lucky. At least she is done. My work seems endless. Funny I should care about what she might think now.) The room became hot and my skin felt clammy. I had never had that reaction when dealing with a man before, at least not since junior high school. I was flustered. He made me nervous. I stumbled over myself to get him the bottle he wanted off the shelf and put it down on the counter with more force than I meant to.

"Easy girl, 'fore you crack op'n my hooch," he playfully reprimanded me as he pulled his wallet out of his pants pocket. He kept eye contact with me the whole time as he pulled out the cash to pay for the liquor, sizing me up from the other side of the counter. My face must have been as red as a berry.

I summoned my guts and spoke, never lifting my eyes to meet his, "Here's your Thunderbird and the bag, but what makes you think I want to give you my number?" The sound coming out of my mouth was more like a whine than a sultry tone. I blushed, my face feeling even hotter than before.

"Why wouldn't you want to give me your number? I look good enough for you, don't I?" He stood back from the counter and cocked open his single-breasted suit jacket. The button down shirt he had on fit him snuggly, grabbing onto to the ripples of his abdominal muscles as thought wet before tucking into his tapered pants. His gold belt buckle glistened in the light given off by the ceiling lights. It captivated me the way a hypnotist's watch would the eyes following it. I couldn't see them then, but he had on saddle shoes, shining like they had just been polished. Spiffy clean. He was a total package for sure.

I didn't have an answer for him. My mouth felt dry, like I had cotton stuffed in my cheeks. He stood there smiling at me, waiting for me to say something, but I just couldn't. Nobody like him had ever walked into the store before, let alone hit on me. He was clean, suave, looked like he was about something. The other men who came to the store were drunks, winos, losers of the worst kind. And they looked like it. None of the guys I had ever dealt with were as put together as Tommy was. It wasn't that he intimidated me. He was just too cool.

Finally he said, "I'll tell you what. Why don't I come back tomorrow and see what you think? Maybe you'll be able to find your tongue then." He smiled as he backed away from me, keeping eye contact until he reached the door. And then he was gone.

I was nervous for the rest of the day, and the next morning, anxious to see him again. Before work, I wasted an hour fishing around my closet for a decent outfit. I curled my hair tight and even put on a little makeup. I thought of all the coy things I would say to him as soon as he came in the door. I would be witty and interesting. I would be all the things I never had to worry about being for the fools I normally went out with. I would be different because this guy was different. Boy, was he. Butterflies fluttered in my stomach at the thought of seeing him again.

The workday went slowly as it usually does when you're looking forward to something. Every time the bell tied to the door clanked against the glass, I looked up, thinking it might be him. But it never was. At around 5:00 p.m., I started to think he wasn't going to come at all, that he was just playing a game with me. I made myself believe it too. Why would a guy like Tommy, who could get any girl he wanted, waste his time with me, a hard-assed girl from the corner? He could do better and I knew it. But that didn't make it hurt any less.

My shift ended at 6:00 p.m. and I checked out my till with a weight on my heart. Tommy hadn't come. I had been waiting, sitting on edge all day, but he hadn't shown up. I felt stupid. I chastised myself for not knowing better, for not listening to the voice inside me that told me not to get my hopes up. The doubt from earlier ruminated within me, filling my head. What would a man like that want with a girl like me? I asked myself for the umpteenth time. I wasn't fancy. I didn't dress up in flashy clothes. My hair wasn't done perfectly with every strand in place, like the women I saw up on 5th avenue; my hair didn't even have a style to speak of. Hell, I didn't even have a perm. I just pulled my hair into a messy bun most of the time, just to get it out of my way. I didn't wear makeup, didn't wear nail polish. I didn't care about that type of stuff. Even when I was all dolled up, I didn't look half as good as the women I was sure he was used to. I wasn't a small woman even then, but I wasn't big either, even though my bones were covered with a generous portion of fat. I guess you could have called me thick. All the men I dealt with liked a woman with some meat on her bones, so my weight never bothered me. Anyhow, I liked pig feet and collard greens with some cornbread on the side too much to let it go. Leave the dieting to those White girls uptown. They liked looking like sticks: no hips, no behind, no breasts. They think their men like them that way, flat as a board. Well, I saw my share of White men right there in Harlem stealing a peak at us Black girls, checking out our round behinds and ample breasts as we walked down the street. I even saw them trying to get a piece.   As I walked out of the liquor store, a wino held the door open for me. He slurred some compliment and coughed wetly before going inside, tripping up the steps as he went. I sighed as I watched him go in. He was the epitome of every man I'd ever been with. Handsome, if he'd ever clean up and shave, looking older than his years for all the grime and wear on his face, the weight on his shoulders. I supposed I did too, after all that time in the streets. That was my life as much as it was theirs.

I only lived four blocks from the liquor store so I walked to work every day. No sense wasting money on a bus. I turned right to walk up the block and saw nothing but green and red in my face. I stopped short, the flowers smacking my cheek.

"I'm sorry, baby. I thought you would see me before you started walking." There was laughter in his voice, but he didn't let it out.

Tommy was dressed in black pleated slacks with a white short sleeve Oxford shirt. He had on a black brimmed hat and black and white wingtip shoes. He was as clean as he could be. In his hand he held red roses on naked stems—all the thorns had been cut away. The bulbs had just bloomed and their open, velvety petals basked in the afternoon sun. They were so beautiful—him, everything was so perfect, I almost cried. Tommy's lips curled into a smile while I watched through watery eyes. He was just so handsome. I couldn't take my eyes off him.

"You ready to go on our date?" he asked with a playful lilt in his voice. I tried to brighten my face, tried to get over my embarrassment with the flowers, but the humiliation I felt when I walked out of the liquor store still stuck with me.

"What's with the long face?" I guess he noticed. "You didn't think I would stand you up, did you?"

I didn't say anything. I just concentrated on trying not to fidget. A woman dressed in work slacks brushed past me and went into the liquor store. I could smell underarm odor in her wake and I panicked, afraid it was coming from me.

"You did, didn't you?" Tommy continued. "You thought old Tommy would leave you standing here, waiting for me to come by. What would I look like standing a pretty girl like you up? Do I look like some kind of fool to you? 'Cause I'd have to be to do something stupid like that."

His voice was like a beautiful song, full of highs and lows, and as smooth as silk. I melted. It was like his words caressed my soul; his rich tenor made me feel sensual.

I could feel my guard breaking, cracking under his smile. My face reddened as he looked at me, lavishing more attention on me in that moment than I had ever received from any other man.

"Don't tell me you still ain't found your tongue, girl! You bes' start talking or I'm gonna think you a deaf mute."

He was so giddy, seeming to genuinely enjoy himself. I broke. I smiled. It was small at first, then it grew into this radiant beam I never knew I possessed.

"I found my tongue all right. I just ain't got much to say."

"You could start by telling me your name."

I clammed up again. His stare was both hypnotizing and frightening.

"Okay then, I'll start," he said after a long, uncomfortable pause. "My name is Thomas. Thomas Kettering. But my friends call me Tommy. It's your turn now, my flower."

He handed me the colorful bouquet that had struck me in the face with such delicacy, it made me weak in the knees. Their sweet aroma filled my nostrils and made me feel lightheaded. Tommy had me swooning for him. I was on cloud nine.

"My name is Lucerne," I started with a low voice. I hated my name, and still do. "But people call me Lucky."

"Lucky," he said, his voice rising to an exclamation that was quickly followed by a hearty laugh. "I'm the one they should call Lucky! *You* goin' out on a date with me!"

I smiled again. He knew just what to say. Boy, he had won me over.

"Why don't you call me Lucky and I'll call you my flower, 'cause that makes more sense to me. How does that sound to you?"

I felt glued in place. Everything about Tommy threw me for a loop.

"Huh?" he asked, sticking his arm out comically, shoving his elbow toward me. He looked so silly, yet regal. He was a character if ever there was one. I started laughing as I hooked my hand onto his forearm. All I could do was nod and go along with him. He chattered about how lucky he was to be with me for at least a block, all the while filling me up with emotions I had never experienced in all of my twenty-two years. I might have fallen in love with him that day, right there on the sidewalk near R.J.'s liquor store. I don't know for sure, but it might have been then.

That night was magical. Tommy took me to Lloyd's Theater to watch a movie that had just come out, "Dial M for Murder", then we had dinner at Carlton's on 5th Avenue. The movie wasn't my speed—I didn't care what happened to the girl, and the 3D effect they used bothered my eyes—but dinner was a different story. I had never been taken to such a fancy place before, where the tables had tablecloths on them and a flower in a vase in the center. My dates were always in somebody's house with the radio blaring in the background. But not for long. We always ended up in the bedroom within an hour. No wining and dining. Just cursory talk and sweaty sex. But Tommy was different. He wasn't like the guys I usually went out with. He was sophisticated. He knew Harlem like the back of his hand, getting us to and fro without the slightest hesitation. He'd been outside of Harlem too, over the George Washington Bridge and up into the country. Being with Tommy made me feel like I belonged. He paid attention to me when I talked, cared what I thought about things. I mattered to him. And he had a sense of humor! While we were on the bus on our way to the theater, he cracked a joke about the bluehairs sitting up front all prim and proper. I laughed out loud as he pursed his lips and tried to look uppity. We were laughing so loud, the bus driver threatened to kick us off before our stop.

It was like a dream. Like I had stepped into someone else's life.

Tommy showered me with attention the whole night. He opened the door for me to walk in and out of the theater and the restaurant, he pulled out my chair, he raised his glass to toast what he called our first date of many. Tommy seemed to be into me. Really into me. And I enjoyed every minute of it.

He took me home and kissed me at the door like we were school kids. I leaned in, my shyness gone, and pressed my lips onto his firmly. He pulled away and said,

"Lucky, are you sure? I don't want to take advantage of you."

I couldn't help but smile at his words. No one had ever been concerned about that before. Never. Not even my first cared if I was ready or not. I didn't answer him. I just kissed him again, harder this time, opening my mouth and letting my tongue play at his lips.

The next time he left my house to go any place other than to work, he was in a body bag.

Tommy and I made love that night. I mean, really made love. He wasn't just some guy using me to get off. Tommy paid attention to me, took note of how I reacted when he touched me. He was slow, gentle, sensitive to what I wanted. He made me feel like a woman. I didn't have to be aggressive to get what I wanted, what I needed. He was going to give it to me anyway. I didn't have to worry about him coming too quickly. He had control over himself like no other man I had been with.

Over the next couple of weeks, he showed me things, taught me things I never thought I'd try. I was used to oral sex; sucking a dick wasn't anything new to me. Most of the bums I dated wanted that anyway, sometimes instead of sex. It was just something women did, as far as I knew. It was easy, after you got used to it. But Tommy didn't ask me to do it for him. He didn't force my head and press his penis against me. He didn't mind if I didn't do it when we had sex. That made me want to do it all the more. Then he did it to me.

At first I was afraid. I felt dirty at the idea of him putting his mouth on me that way. It was something I had never experienced before, something that I tried not to wonder about. When he started kissing me that night, I hoped he would forget all about what he said he wanted to do. But as he kissed my neck, my breasts, my navel, then my thighs, spreading them as he did, I knew he was determined to do it. I tried to get up from the bed but he held my hips in place.

"What's the matter, baby?" Tommy asked. "Ain't nobody ever tasted you before?"

I hesitated, averting my eyes. His gaze was steady.

"You ain't supposed to do that," I said finally. He was so close to me, I could feel the heat from his mouth as he exhaled. I felt myself getting excited, even though what was about to happen was taboo in my mind. I could almost imagine what his tongue might feel like on me. In me. I wanted to let him do it, God I wanted to, but it was wrong. It was nasty. It just wasn't supposed to be done. I remembered what the old ladies from the South used to tell us young girls.

"Any man who wants to put his mouth on you got a problem," my grandma said as she rocked back and forth absently, fiddling with the stitching on the blanket that covered her immobile legs. "They nasty chile. Might e'vn have something. Don't you never let a man do that to you!"

But I wanted to. I was throbbing as I lay there with his mouth so close. The way he looked up at me riled me up even more. His eyes looked so perfect in the dim light, soft brown and expectant. I felt my legs trembling against the bed.

"Why not?" Tommy continued. "Because some old biddy told you it was nasty?" The reverberation of his words against my labia was mind numbing. It took everything I had not to press myself closer to his willing mouth.

28

How it was. How it won't ever be again.

I was stunned that he knew my reason. For a second, I wondered if what the old women said was true. How else could he have known?

"It's dirty." My voice wasn't louder than a whisper.

"You believe that?" I nodded. "Is doing what you do for me nasty too?" he asked.

The room was noticeably silent, as though music that had been playing was suddenly turned off. It was the same thing, wasn't it? Why was it all right for a woman to give attention to a man, but bad for her to get some back?

"Don't believe what those old women told you," Tommy continued. "They're the same ones that let their men screw them in the butt so they could still call themselves a virgin when they got married. Me kissing you down there is not nasty. It's part of what we've been doing. Making love."

His words sounded like poetry to me.

"Let me show you."

I didn't stop him that time. I never tried to stop him from doing anything to my body again.

Tommy moved into my place pretty much the day after our first date. We were inseparable. He would walk me to work before going to his job uptown, and would pick me up after my shift was over. I stopped stealing and pawning and he gave up whatever had occupied his time before meeting me. It was as if I had been dead before, like life was just beginning for me. I looked forward to waking up every day and seeing his handsome face on the pillow beside me.

Sometimes we'd grab a bite to eat after work, other times he'd cook for me. He blew my mind the first time he did it. He came by the liquor store two hours earlier than usual and told me he wasn't going to walk me home that night. He said I should come straight home and not to stop and get something for dinner, because he had all that taken care of. I came home to find fried pork chops, macaroni and cheese, and collard greens waiting for me on the table. I turned to lock the door as he reached into the oven and pulled out a tray of cornbread.

"Tommy, you did all this for me?"

He nodded as he put the cornbread on the table.

"But it's so much."

"Nothing's too much for my baby," he said.

He always had a way with words.

Months went by with us living like we were married, shacked up, as the old folks say. He seemed fine with it, but I was ready for more. I was giving the milk away before he bought the cow. I couldn't help being old fashioned sometimes. I wanted to get married.

I think he knew it too. Maybe that's why he did what he did. Maybe he thought it would make me break it off. Maybe he thought I would leave him so he could escape the ball and chain without having to say he didn't want to be married. He probably thought he'd only get a beating in the process, a smack or two, and then it would be over. Or maybe he was just a nasty dog, like all the rest of them. Maybe he had been doing it the whole time we were together because he thought he could get away with it. If he didn't want to marry me, he should have just left. He didn't have to do what he did. Tommy messed with the wrong woman that night. He underestimated me and ended up paying the ultimate price for it.

I worked the late shift a couple of nights at the liquor store, closing up around 10:30. The night everything changed was a slow one for the store. I had maybe five customers, and only two of them bought anything. So, I decided to close up shop early, around 9:30. I took in the night sky as I walked home. The stars were out. I remember that I could see the little dipper. Funny the things that stick in your mind.

It was a warm night, not too hot, not too chilly. One of those summer nights when you could sleep with your windows open and let the air flow over your naked body. An image popped into my mind: me lying naked next to Tommy, spent, looking out of the window and over the tops of buildings at the night sky, the roofs glinting like foil under the moon's spotlight. I hurried my step so I could get home and get started on the fantasy.

I opened the door to the apartment and heard Tommy laughing in the bedroom. Without pausing to drop my purse on the table, I ran through the living room and into the hallway that led to our bedroom.

"Baby, I'm home early," I shouted as I made my way to the bedroom. I was so excited to see him, so ready to feel his arms around me. I could almost taste his lips on mine.

"I was just thinking that we could strip and look—." My words died in my throat. A woman sat on top of Tommy, straddling him, riding him. Tommy's eyes were open wide as he pushed her off hurriedly, revealing his erect penis glistening from her juices. I was so angry I couldn't feel my hands or my feet.

"Baby, I-," Tommy started, the words catching in his throat.

"What?" I cut in. My blood was boiling, flooding my ears. Deafening me.

"Listen to me. Let me—."

I stopped hearing his voice. His mouth was moving, but to me, the room was dead silent. The girl he was screwing stood up, trying to look like she was tough. She stared at me like I was the one in the wrong, like I was the one with the problem, not her. Suddenly all I saw was her, her naked body, her hands on her hips, her lips twisted up in a grit, her eyes rolling, the sweat on her forehead. I couldn't believe she thought she could break bad with me. I was going to teach her a lesson, one that would replace that sweat on her face with blood.

I walked toward her, my hands clenched into fists at my sides. She took a step backwards as I approached, flinching just enough for me to see what she was made of. I remember thinking that somebody better stop me before I killed her.

Tommy stood up and took a step toward me. I looked at him and was sickened. There he stood, the man I was in love with, standing up to me to protect some bitch he found on the street. His penis, once hard and pounding into the whore standing in front of me, had gone soft and shriveled, seeming to cower away from my anger. I couldn't help but chuckle at the idea that he was afraid. *Well fuck him*, I remember thinking. *He should be afraid.*

Tommy stood on my right, still talking. He was asking me what I was thinking of doing. A smile that frightens me now to think of it spread across my face.

Just watch, motherfucker.

In the second I spent looking at Tommy, the girl sucker punched me. She hit me pretty good too, turning my head completely over to the other side and almost knocking me down. But my legs held and I straightened up. I smirked before returning the favor. I was so angry, I felt like I could take on ten men.

I threw a punch that connected with her mouth flush; I felt her teeth cut into my skin as my knuckles passed over them. I jumped on her when she fell, pummeling her with punches, and beating her head against the floor. Her hands pulled at my forearms weakly, the strength knocked out of her by the first couple of blows. It didn't take long before blood rolled out of her mouth and down her chin to mingle with the blood on the floor from the back of her ruined head.

I rammed her head on the floor one last time for good measure. Sound was starting to come back to me, bursting through the bubble of silence that had surrounded me since I saw them together on the bed. Tommy was on his knees to my left, checking the woman's pulse. His face was wet with sweat and his mouth was open, taking in deep gulps of air.

He looked at me with panic in his eyes. "She's dead, Lucky. You killed her!" I didn't say anything as I rose to my feet. He stayed by the dead whore's side. It made me ill.

"I can't believe you did this!" he screamed, his voice bordering on shrill. "This is crazy." Tommy stood. "Lucky," he called out. I remained silent. "Lucky," he said again. He put his hand on my shoulder and shook me. "Lucky, this is serious."

His touch made my skin feel hot, like it was being burned by the heat of a flame. I shrugged his hand off violently and he put it right back in place. "We gotta call the police and tell them something," he sighed; his voice sounded panicked. "They're gonna ask a lot of questions that you have to answer. You have to tell them the truth, Lucky. There's no other way."

I couldn't help but laugh at him. He was talking like he had nothing to do with what happened, like he hadn't driven me to it. He was acting like everything between he and I was forgotten in light of the dead body in our apartment. His whore's dead body. He seemed to have no fear, no concern for what I might do to him. It was as if he didn't think I was *capable* of doing anything to him. Like I had taken all of my anger out on the girl and I was done. The cops would come and ship me off to jail and he'd be rid of me, just like he wanted. All's well that ends well. I could feel my stomach turning over at his confidence.

"Lucky, you gotta get yourself together—."

I smacked him harder than I had ever smacked anyone before he could finish his sentence. The blow surprised him. His eyes opened wide as his head turned from the force of the blow. But he recovered quickly. He grabbed my neck to hold me in place, and smacked me back before throwing me to the floor like a rag doll. I landed right next to the girl—she was pretty, I had to give him that much— getting some of her blood on my hands.

He chuckled and said, "You think you 'gon punk me like you did her? I ain't some bitch you can just take over."

He strutted, actually strutted, to the dresser on the other side of the room and pulled out some underwear. As he put them on and pulled them up to his waist, he finished, "Now pick your ass up off the floor and let's call the police."

I got up from the floor, staring at him the whole time. Tommy was putting on his clothes like he didn't have a care in the world, taking time to button up his shirt and smooth the creases in his pants like we were going out some place nice. I knew then that he would never see the outside of the apartment again.

My cheek stung from the smack he'd given me. I rubbed it absently as I walked briskly out of the room, down the hall, and into the kitchen. Tommy realized I had left the room a second too late.

"Lucky," he called out as he ran down the hallway. I hid in the shadows of the kitchen, clutching the knife I had taken out of the sink. He had been cutting vegetables with it before falling into to bed with that hussy off the street. I was planning to use it to cut some vegetables of my own.

"Lucky? Girl, you better get out here," he said as he ran past the kitchen

and into the living room. The lights were on in there and I could see
Tommy's neck craning from side to side, looking for me. The drapes
billowed in the breeze, ballooning outward. It caught his eye. Tommy
started to walk over to the window. I snuck up behind him; two paces
was all it took to get close. I reached for his balls and held them lovingly
in my hand, disarming him for a second. I could feel his body tense from
my touch, then relax as I rubbed them. I thought of cutting them and the
offending dick off too, but decided against it. Either way, he'd never use
them again.

A second after fondling his testicles, I raked the knife across his throat
with my other hand, cutting him open. His hands reached for his throat
as he spun towards me. Blood wet the front of his shirt, spewing from
the wound in torrents, spurting out with the beat of his heart. He took a
step toward me, reaching out with one of his bloody hands to grab me.
I stepped backwards, just out of his reach. His face was contorted in a
painful grimace as he fell forward, hitting his unguarded face on the floor.
His feet tried to push him forward, to worm him in my direction, but they
gave up as quickly as they started. After a minute or so, he stopped moving
all together.

I stood there for a long time looking at Tommy lying dead on the floor. So
much for love. So much for the happiness that life offered. My happiness
lay in a bloody mound in front of me, dead by my hand.

I was sad for Tommy, sad for us. Why did he have to betray me? I was
content to go on the way we had been for a while, marriage or not. I
couldn't see myself with anyone else. I couldn't see myself going back to
the life I had before he walked into the liquor store. But he took all my
dreams, dreams I never knew I had before him, away from me. So I took
his life away from him.

Someone in the building called the cops. I never found out who it was.
They came in a rush of blue and took me out of the house. I still had the
bloody knife in my hand when they broke down the door.

 That's how I ended up at that godforsaken jail with Angie. It was the spark
that led to where I am now.

How it was. How it won't ever be again.

Talking about the old days makes me feel like I'm back in them. I can hear the sounds of the street, cars driving by, people yelling out of their windows. New York is New York is New York, always has been, and always will be. My old tongue comes back, uneducated and crass at times, but real nonetheless. I miss her, the old me. She was replaced by a different person, a me who is what the old me wanted to be. I now have style to my haircut and in my dress, I've traveled the world and learned about other cultures, I've experienced their languages and made some of them my own. I have everything I once coveted, what I was envious of. I can't help but think about how I got here. If I had never done what I did, if I had never given Tommy the time of day, I wouldn't be where I am now. Life is bittersweet that way, isn't it? I'm the person I always wanted to be, yet all I want now is to be that streetwise girl who should have died in the electric chair decades ago.

By now I'm sure you're wondering why I wrote all of this down. You're probably asking yourself why I would ever want to remember what happened in my life that caused everything to go to shit. The honest truth is that, were it not for those memories, those images playing themselves over and over in my head, I would go crazy. I know I would. I was real then. Alive in every sense. Sure, I was one mean son of a gun, but it was real life that I was living. I'm not living now. I'm an abomination, an affront to what life really is, what it stands for. I exist now, in this shell of human skin, mocking the life I once lived. So you'll forgive me, then, if I allow myself the pleasure of writing in my old tongue every once in a while, won't you? Or if I digress into a time that is long past and where every person I speak of is dead. It feels good. Almost like I'm that girl again. Still, why? Why should all this matter to you?

Because what Angie said was true. Even though I didn't believe it then, wouldn't believe it now if I wasn't living it myself, she was telling the truth, and you need to know what's in store for you, come Hell or high water.

THE JOINT

When I met Angie, she had been in the joint for three months already. I never really met her, at least not formally where we could shake hands and exchange pleasantries face to face. We talked through the walls mostly. You didn't see people much in The Death House. Either they roomed with you, which was rare by the time I got there, or they walked in front of your cell just before they died.

I had just been processed. My skin was raw from the delousing chemicals and I was ticked off by the strip search, which I thought was nothing more than a way for a few muff divers to get their kicks. The smell of the receiving area was almost unbearable. The dingy walls were covered with old, pocked wallpaper and stank of rot. Adding to that was the guard's body odor and the feces in the corner, a present left by the last inmate. I was afraid to bump against the walls or take a deep breath. The thought of someone else's shit getting on me made me sick.

The whole thing was like a horrible worst nightmare. The rough handling by guards who despised people like me, the fingerprinting, the mug shots, the degradation. And I had a whole new hell waiting for me when I got to my cell. The lack of sound and the absence of natural light drove me crazy. Who would ever have thought that not seeing the sun, not even just a ray of it shining on the floor, could make a person feel as if the darkness was crawling inside them, festering, growling there like gangrene. Or that silence, the very quietness of it, could drive a person to create voices in her head and beckon them to speak until they became entities independent of her, independent of themselves. I had never considered such things when I was on the outside walking the streets, but it hit me hard on my first day. I'm surprised, even now, that I made it through.

My cell was eight-by-eight with cinderblock walls painted a cheerful gray. There was a lidless toilet in a dirty corner, a concrete slab with a thin mattress on top of it for a bed, and a concrete shelf jutting out over the bed, meant to hold personal items. All of my belongings had been confiscated at check in, so I had nothing to set on top of the shelf. For some reason that fact bothered me more than anything else in my first couple of hours, and I found myself feeling depressed. I curled into a ball on the thin mattress and cried into my hands, first over the empty shelf, and then over my situation, my life. Later in the evening, the lack of privacy the toilet afforded sent me into a tizzy and I yelled, cursed, flung myself around my cell protesting it. The only response to my shouting was the threat of a beating from a big male guard with a gut hanging over his belt. On the streets such a threat would have whipped me into action, would have made me challenge the person issuing it, man or woman, big or small. On the streets, I knew how to take care of myself. Nobody frightened me out there. But within the cold interior of The Death House, everybody scared me. Everybody and everything. When I saw the guard approaching my cell, his mouth curled into a vicious grimace as he yelled his obscenities about where he could shove his billy club if he so desired, I felt the chill of fear creeping up my back, washing over me like cool water. The clanking of the billy club as he banged it against the bars, the heavy thud his heel made as it met with the floor, even the jingle of change in his pockets shot rivulets of fear through my body. I ran to the opposite side of my cell, the escape taking no more than a step and a half, and squatted there, trembling. My sudden silence pleased the guard and he walked away from my cell, giving its bars a bang for good measure. I shivered, and hugged my knees to my chest. I had never experienced such fear, such a lack of confidence in myself. I had never felt so alone. I was humiliated and embarrassed, angrier than I had ever been, but there was no way to express my feelings. And no one to tell.

The silence of the room made me feel as if I had grown deaf; the only sounds I could hear were my breathing and an incessant hum coming from above me, beneath me, from either side: from all around. I found myself mumbling aloud just to break up the monotony.

On that first night in The Death House, my will, the one basket in which I had placed all of my eggs, was broken.

"Shh. They'll hear you."

I heard the voice break through the silence and I wondered if I was imagining it. I grew silent and still, straining to hear something, any sound that I didn't cause. After a couple of seconds, she spoke again.

"They'll think you're crazy and take you to the basement. You think it's dark here? This doesn't even come close."

"How do you know?" I asked because I wanted to talk, I wanted to use my voice. I felt like I had been quiet forever.

"I've been there," she responded. "Trust me. You don't want to see it."

I smiled in the darkness. I wasn't alone. There was someone just like me sitting on the other side of the wall, stuck here in the dark. I got excited. There was a small hole in the wall just underneath my bunk where some of the mortar had fallen, or had been picked, away. It stretched all the way through to the other side. Later, when the solitude would crowd me like death itself come calling, I would get on my hands and knees and look through the hole. I would only be able to make out a part of a leg or a foot, but it was better than nothing. It made all the difference in the world those nights when the thought of being the only person alive took over, covering my heart and soul in blackness, devouring it.

"How long have you been here? What did you do? Where are you from?" My voice elevated a notch or two as I shot a barrage of questions at her.

"Shh, not so loud," the woman admonished. "You'll get us both in trouble."

I wanted to apologize, but I thought it might make me sound weak. Truth was, I was starting to feel that way anyway.

"My name is Angie," she said after a pause.

"Where are you from? How'd you get here?" I continued with my string of questions.

Keys jangled in the distance, growing closer every second.

"Shut your mouth now and act like you're asleep."

I did as she said and shut my eyes until the guard passed. Angie waited a minute longer before she spoke again.

"They'll be on this floor now for an hour or so. Be quiet until they leave.

Then, maybe we can talk."

"Okay," I whispered back, eager for the hour to pass. My spirits had been lifted during that short conversation, and I feared they would sink right back down again after too long.

After what seemed like forever, I heard her voice again.

"What's your name?" she asked.

I laughed bitterly and replied,

"Lucky."

It was hell. Day in and day out there was this nothingness. There isn't anything romantic about jail. The images of it portrayed on the big screen couldn't be more make believe if you colored them in hues of orange, red, and yellow. It's tough, not because of anything the guards did to us, and they did plenty, but because of the absence of independence. We got up when they told us to, ate when they said we could, went to sleep when they turned the lights off. We filled the time in the middle with our thoughts, our regrets, our desires.

I wanted sex so bad the first couple of weeks, I would have fucked the first swinging dick that gave me the eye. But none of the guards looked my way. And why would they? I looked raggedy. My hair was wild and unkempt and the nail polish I was wearing when they brought me in had chipped something awful. My face held a permanent scowl; I could feel my down-turned lips and furrowed brow burning creases in my skin. And I didn't care. What was the use? I was going to die soon anyway. What did it matter how I looked when it happened? I tried to take solace in the fact that it would all be over soon. I only hoped that, when I shut my eyes for the last time, I wouldn't see Tommy's face on the back of my eyelids. I satisfied myself and let the rest of the world be damned. They'd be rid of me soon enough.

Or so I thought.

I had been sentenced to death by electric chair for the murders of Thomas Kettering and Sharon Crawford. It was a crime of passion, impulse rather than pre-meditated, but that was splitting hairs. I was going down for their deaths no matter what fancy wording they wrote on the paperwork. Death is death and murder is murder.

I hadn't gotten my date yet, but they said I would get it soon. I didn't appeal to the courts, didn't beg for my life like so many of the poor saps in the House did. I knew I did what they were accusing me of. If I had the chance to do things differently, I could honestly say that I would do it the same way. If you told me I could avoid ever meeting Tommy, I would do everything I could to be sure we met anyhow. Tommy brought the life out of me. That my newfound sense of being took his life from him was part of the tangle that made up 'us'. It was bound to happen. You can't change what's in the cards.

Knowing that I couldn't have changed what happened didn't make it any easier. I missed the things on the outside. Drinking soda out of a cold bottle, playing Tonk with the men on my block, feeling the night air on my face, hearing the squeaking of bedsprings underneath me while I had sex; those were the things that sat on me, vexing me, pressing me until I burst. I sat in my cell remembering those things, crying at times, laughing at others. But mostly, the memories made me angry. At that point in my life, I never thought I would experience any of those things again. I was convinced of it. I was scheduled to die in the chair and soon. I wouldn't set my feet on my block ever again.

I didn't miss the people.

My mother and I didn't get along. It wasn't anything she or I did, really. It was just us. We were opposites in every sense of the word. When she said up, I said down. When I said the sky was blue, she'd swear up and down that it was red. Opposites like us didn't attract. We pushed further and further away from each other as the years dragged on. After I moved out, she went back down south bought a trailer, and set up house on land that had been in her father's family for over fifty years. I hadn't seen her in a year and had only talked to her a handful of times before I got arrested. We seemed to get along better that way, and that was fine by me. We never made the mistake of thinking we were more than what we were. She was my mother and I was her child. End of story. All the nice little frilly things in between were nonexistent for us.

I wasn't surprised when I hadn't heard from her after I went inside, even after I knew my aunt had told her about what I did. Either she was ashamed of me, or she was avoiding the issue in the hopes that it—I—would go away. It doesn't matter which was true. What mattered was that the moment I stepped into that jail cell, she considered her obligation finished. Her child was dead in her eyes. I imagined her rocking in a wooden rocking chair looking out at the vast expanse of land her trailer sat on. Beautiful country, or so my aunt told me, lush and green. I imagined the sun setting on her bronze skin as she chewed and spat tobacco into a stained mason jar. In her mind, she would be putting me to rest, picking out her dress for my burial, accepting the sympathy of the folks that lived on her old block, 'Oh, I'm sorry, Loretta. I know how special Lucky was to you.' Empty words spoken by people who feel the need to say something, anything. She'd nod and accept their kindness, no matter how forced the sentiment might be. After putting me in the ground, she'd have dinner at my aunt's house. Everybody on the block who wanted a meal would come and eat at my expense. They would talk about old times, most of which didn't include me. They would drink and take out what little bit of money they had and play poker. The shindig would end the next morning, and after everyone left, my mother would trudge off to bed, leaving the dishes in the sink for my aunt to clean. The next day, she would make her way back down to Georgia to her new house and her new friends. I would be nothing more than a picture on her wall, a child in her memory that she could tell stories about. I didn't expect anything more from my mother. She had probably written me off the moment she rode out of town.

I couldn't blame her, really.

SOMETIME IN NOVEMBER 1954

After a while, all I had were Angie and another girl in the joint named Marcel. We would talk every day, covering our faces with pillows to muffle our laughter, dangling our bodies off our beds to get closer to the holes in the walls. The guards didn't bother us too much during the day, but at night they got after us. "This ain't no social club," they would yell and beat their billy clubs against the bars. I didn't much care if they decided to beat me over the head with it one day. It would take me out of my misery. But I didn't want the other girls to suffer. So we kept quiet at night, for the most part, replaying the day's conversation in our heads until we fell asleep. If we were lucky, the banter would be enough to block out the pain. Day in and day out it was Angie and Marcel's chatter that keep me connected to the world, that kept me from filing my nails to points and clawing at my neck with them.

We talked about our lives outside and the things we missed. We reminisced about the sun shining on our faces, and the wind blowing against our backs. When we couldn't avoid it anymore, we talked about the place we found ourselves, the sempiternal nature of the time we were doing. None of us had received our dates yet, and the waiting was as bad as the notion of death itself. It lingered in front of our eyes like a treat for a dog, baiting us to cry, moan, lash out: to bite the hand that fed us. Angie and Marcel gave voice to all of the things I had been feeling since getting locked up; every sentiment they expressed mirrored my circumstance. I heard the despair in their voices and felt their hearts bleeding like my own did. We were kindred spirits, damned together on our road to perdition. We never talked about what we had done to end up there. We didn't dare speak of the indiscretions aloud, not even when we knew we were the only ones in the world who gave a damn about each other. Marcel missed her boyfriend something awful. That day was no different. She talked about him when we reminisced, building him from her memory in such detail that he was a real thing to me. The man she described was a dream, a fair-skinned, hazel-eyed angel with good hair and a goatee. Her man was a number runner, but the man in my dreams was a banker up on 125th street. He dressed in three-piece suits and wore Bucks on his feet. He kept his nails neat and wore a Stetson on his head as he walked through the busy streets in Harlem. My man lived uptown, mingling easily with the White and Black folks that neighbored his brownstone. I nurtured my dream man, adding little things as the days passed, a briefcase one day, a gold pocket watch another. He was perfect. I found myself lost in thought most nights, watching my man, whom I refused to name, walk toward me with a bouquet of blood red roses. I would be dressed in a short little black and white number that fanned out just above my knees. My hair would be pulled up in a beehive in those fantasies, my nails painted Carnival Red. I had never owned such a dress, nor done my hair in that particular style, but in my dreams I was positively regal.

Marcel told us about her guy and how he always did nice things for her. She said he bought her whatever she wanted and took her places she had never been before. She told us over and over again about their trip to Atlantic City.

"Ralph and I were on the colored side of the beach, you know, down past Pennsylvania Avenue," she always started. "He had brought a picnic basket and a blanket and set it all up when I took a dip in the water. Ooh, you should have seen my bathing suit, chile. Black with white trim, low-cut cups, thin straps," I could almost see her shaking her head, "Umph, chile, you couldn't tell me nothin'!" Marcel would laugh then, the sound filling up hers, Angie's and my cell. "Ralph used to love the way the water made my bathing suit stick to me." She would get lost in the memory then, like she always did, thinking of what Ralph said to her when she came out of the water, dripping wet. She never told us. I guess some things aren't meant to be repeated.

"The beach was so crowded, I'm surprised he had enough space!" Marcel said when she started back up. She was laughing, but this time it was a sound filled with sorrow. It was times like those when I wished the cold cinderblock walls didn't separate us.

"Anyway," she continued, "By the time I got out of the water, Ralph had set up our blanket and laid out all the food. Chile, he had turnip greens, cornbread, fried chicken, and potato salad. He said he cooked it but I know his momma's cornbread anywhere!" We would laugh at that point, no matter how many times we heard the story. For me, the laughter was more an acknowledgement of good times, of life on the outside. It felt good coming up from my chest and through my throat. I felt human again. "Frank Sinatra was on the bill at the Steel Pier that day," she'd finish. She never said if she got the chance to see him, but we all knew she hadn't. The Steel Pier wasn't a place Blacks could go back then. I look at it now and wonder what the big deal was. The whole thing is nothing more than a rickety old fishing pier with splintering wood that is covered with bird shit. It looks nothing like it did back then, with a carnival on one end, a makeshift stage in the center where headliners performed, and a low-scale circus at the mouth of beach. The pier was always dotted with well-dressed onlookers waiting for a glimpse of the dancing bear or groupies waiting to see their favorite star. But not anymore. Now it's just a forgotten piece of history, left to rot in the salty breeze. The last time I was there, I wondered how it was still standing.

I heard Marcel sniffle before she spoke again. My own cheeks were wet from the tears streaming down my face. Why did I cry when Marcel told that story? I've always wondered about that. Maybe I wasn't crying for her at all.

"What about you, Lucky? What do you miss most about the outside?" Even though Marcel's voice sounded faint coming through cinderblock walls, the question rang loudly in my head. My mind brought Tommy's face into view in brilliant color. His beautiful smile and his appealing body flooded my head. I blinked trying to wash him away as fast as the thought appeared in my mind. His image still haunted my dreams, sometimes seeming to stand in the cell with me at night under the cover of the shadows. To think of him no longer brought anger, remorse, sadness, or loss. It brought only fear. His would be the last face I would see before my death, I was sure of it, and the thought frightened me more than death itself. That he might be waiting for me on the other side to exact his revenge was the only thing that scared me more. I never told the girls about that, never mentioned that the ghost of my dead lover was coming to visit me at night. I didn't want them to think I was crazy, or that I was losing my grip. Even though I was.

"What do I miss most?" I said. "Getting laid."

The girls laughed as they always did, my admission touching upon their own desires. I answered that way to any variety of questions—"If you were on the outside, what would you be doing right now?" "If you could do anything you wanted on your last day, what would it be?" It was an easy answer, one that didn't require me to tell more than I wanted to. And it was true. I did miss getting laid, feeling a strong body on top of mine, moving in tandem with me. The release. I gave myself satisfaction many times while in the joint, but it never felt the way sex did. So I wasn't lying to them when I said I missed it. I just didn't admit that the sex I missed, and the body I craved belonged to Tommy.

After the laughter died down, I asked Angie what she missed. My question was met with uncharacteristic silence. Angie usually had a fantastical story to tell. She spoke of places Marcel and I had never heard of, foreign lands we would never see. Sometimes I thought she was making it all up, just to come up with something that sounded good. Other times I thought she was crazy. She sounded so sure, like she really had seen the Colosseum in Rome, or the pyramids at Giza instead of just reading about them in books. Her descriptions made me feel like I was there too, standing in the bowels of the ancient building, the smell of sweat and fear still lingering in the air of the gladiators' chambers, the tangy stench forever sealed in the walls, or in the sweltering desert, the hot sand burning my sandaled feet I didn't know for sure whether she had been to the places she described or not, but I loved listening to her. Her stories told took my mind off my troubles for a while.

"Angie?" I called out to her again, but she still didn't answer. "Angie, did you hear me?"

"I heard you. I just don't have anything to say is all," she said, her voice sounding low and muffled.

"Oh c'mon! You? You always have a story for us! C'mon, tell us about Paris or Rome, Egypt. Anywhere. I know you must miss something from those places." I was pushing. I needed something to tide me over for the night, to occupy my thoughts. That way, maybe Tommy's ghost wouldn't be able to get in my head and torture me.

"I told you, I don't have anything to say!" Angie's voice was forceful and full of anger. I could hear her turning over on the mattress in the other room. I imagined her pressing her face into her pillow and shutting herself away from me. I recoiled, my feelings suddenly bruised.

"Angie, I'm sorry, I—."

"If you all can't play nice, you won't be able to play at all," the guard called out, cutting off my apology mid sentence. I bit my lip nervously. I didn't want Angie to be mad at me. The thought of our afternoon talks going away sent a chill down my spine.

"All right Angie, you can tell us something tomorrow. We'll talk about anything you want, okay?" Marcel said, trying to smooth things over.

Silence.

"Let's leave Angie alone, okay Lucky? Enough's enough anyway, huh?" Marcel said to me, her voice thick with an emotion I couldn't place.

I mumbled my agreement and turned away from the wall. We didn't speak again that day. After I ate the stale leftovers they called a meal, I settled in for the night, willing myself to sleep. I let my mind fill with thoughts of my fantasy man, shut my eyes to my cell, and opened them to a plush bedroom with cream-colored walls and soft bedding. My hand slid into my pants as I saw my man approaching me with flowers in one hand and his dick in the other. I only envisioned it severed, sitting limp in his bloody hand, for a second.

I heard Angie crying in her cell later that night. I'm sure most of the girls in our cellblock did. It was a horrible sound, loud and deep. The kind of sound a wounded animal might make in the wild.

46

It was cold in The Death House that night, the kind of cold that goes through into your body and resonates there, never warming to body temperature. When I woke up, my jaw was clenched so tightly, I wondered how my teeth held up against the pressure. Even through the cold, I was happy to be awake. I had been dreaming that they had just told me my date. June 23, 1955. It's funny how the faces, the room we were sitting in, the color of the suits the men wore, and most of the other details in the dream had faded away, had been embedded in my memory, hidden only to be recalled in the most abstract of ways. But the date was there, bold and unmistakable. June 23, 1955. Even in my dream, I knew how long that meant I had left. Somehow, in my slumber, I knew it was November. Maybe the tree outside the window of the courthouse they sentenced me in was bare and I caught a glimpse of it, maybe I could feel the chill in the room that seemed to crawl into my skin to settle on my bones, making them ache. I don't know. But somehow I knew it wasn't just winter. It was November. That gave me seven months. Seven months to live, to prepare for death, to make my peace. Seven months until I would always and forever be gone from this earth, gone from my body. Gone to where? It was a question I often wondered about. Was there a Heaven, a God waiting for me to run into His arms? If there was such a place and such a being, would they accept me, a murderer? Even though I never said anything to the girls, I was just as afraid of meeting my maker as the next person. Sometimes I cried in my confusion, begging for an answer. Other times I threw my hands in the air, leaving my fate to whatever laid ahead. That fear made me nervous, paranoid, afraid of anyone coming toward my cell, of their footfalls bringing them closer, ever closer. Getting the date, the finality of it, terrified me more than anything else. I knew I was going to die, but so did everyone else in the world. It's only when you know the exact time that mortality becomes real, even in a place like Raskin Correctional. Waking up in the dead of night to the sound of Angie's anguish, made me wonder what would happen to me after death as I had so many other nights. My mind filled with images of the afterlife, from what would happen to my body to what would happen to my soul. I saw myself laying still in the ground, surrounded by the walls of a plain pine box. Bugs would get in with ease, dropping from mis-fitted seams, eating away at the soft wood. In my mind's eye, I saw them pulling at my body, penetrating me through unused orifices to squirm within me, eating my flesh, laying their eggs. Bile rose in my throat as I imagined spiders crawling over my skin and maggots writhing just beneath the surface, inside me. I saw flies and worms moving in and out of me at will, my body like road kill sweltering in the summer heat. Then suddenly, the image was gone. What replaced it was a nothingness so profound, I wanted to cry for release. My body was gone, my physical existence reduced to nothing more than mere wisps of smoke floating in the air. The place was as nondescript as the vastness of space, the backdrop black and unadorned. I was in limbo, alone. The solitude, the very silence of the place seemed unbearably loud. I screamed, a soundless action that emitted from an unformed mouth into a still atmosphere. My soul felt as though it was bleeding from a mortal wound. From above me, below me, all around, an answer to the question of life after death was whispered. It was a presence felt rather than seen, yet my soul grabbed onto it like flesh upon flesh. My soul surged toward the sound of lips parting, of saliva lubricating a tongue in preparation of speech. I was eager to hear a voice, eager to share my lonely world. To my horror, my murdered lover's voice, as smooth as it had been in life, whispered, "Death is only the beginning."

The guard came by and banged his nightstick against the bars a couple of times, telling Angie to shut up unless she wanted to spend a night in the hole, but she ignored the warning and kept on crying. No one came to take her away. They probably felt pity for her the way most of us girls did. Anyone who cried like that was hurting something awful. That might have been part of the reason they kept away, but not all of it. I think they might have been afraid of Angie. A person with that much pain inside them is liable to do anything to anyone. Angie sounded like she had been to Hell and back and didn't care who she took with her on her next trip.

"Angie, what's the matter with you?" Marcel whispered urgently. "Girl, if you don't shut up they 'gon give you somethin' to cry about."

Angie kept sobbing, wailing sometimes, as though a knife pressed against her skin, the tip of the blade breaking through and drawing blood.

"Angie! Quiet down before they put you in the hole for sure."

"I couldn't go to them," she screamed, her voice distraught and rough from sleep. "I wasn't there when my mother died, yet I heard my name escape her lips with her last breath. I had to leave forever or I'd hear her cry every night from the grave."

"You talking crazy, girl," Marcel whispered. "Shut up now before the guards shut you up with that billy club."

I could hear the fear in Marcel's voice as she admonished Angie. I felt fear in my heart too. I always did when Angie talked like that. Her words made my skin crawl.

Angie kept crying and moaning. I imagined her, this faceless woman, rocking on her bed with sweat dripping down her brow. I felt for her then as I did many other times during our stay in the house. The story she told that night is one of many that tug at my heart to this day.

"My first night on the other side, I went back to my mother's house," Angie started. I'm almost ashamed to say this, but I settled in to listen just like I used to when I was on the outside and skits played on the radio. I nestled closer into the thin bed covers and pressed my ear closer to the wall.

"I had to see them one more time," Angie continued, emotion threatening to take over her voice with sobs. "I knew I could never go home, that I could never be a part of the family the way I once was. Things were different. I was gone to them forever and them to me.

"I walked up the dirt road from the cemetery to my house in the shadows. My white dress gleamed in the dark so brightly I thought of stripping myself naked to keep hidden. But it was late, after midnight, and no one in my village would be awake at such a late hour, let alone be on the road.

"When I reached my house I was shocked to see that the lantern was on in the front room. I crouched in the bushes that rimmed the yard so they wouldn't see me. My vision was keen, much sharper than it had been when I was alive, so I could see them from that distance as clearly as I see my hand in front of my face now. My mother and sister were sitting in the room, both of them staring off in the distance at some unknown sight. I could see the back of my mother's head, could tell that she was nodding absently. I could hear the song she was humming as she tried to soothe her nerves. My younger sister Oni was crying. I could see her tears gleaming like crystals on her cheeks. How I wanted to take their pain, their sorrow, and cast it away. They were broken and I knew then that they would never be the way they were before this terrible thing happened. But there was nothing I could do to help them. It was for me that they spent their tears."

Angie was silent for a while before continuing. The pause gave me time to reconsider the question perched on my tongue. When she started to speak again, her voice was choked with emotion.

"I wanted to leave, to run away from the house where I had grown up, and never return. I caused them the suffering, the pain they were embroiled in. My death was the reason for it all. But I couldn't leave. I was rooted in place by some force beyond my control. I tried to shut my eyes to them as they sat in our small front room, but I could not. I couldn't shake it, the entity that paralyzed me. I couldn't budge. I was forced to stay there. To watch them.

"I fidgeted, tried to calm my shaking hands by wringing them and clenching and unclenching my fists. Nothing worked. I didn't want to be there, standing outside of my house like a stranger. It made the truth all too powerful, too real. I was gone to them. I was a stranger to the world they lived in because I was among the dead.

"My sister rose onto the balls of her feet suddenly, all the while peering out into the darkness of which I had become a part.

"'A fon?' (*Hello?*) she asked, drawing closer and closer to the window. I unglued my feet and moved to my right, ducking behind the bushes skirting the plot of land where the house stood, squatting deeper, closer to the ground. She was in front of the window then, sticking her head out of it and craning her neck around the corner.

"'Me we?' (*Who is it?*) she called into the night. I covered my mouth with my hand, the urge to answer her mounting. But I couldn't answer. I knew I shouldn't.

"'Zaji?' she called. To hear my name spoken with such sweetness again, to hear it dip and crest in the wind, was magical. I felt like crying. I wanted to sit down and weep loudly, mourning myself, but I could not. My tear ducts were dry, my eyeballs no more moist than the dew-laden leaf that lay upon the ground before me.

"'Zaji,' my sister called again, this time her voice breaking under the weight of the pain she tried to suppress.

"My mother rose from where she sat and turned to Oni. I could see the pain in her eyes as she spoke to her. The fact that I could both see and hear them as though I stood in the room with them struck me as odd, such a phenomenal spite, but there was no room for contemplating that then. I had to focus on remaining hidden from them. They could not see me, could never lay their eyes upon what I had become.

"'Eho, viche. E' ku.' (*No, child. She is dead.*) My mother spoke with such anguish I thought I might collapse. My heart leapt out to her. With a sigh, she said, 'Oni, vlavo nu ci ko nu we. Ete wutu a no yi mlayin à?' (*Oni, maybe you are tired. Why don't you go to bed?*)

"'Eho!' (*No!*) Oni raised her voice in exasperation, something rarely done in our home and never done by a child. But my mother ignored it, choosing instead to follow my sister's finger as she pointed out of the window toward the spot where I was hiding.

"'Mo fine?' (*See over there?*) she exclaimed, her voice a mixture of panic and sorrow. 'Mama, nuviche jawe. Mawu! E gosin kutome!' (*Mother, my sister is coming! My God! She returns from the grave!*)

"I could see my mother peering out into the night, looking for something, anything that might have caused Oni's outburst. She looked past the two boulders that marked the end of our land, over the makeshift fence my father had put up to keep the chickens in, but saw nothing. She was about to turn away when a cloud shifted, fully exposing the moon. Its light glinted off my eyes for only a second, but that was long enough for her to see me. My body froze in place.

"My mother's eyes widened when she saw me. My sister had begun to cry again, finally giving into the grief that engulfed her. When the moon revealed my countenance to her, she screamed. It was a most piercing sound. I felt as if my head might split in two from the pitch of it. Oni's screams subsided into venomous words spilling from her mouth in torrents,

"'Asiman! Asiman!' Vampire. To hear her call me by my name, for her to give voice to the craving within me, the inhuman longing that I felt tugging at my insides even as I stood before my family, scarred me like nothing before had. I cringed, curling within myself as she repeated it over and over again. With every repetition I hated her more. With every pause I forgave her.

"'Ete wutu a do fi?' (*Why are you here?*) Oni asked, her voice belligerent and raw. 'Bo yi! Ton sin houe tchegbe! We o a ku!' (*Get out of here! Leave my house! You are dead!*)

"'Dedeme,' (*Calm down*) my mother said to Oni in the quietest of whispers. My sister's chest was heaving from fright.

"'Ete wutu e' do fi?' (*Why is she here?*) Oni asked. Her voice was shrill.

"'Un tuun a,' (*I don't know*) my mother replied. Her eyes were wide with fright.

"'Un do hessi de ne we,' (*I am afraid of her*) my sister said, her voice taking on a whining quality that I had never heard from her before. Mother could only nod at her, unable to come up with words to console her only living daughter.

"Mother motioned for Oni to leave the room, to leave her alone to talk to me. Oni nodded and ran out of the room, bursting into the most terrible sobbing. I wished I had never come back to them. They would have been spared such pain.

"Mother walked out of the house and into the dirt yard in front of the window. A night breeze caught her gown and swirled it around her ankles. I felt such sorrow then, looking at her. She was the same yet different. She looked as though she had aged since I laid my mortal eyes upon her only days earlier. Her skin was creased around her eyes where there had once been smooth skin. The lines of worry etched into her forehead were deeper and wider than they had appeared before. She looked tired. Weary.

"Mother was silent for a long time. I remained crouched behind the bushes. I didn't want to show my face, my paled skin, my eyes wild with hunger. I wanted to spare her that visage.

"When she finally spoke, her voice was strong and controlled. I felt young again hearing her speak to me, like a girl of ten or twelve being reprimanded for lingering too long at the well.

"'Zaji,' she said taking in a deep breath, 'Un mo we, yokbova. Assi hounwla do sun a. Wã.' (*I see you, girl. You can't hide from the moon. Come here.*) Even though she beckoned me to come, I stayed where I was.

"'Ete ba a di?' (*What are you looking for?*) she asked after a long silence. 'Doho nu non towe!' (*Speak to your mother!*) Still I did not speak. There was something wrong, something evil about responding to her, though my heart wanted to. I had already mixed the living with the dead by going there. I didn't want to mix the two any further.

"Mother stood looking at me in the bushes, seeing but not seeing, sensing my presence. More in sorrow than in fear, she whispered, "'Asiman.'

"The very word turned the blood that stood stagnant in my dead veins cold and drew a gasp from me that was all but imperceptible in the night. But my mother heard it and the sound drew fresh tears from her swollen eyes. To hear the word spoken again in my mother's rich alto made me ill. The word was ancient in people's tongue, but its definition was precise. It named my sickness, one that was beyond the cures of mortal medicine or prayer. It was the discontent of the afterlife, the disgust of my being that tormented me, springing to from the whisper on her lips.

"She knew what I had become, had known it since she came into my room to find me dead, my skin still warm. She hadn't allowed my father and the men of the village to carry my body to the pyre to burn as was the tradition of my people. They questioned her decision to bury me in the ground next to the wanderers and outcasts: the forgotten. She told them that it was what she wanted and they let her word stand. A mother's wish was not to be unheeded, especially when a child died pure. My mother knew that to be untrue as well. She checked me before dressing me in my burial dress, her eyes watering with tears of shame at my wantonness.

"She knew I was undead, that I had been touched by evil and made to walk the earth for eternity. She knew. And still she prepared me for an earthly grave, knowing well that I would not rest there. Some part of her must have believed I might come back, that she might see my face again, even if it was reanimated and twisted. That possibility was too enticing to ignore, even knowing what I would do, who I would be, once I was reborn.

"I cried for my mother, for the decision she made against tradition, against the Gods. She would have been killed for not turning me over to the men folk if anyone ever found out. The punishment of an afterlife as an *asiman*, a bloodsucker and killer of men, women, and children alike was only bestowed upon those who killed themselves, snuffed out their life to spite the Gods as punishment for their sins. The people in my village chose to believe that was the only way, even though witches could make zombies out of men, controlling their bodies after death to do their bidding, even though our ancestors had entertained the idea that a select few were born *asiman*, like it was some incurable disease. Even when they saw the demon for themselves, traveling by water under the cover of night, the fog that concealed it glowing with a beautiful yellow light, they ignored the evil that dwelled among them. And had for centuries. The people tossed aside what they saw with their own eyes and prayed to the Orisha to watch over them. They made grand offerings of fire-grilled meat and vegetables on tables draped with green and red cloths to appeal to Legba the day after an appearance of the unexplained, asking that he open the gate to the loas and that he interpret the information the loas gave in return. They offered goat meat to Sobo Kessou so that he would protect them from harm. They sacrificed a hen and cock to Dumballah in the hopes that he would deliver an explanation of the occurrence, no matter how cryptic the message. They did all of those things to gain closure to the event that had shaken them.

Sometime in November 1954

They prayed to their gods for protection and guidance and closed their eyes to what they saw. They believed what they perceived as answered and did as they were told because to defy the gods was to slit one's own throat. It was a way of life for them. The only way of life. I knew that I had to disappear if I wanted to keep my mother from the pain she would surely feel for her blasphemy. For her protection.

"Her sobs called out to me, floating gently on the silence of the night, as though carried by the air. She beckoned me to answer her several times, but I remained silent. I was too afraid to show myself to her, to allow myself to see her in full view. We were no longer mother and daughter. Now she was prey that could easily be taken in the quiet of night. I could never live with myself if I succumbed to the hunger that dwelled within me.

"She repeated the word once more, the loss weighing on her voice so heavily, she would not have been heard had I not been so close.

"'Asiman.'

"The folklore of our people talked about the *asiman*. The Elders of the village told the children stories about it for a good fright, but they did not understand it. Sometimes a chicken thief, sometimes a spook, most times one who stalked the infirm and dying, the asiman was never completely described, its powers never explored. I laugh inside now when I remember the descriptions I heard as a child, at the naiveté of the people passing the story down from generation to generation. Their tales of woe, meant to keep children close to home before puberty and pure afterward, never talked of the desire for human flesh the *asiman* had, from the frail or firm—whichever. They never talked about the newfound agility or the magnified senses they possessed, the taste for living blood. No one was safe from the creature of the night that I had become. I was neither witch nor beast of the night. I had become a devil.

"After several minutes had passed Mother said, 'Edabo viche. Fifa na noxa mi.' (*Goodbye child. May peace be with you.*) Tears fell from her eyes as she walked back toward the door of our house, a place that I would never again enter. Before going inside she turned back to where I crouched in the bushes, kissed her hand, blew a precious kiss, and said, 'Un nyi wa nu we.'"

(*I love you.*)

Angie's words sounded like gibberish to me, as they always did when she talked in those strange languages she used every once in a while. I had learned the difference between French and Spanish, Kreyol and Italian by then. Angie used those languages on days when she felt carefree. She took pleasure in translating it for us, in trying to teach us words. Fon, the language of her people, was one she only used when she was feeling down. It was the language she used that night.

There was another language she spoke every once in a while. She called it Papiamento. She said it was a mix of many languages like Spanish, Dutch, and Kreyol. Marcel told her it sounded made up. I thought the same thing. Angie laughed at her but the sound wasn't mean the way the guards sounded when they laughed. It was full of joy. I don't think I had ever heard her laugh that way before. I only heard her laugh that way one other time, but I'll get into that later. Angie said that White people in the Caribbean spoke Papiamento too, and that it was a language that slaves made up to speak to each other when their tribes were mixed on the ships and on the plantation. Marcel asked her how she knew so much about it, but Angie didn't answer that day. When she did answer, I didn't believe her. Not in my heart, at least not for a long time. But now I have no choice but to believe what she said, to know what she had been talking about the whole time was true. Now I live the life that she had long ago.

Angie's voice sounded dull and lifeless when she spoke those last words on that cold November night. She said, in an eerily monotone voice that sounded miles away, "That was the last time I saw my mother alive."

Marcel whispered, "I'm sorry, Angie," but there was no response. Marcel kept at her, asking questions about what happened to them, if she ever saw her sister again, how long ago all of it happened, but Angie ignored her. The only sound that came from her cell was the rustling of covers as she turned her back to the wall.

I struggled to go to sleep, but Angie's story kept coming back to me. Had Angie said she was dead? I felt like my mind was playing tricks on me. I couldn't have heard what I thought I heard. Marcel didn't seem to hear the same thing—for all of her questions, she didn't ask about that. I wished I could have spoken to Marcel without Angie hearing, just to be sure.

The next morning Angie apologized for causing a ruckus. I breathed a sigh of relief—I wanted to talk about the night before, wanted to ask more questions, but I was afraid Angie wouldn't be in the mood to talk. I was glad she was. We asked her where her people were from, trying to get her to start from the beginning. When she named her homeland none of us knew what she was talking about.

"Dahomey," she said, her voice sounding dreamy and far away. "My village isn't far from the shores of the Gulf of Guinea."

Her voice was met with silence. After a while, Marcel spoke with humility, "I ain't educated like you Angie, and I don't know the places like you know. Where is this Dahomey you're talking about?"

I pressed my ear to the wall, straining to hear her answer. I wanted to know as much as Marcel did. It sounded mystical, some far away place where the people were Black and proud and educated.

Angie answered, sorrow replacing whatever emotion had risen before. "It's a place I will never see again. It's so far from here that you can't see it from any shore. Dahomey is so foreign to me now that I should be damned to speak its name."

Angie turned over then and didn't speak again for the rest of the day. Marcel and I never did find out where Dahomey was but it stuck in our minds. Marcel talked about it in the days between hers and Angie's death. She would whisper to me,

"Did you hear her say it, Lucky? Dahomey, that's where she said her home was." I would mumble my response to her, but I couldn't do much else in those days. My number was coming up a week after Marcel's was due and I was preoccupied with it. First Angie, then Marcel, then me, all within three weeks of each other. I was supposed to check out on June 23rd. Just like the dream said. If only I had been that lucky on the outside. I could have hit the number and made a fortune.

I was taking it hard and had withdrawn into myself, shutting everyone and everything else out. It was also around the time that I started having the strange thoughts that led me to this point. I would hear Angie's name spoken over and over in my head. Not always in my voice either. Sometimes it was spoken by male voices of varying pitches, deep baritones and rich tenors, sometimes in her voice. I didn't mind it at first. In fact, I thought it was my way of not forgetting her. I had always loved her names: Zaji and Angelique. Back then I didn't know what it meant. The voices were soothing at first, their incessant repetition comforting. But then it changed. The voices took on a haunting cadence; they became scary in a way that not much else had ever been to me. Now I only wish I had pushed the voices out of my head, had denied them entry into me. Maybe if I had, I wouldn't be in the position I find myself in now.

The day before Marcel died they took her out of her cell and into another section of The Death House called the Rest Room, her last stop before execution. When they were taking her away she passed by my cell. I stood to say goodbye to my friend, to a woman who I had never laid eyes on before. Marcel was a short, fair-skinned woman with a plump body. Her hair was long and matted like a Rastafarian's dreadlocks, dark brown at the root and Lucille Ball red mid-strand to the end. She offered a weak smile revealing the wide gap in the front of her mouth. "Lucky," she said as the guard tugged her away, "find out where Dahomey is, hear?"

I just looked at Marcel, shocked by the words she spoke. I didn't know Angie's stories had affected her the way they had affected me. I nodded my head at her, never uttering a sound as my friend was led off the cellblock to the Rest Room, to her death. I wonder sometimes if she knew how much I hated to see her go.

JANUARY 27, 1955

That day is as clear to me as if it was happening now. Maybe that's because of my mind and its ability to play my memories back like movies on a picture screen. Everything about my life before the change is clear to me, whether I want it to be or not. Since that night I've had my own dream, a mirror of the one that woke Angie up screaming in her sleep. It caused the same reaction in me. I found myself covered in sweat and sitting up as straight as a board in the middle of my bed the night I had it. That was just before he came to me. I can't shake the memories of those last days of normalcy, those last days of being the Lucky I used to be. If God wanted to show me mercy, He'd wipe those memories from my mind, clear them away. But this doesn't have anything to do with God, does it?

It was barely morning when Angie woke up, yelling in her strange language. It was becoming a common occurrence, Angie screaming in the night, so most of the girls didn't bother to react. Her voice was wild and shrill. She sounded like she was speaking in tongues, not because I couldn't understand her words but because her voice was so primal. The springs in my thin mattress squeaked as I sat up. Squinting in the darkness of my cell, I wondered how many more nights I'd be awakened by the sound of Angie's screams.

"Bo yi, dèmon! A na ze vice ã!" (*Get out of here devil! You will not take my child!*) she screamed. The rustling of the covers made it sound like she was striking out against something, trying to fight the thing in her dreams.

"Angie, what's the matter?" Marcel asked, whispering so that the guards wouldn't hear her talking.

Angie went on hollering, sometimes in English, sometimes in Fon. She was starting to calm down when the guard knocked his billy club on the bars to her cell and said, "You better shut that noise up darky, or I'll have to come in there and shut you up. Is that what you want?"

Angie didn't say anything to the guard. I imagine she just looked at him, daring him with her eyes. That seemed to be the type of woman she was. She didn't put up with anybody's shit.

"She's okay," Marcel piped up, trying to save Angie from a beating or worse. "She just had a bad dream."

There was an uncomfortable silence. The guard was probably glaring at Angie through the bars, daring her to say something. Satisfied by her silence, the guard walked away, throwing a warning over his shoulder, "You bitches better shut your mouths, or come morning you'll find yourselves without your Thursday privileges."

Marcel uttered a weak, "Yes sir." The guards always threatened to take away Thursday privileges: visitation, letter pick up, laundry pick up. They'd say anything—do anything—to keep us in line.

Marcel waited a minute or two before speaking again, trying to give the guard time to get out of earshot. I pinned myself as close to the wall as I could so that I could hear them talking, as I always did. I don't know why Angie interested me so, but she did. I wish she hadn't, though I'm not sure it would have mattered either way.

"What's the matter Angie?" Marcel started. "You have a bad dream or something?"
Silence.
"You must have," she continued. "You were speaking that language again, the one you only talk when you're feelin' the blues. What's the matter?"
Still nothing.
Marcel chuckled uneasily and said, "C'mon Angie. You can tell me. After all, it was only a dream. It might do you some good to get it off your chest, huh? C'mon, tell me what happened."
I didn't think Angie was going to respond, she waited so long to say anything. I could hear Marcel shift on her mattress. It sounded like she was scooting back down into the flimsy covers we had, getting ready to go back to sleep, giving up. But then, after a minute or two of complete silence, Angie said something, her voice filled with a dread so thick, I felt it creeping along my bones, strumming them like icy fingers.
"He's gonna find my boy. He's going after him."

"What boy? Who's going after him? What are you talking about?" Marcel asked as she sat up. Her voice was louder than she meant it to be.

Angie paused, the halt almost tangible in the dark. The silence was killing me.

"My son."

My mind reeled. Marcel peppered Angie with questions, shooting them one after the other in rapid succession, but I didn't hear any of them. The phrase just kept repeating itself over and over in my head. I didn't know why then, but I do now. It was his way of making me see, making me hear, making me remember.

"Angie, it was just a dream. Nobody's after anybody. It was just a nightmare," I heard Marcel say when my head cleared.

"It wasn't. I saw it."

Marcel sighed just loud enough for us to hear her. I imagined that she was shaking her head. "You're not making any sense, honey," she said, pity lacing her voice. Marcel was genuinely concerned, bless her heart.

"I know it's true. Marcel. He showed me. God damn him, he showed me!"

I'll never forget the dream she laid out for us, the way she painted the scenery with a trained, steady hand. It was so vivid and horrifying, so incredibly real. She described a scene so terrifying the image emblazoned itself on my mind, revisiting me when I least expected it.

In her dream, the day was so bright it was nearly colorless. The sun sat high in the afternoon sky, white clouds melted into the cerulean backdrop that had been muted by the sun's brilliance. Only the faintest of color could be seen. Just the hint of blue, powdery and light, bleached of its rich hue, colored the landscape and added a hint of depth in an otherwise flat sky. Jared and Stephanie traveled along the road. As Stephanie gazed out of the passenger window of the SUV her husband was driving, she daydreamed of a bustling young boy, no older than five, kicking a soccer ball in plush, green grass. Her mind strayed to images of Golden Retrievers, two of them, running beside an older boy of eight or nine, as he sprinted on the concrete path, racing them to the finish line that was the edge of the neighbor's driveway. A smile formed on her lips and her hand absently caressed her protruding belly. It would only be one more month before she laid eyes on her son's face. Her mind repeated the timeline in her head, her inner voice sounding singsongy to her ears. *One more month, my love. Only one more month.*

Jared's eyes stayed on the road. He didn't notice how at peace his wife looked as she fantasized about the future, the look of her son, his hair, his smile. Stephanie had begun to wonder how tall he would be, whom he would resemble more. Jared's father was a tall man with broad shoulders and complimentary girth to accent his six foot two inch frame. Jared took after his mother's side of the family though, with his short legs and penchant for Italian food. She turned her head and smiled wide at Jared's muscular arm propped on the base of the driver side window. Her eyes scanned his body and she nodded her approval. Jared loved to eat pasta—fettuccine alfredo and ricotta and herb-filled ravioli topped his list, alongside lasagna and manicotti—but he loved to sculpt his body too, and he worked hard at perfecting it. Jared spent five nights a week in the gym, and a half hour of every night on the floor beside their bed doing crunches and leg lifts. His breathing would increase in the thirty minutes he spent working his abdominal muscles, and by the time he slid under the covers with her, the panting—the hot, desperate sound of it— would make her stomach quiver, as it always did. Stephanie's eyes cascaded over his chest and arms, thinking of their child's chest, wiry and flat at first, but then growing into that of his father's when he hit his early twenties. How the girls will love him, she mused. They'll trip over each other to be with him. Much like she had with Jared.

Motion stirred in her stomach beneath Stephanie's gentle caress. She stilled her hand on top of it, feeling her child move inside her. She shut her eyes, speaking to him, feeling him. *Hush little baby, don't you cry…*

"We'll be there in no time," Jared said, not looking away from the road. "I know Mom's looking forward to seeing us."

"Maybe she can help us decide on a name," Stephanie added.

"David is nice. Or Michael. Good traditional names, I guess," Jared offered.

"I don't know," Stephanie sighed. "I was thinking about Jared. Jared Christopher… Junior," she sang, a smile forming on her lips and seeping into the lilt in her voice.

Jared beamed. A junior. He had wanted one, but didn't know it until Stephanie rejected the idea months before. "I want our child to have his own identity. I don't want him to have to live under the pressure of being your junior," she said then. "I want him to do what he wants to in life, and not feel like he has to fill someone else's shoes." Before then, before she had reacted negatively to the idea of it, Jared hadn't given the naming process much thought. Before they found out that Stephanie was pregnant Jared hadn't thought much about children in general. Sure, he and Stephanie had talked about having kids before they got married five years before, and yes, he said he wanted them. But what he meant was that he wanted them at some point in the future. The distant future. There was no place for children in his life yet, at least he hadn't thought there was. It was full enough already, stacking work on top of going to the gym, and enjoying married life. He and Stephanie enjoyed each other's company more than most people did in their marriage. They were always together. On the weekends they could be found at the movies, the beach, on an impromptu trip to the Caribbean, anywhere. During the week they typically cuddled up on the sofa and watched a movie snuggling in each other's arms. He liked his life the way it was and didn't want it to change. No encumbrances, no strings. It wasn't that he didn't want kids. He just didn't want them any time soon.

But then Stephanie got pregnant. Life changed in that instant, that semi-second of time when his overactive sperm took it upon itself to swim and swim and swim until it found her egg, penetrated it, and created a life. He was numb.

It took a while for him to grasp the idea that he was going to be a father. In that time he mourned the loss of his carefree, answering to no one lifestyle and embraced the concept of parenthood. It wasn't the same as caring for a pet. It was different. A living, breathing product of the two of them would enter the world in eight months (Stephanie was six weeks pregnant when she told him). The baby would look to them for sustenance, for understanding, for love. It would mimic them to learn, would develop oratory skills at their instruction, would learn to reason at their insistence. The child's very being, its sense of self and place, would be molded by them. The magnitude of the job was staggering.

Yet, Jared didn't sway under the pressure. Instead, he felt it build within him, lifting him up. It straightened his back and made him hold his head high. He was about to embark on the most substantial role in his life. He was about to be a father.

So when Jared and Stephanie discussed the naming of his son, he mentioned the prospect of having a junior, offhandedly, at first. But the desire grew in him with every second she hesitated, forming her answer in her mind before uttering a sound. He felt deflated when she said, in effect, no. Over the months he willed the desire away, pushing it down in his subconscious never to be mentioned again. And it had worked. He'd forgotten about it until then, when Stephanie mentioned it from the passenger seat of their SUV on that inordinately clear spring day. Mostly.

"What? I thought you didn't want a junior? Individuality, and all of the other stuff you mentioned." He couldn't keep the giddiness he felt out of his voice.

"Well, I was thinking about the whole naming thing and why it's so important. I wanted to make sure our son had a strong name. A name that he could take pride in. It's the one thing we can give him that will be his forever and I want it to be special. What better name to give him than his father's?"

Jared's smile was genuine. He reached over to hold Stephanie's hand. She put his hand on her belly so he could feel his son, his junior, kick against it. His rich laughter filled the car as he relished in his son's movement.

He said, his voice full of pride, "I think he likes his name."

Charlie's engine light came on as he switched lanes. The car had already been sluggish, laboring so hard, he thought he could hear it straining. He had been trying to make his way over to the next exit when the indicator light lit up on his dashboard.

"Shit," Charlie said and banged his hand against the steering wheel. Traffic was moving steadily making it difficult for him to move from the middle lane into the one on the far right. The car was slowing down, going much slower than Charlie wanted to go, much slower than the law allowed. He was afraid that if the car stopped, the engine would never turn over again.

"Come on, baby," he begged the aging Buick Regal as he led its nose into the next lane, waiting for his opportunity to move over. Charlie felt it before it happened. He could tell the engine would die by the sudden smoothness of the ride. The tires seemed to glide on air instead of on cracked asphalt. He couldn't feel the grooves in the road anymore, or the tension in the steering wheel. He was riding on a cloud. Charlie jerked forward when the car stopped abruptly, the nose far enough in the right lane to tie up traffic. The keys on his key ring clanked together as they collided against the steering wheel column. Sighing, Charlie grabbed at them, his fingers curling around the one in the ignition. He turned the key. The raspy whine of the starter filled his ears as the gear stood motionless, unwilling to engage. He tried again, pumping the gas pedal this time, urging the old girl to start up, to turn over for daddy just one more time. Nothing.

"Shit!" he yelled in the empty car and released the key reluctantly. The engine was dead. He turned on his hazard lights and looked sullenly at the cars speeding past him. He jumped out of the Regal during a break in traffic and lifted the hood. It was only for show though. Charlie had never been all that handy when it came to cars. He looked at the innards of the car but the radiator, spark plugs, belts, and hoses all seemed to run together to him. The only thing he could readily identify was the engine block, and that was only because of its size. Charlie leaned closer, the raised hood shading him from the high sun. He thought about jiggling one of the hoses coming from the engine, had actually extended his hand toward one, but thought better of it. It could have been connected to any number of things, none of which he knew how to fix if he broke it. It would be like banging the side of a snowy television set: it might work, but who knew what kind of internal damage the quick fix would cause. Returning his hand to the side of the car, Charlie shook his head and, not for the first time, cursed himself for not paying more attention when his brother tried to teach him the tools of his trade. *Walt would know how to fix this*, he thought bitterly and slapped his hand against the car's side panel.

Jared turned to look at Stephanie. Her face, backlit by the sun, was soft and beautiful. She was radiant. Her skin was resplendent with a glow known only to expectant mothers. She was dozing; the licks of Charles Fambrough's upright bass mixed with the gentle rocking of the drive had lulled her to sleep. Jared loved looking at Stephanie when she was unaware of his adoring eyes. Wisps of hair fell in her face, pulling away from the upswept ponytail she often wore. It softened her features, rounded them, showcased the shape of her eyes. She looked peaceful.

Stephanie was caught between two worlds; the waking and the dream. Her thoughts, at times, were conscious, *Did I turn off the oven?*, *Did I remove the price tag from mom's gift?* They were normal, rational, common. They tricked her into thinking she was awake, just resting her eyes. But then the dream intertwined with her thoughts, skewing them, distorting the words and adding misplaced images to them. It was interesting at first, the worlds merging, colliding, melding together like colors mixing on a painter's palette. The hum of the road the undercurrent, the random thoughts running through her head embodied in an expression more felt than seen. She was enthralled by the way they danced together, circling and weaving. But then the dream world took over. She knew it had happened, even though nothing had changed. She was in the car, sitting in the passenger seat as she had been when she was awake. Jared was driving, but she couldn't see him. There was no traffic on the road, which in and of itself wasn't odd since traffic had been light before she shut her eyes. Yet something was different. She could feel it.

The air was cooler, just enough to make a chill stand on her skin. Stephanie opened her eyes to a dream world that was very much like the waking world she was accustomed to, but with differences that were palpable and left the tinny, metallic taste of blood in her mouth. The day, though bright before, was brighter still, without a cloud in sight. The pale blue sky was blanched as the sun overpowered it with blinding white light. She found herself squinting against the glare it cast against the glass.

The sun was relentless. It seemed to bear down with force, targeting her as she sat in the passenger seat daring her to stare back at it. She raised a hand to shield her eyes. Through the slits of light her fingers made, she caught a glimpse of a figure standing on the road in front of the car. Stephanie only saw it for a second, the silhouette of a man's frame backlit by the blazing sun, the effect akin to the blackening of the sun during a solar eclipse. The fringes of the man's body were made bright by the light behind him. The light seemed to come from him, to be controlled by him. Its rays didn't shine on him, didn't blind him to the world beyond. Instead, it stayed obediently behind him, bending to his will. Stephanie pulled her hand away quickly, shaken by the faceless man standing in the street. She blinked against the sun and squinted, looking out at the street again, her eyes needing to see him clearly, needing to understand.

Stephanie could feel the air standing around her now, cooler still as it coursed through the openings of her jacket and blouse. She thought distantly of how uncharacteristic the weather felt, even for a moody April in Virginia. She felt the ground beneath her feet before she realized that she was outside of the car, standing on the asphalt that paved the highway—that, moments before, she had been riding upon in the comfort of the SUV. She looked around herself incredulously once she realized she was outside, her mouth slack and questioning. Panic gripped her when she saw the white lines of continuous traffic painted on the pavement. She spun to look behind her then again to look ahead. There were no cars on the road for as far as the eye could see.

Stephanie let out a sigh of relief. Her hand rested on top of her stomach as it often did when she was thinking. *How did I get out here?* she asked herself. *Where is Jared?*

"You'll see him soon enough," a voice said from in front of her, behind her, all around her at once. Stephanie's heart jumped into her throat as she turned to face the man she had seen through her interlocked fingers. He stood drenched in shadows that were impossible given the high sun. His face was hidden to her, but she could see the shape of his head. It was elongated and slender. Where hair would normally rest stood protrusions, two of them, on either side of his skull. They were thick at the base and drilled to fine points at the ends. They were rigid and solid, like horns. His face had a gray haze in front of it, much like smoke. It seemed to writhe as he stood before her, moving of its own volition as though a breeze made it sway and swirl. His chin was split into two fleshy sides forming points similar to those on his head at their tips. They moved independently of each other, like worms rising from damp earth. Stephanie gasped and took a step backwards.

"Who are you?" she asked, her voice betraying her fear.

The man laughed in a deep baritone that shook her to the base of her spine.

"You know who I am, but your mind won't allow you to say my name aloud. So limited. So puritanical in your thinking. I'll relish introducing you to the depravity that is my world."

The words, spoken by a voice that was neither male nor female, resonated in her ears like knives drawing warm blood. She began to tremble where she stood, her body quivering in the face of the evil that commanded her in silence. Her mouth opened, but she said nothing. She was trapped inside herself. A scream borne of a fear that was as smothering as a winter overcoat tickled her larynx and rushed out of her mouth, pushing free of her and out into nothingness.

"Wise choice Brian, to hide yourself in the woman," he said, his voice penetrating her body like daggers. "Her blood is on your hands."

Stephanie's body quaked as he spoke. His voice wasn't a singular tone, rather it was a mixture of many; several tongues speaking in tandem. Each utterance was thunderous in its base and piercing in its treble. The contrast was unnerving. Stephanie put her hand on her stomach in an effort to shield her child from the being that stood before her.

"Did you think you could hide from me forever?" the man asked.

Stephanie felt naked in front of the creature, exposed. He spoke as though he was talking to someone else, but she knew he was staring right at her. Through her. His countenance was indecipherable. She peered past the smoke with reluctant eyes, trying to see the thing that stood behind it. His nose, cheeks, and mouth were lost to the blackness that surrounded him; the darkness itself embodied his very being. The entity was the epitome of her fears, climbing out from Hell to claw at her in the beautiful light of the noonday sun. Stephanie forced herself to look at it, knowing that she had to, knowing that she didn't have a choice.

The blackest eyes glowered at her through the haze. They were distinct, backlit from his face just like his form was backlit from the landscape that surrounded him; a white ring of light separated them from the blackness within. His pupils were black, accented with an almost imperceptible dot of red right in the center. The color of blood. She stared at the illuminated edges as they pulsed with the rapid beat of her heart, lightening, darkening, lightening, darkening. He was watching her, enjoying her fear, feeling it as one might a soothing massage.

"Who are you?" she asked again, her voice barely above a whisper. "Who is Brian?"

He seemed to readjust then, to look at her more intensely than he had before. The force of his stare weakened her knees.

"Ignorance is bliss, child. Rejoice in it now, for it is a luxury you will soon cease to know." The finality of his words was crushing.

Stephanie's breath caught in her throat.

"You are mine, Brian. She can't help you anymore." His tongue licked fire with the words he spat at her, at Brian. Stephanie's fear and confusion was driving her mad.

"Now," he finished, "come to me."

The man extended his arm, as dark and shaded as the rest of his form, toward Stephanie. His fingers, inordinately long and skeletal, unfolded from his palm and splayed against the air. The heat from his hand caused the air to rotate beneath it, to shimmer as it did on hot summer days above paved roads.

Stephanie wanted to run. She wanted to recoil, to back away from the thing in front of her, but she couldn't move. She couldn't feel her feet or her legs; her whole body was numb. She could only feel the unbearable heat emanating from his hand, its torridity seeming to burn her flesh as it drew closer.

His hand, only inches away from her protruding belly—her child—seemed to shake with anticipation.

"What do you want from me?" Stephanie pled, her voice cracking and hoarse. The man looked at her with his horrid eyes and answered the question without moving his mouth. His voice rose within her, crescendoing the scale between whisper and scream. His words were spoken with numinous calm. Before the hand that would melt her skin and muscle away to reveal the unborn child she carried touched her, the man said, with an almost imperceptible sensitivity,

"It is the child I want. But his cowardice bids me take you as well." Stephanie's screams deafened her as his hand ruptured her amniotic sac and tore through the protective spongy tissue to rip her child from her womb.

Stephanie awoke with a jolt, her hands clawing at her stomach. She relaxed as they rested on her swollen belly, breathing deeply and releasing her tense shoulders. Sweat had formed at her temples, dampening her hair and making it stick to the sides of her head. She wiped at it absently as it threatened to drip into her face. Her mind was still troubled by the images in her dream.

Jared looked over at her and asked, "Honey? Are you okay?"

"I had the most horrible dream," Stephanie started, her breathing still accelerated and irregular. "It was the most terrible dream I've ever had."

"Wait," Jared cut in. "Don't try to talk yet. Take a couple of deep breaths to calm down."

"The baby," Stephanie said, ignoring Jared's suggestion. "Someone took the baby from me."

"It was just a dream, honey. Don't worry about it."

"I know, but it seemed so real. I was standing on the road—this road—and he reached his arm toward me and took the baby out of my stomach." Stephanie's back had stiffened so much that she found herself sitting board straight in her chair, her body leaning forward from the weight of the dream. She tightened her hand on her stomach.

"What?" Jared asked as he cast a quick glance back to the road.

"He took the baby out of my stomach, Jared. He just reached in and pulled him out."

Jared paused and let her recollection of the dream sink in.

"That is horrible, honey," he said with sincere emotion. The mere thought of something like that happening was enough to make him sick. "But it was just a dream," he continued. "Nothing like that could ever happen. You know that."

Stephanie sank back into her seat and looked down at her stomach.

"It just seemed so real."

"I know. It's probably brought on by all the stress of the pregnancy and the fact that you'll be delivering our son soon. This is a huge thing, Steph. You're probably just nervous about it all. That has to be it." Jared hoped that was the only thing that was bothering Stephanie. He suddenly felt very uncomfortable.

Stephanie nodded, but only to pacify Jared. She wasn't nervous about being a mother. She knew she wanted to have children since she was a young girl. Stephanie couldn't wait for her son to be born. Nothing about it frightened her, not even labor. That wasn't it. She fretted, furrowing her eyebrows deeper in thought. What could bring those horrible images into her head?

"Okay hon?" Jared pressed. He put his hand beneath her chin and raised her face to his eye level. He made eye contact with her, holding it for a few seconds before saying, "It's nothing, okay? I'll never let anything hurt my little soldier or you. Okay?"

Stephanie nodded and offered a weak smile. Jared smiled reassuringly and turned back to the road.

Charlie stretched his back in front of the raised hood of his stalled Regal. It was useless. He didn't have a clue what was wrong with the car. Sighing, he patted his pants and jacket pockets in search of his cell phone.

"Oh hell," Charlie said as he realized the phone was still in the car, sitting on the passenger seat. Charlie started toward the passenger door and glanced up the road, looking for oncoming cars. Only one had passed him since the old girl stopped, and traffic was still very light. There were only two cars coming, one in the right lane he had been trying to merge into, and one in the lane the stalled Regal occupied. The car in his lane was close and didn't show any signs of stopping.

"Hey!" Charlie yelled futilely as he waved his arms above his head to try and catch the driver's attention. The car in the right lane slowed, pressing the brakes suddenly. The driver beeped the horn, the shrill sound of it piercing the otherwise quiet day. It was like the eye before the storm; the very silence before the inevitable was louder than the screeching tires of the car in the right lane as they slowed to avoid the crash.

The car in his lane drew closer and closer, never slowing. With unaccustomed agility, Charlie maneuvered around his vehicle and ran to the shoulder on the left side of the highway, praying for the lives of the people in the SUV while he did it.

A car stood still in their lane, its hood raised and its emergency lights blinking. Jared and Stephanie were bearing down on it.

"Oh God!" Jared screamed and slammed on the breaks. Stephanie whipped her head toward the windshield and saw what lay ahead. Her eyes widened as the already small gap between their SUV and the stalled car closed in. She screamed from her diaphragm, emitting a deep, guttural sound that resembled a moan more so than not. Her arms ached as they encircled her stomach, holding her child for the last time.

Just before the collision, before the glass flew and the metal twisted around them, the world was silent. Stephanie's scream died in her throat and the restriction of her seat belt loosened. She sat back in her seat and looked at the car they would soon hit, at the road upon which she would breathe her last breath. A tear fell from her eye as she realized that she was living her last moments. She looked over at her husband, poor, sweet Jared, whose mouth was contorted in a terrified scream. The veins in his neck and forehead were distended painfully; they looked as if they might burst from the pressure. His fingers gripped the steering wheel tightly as he turned the wheel away from the stopped car. His right leg was fully extended as his foot pressed the brake to the floor pad. The accident was imminent and Stephanie knew it. Jared's efforts wouldn't save them. The car was too close. With love, she kissed her hand and rubbed it against his.

Stephanie looked out of her window for a last glimpse of life. The trees swayed slightly in the breeze, waving a solemn goodbye. The car to the right of their SUV was swerving away from the impending accident, the driver's face a mask of fear. Stephanie smiled at the woman behind the wheel as tears dropped into the corners of her mouth.

She was about to turn and face her mortality, to look the beast that would take her life in the face, when a flicker of movement caught her eye. Standing to the left of the car was the man from her dream. He was dark, his frame was still hidden in the shadows that seemed to emanate from his very body. Stephanie couldn't see his face nor the outline she had glimpsed before, but she knew it was him. He was watching. Waiting. The scream that rose in her throat was borne not only of her ineluctable death, but of her fear of the man delighting in it.

Maybe if I hadn't heard about the dream, if I hadn't listened when Angie talked, I wouldn't be the way I am now. Her words opened a door inside me, tearing it off the hinges and baring the vast emptiness within.

That night I had the most horrible dreams, one of many that haunt me to this day. There were two of them, demons dancing in tandem with one another like partners. They spiraled towards me, showing their hideous faces, faces like those of an animal gone to rot in the hot sun mixed with the innocence of a child. Their bodies were deformed, slabs of meat with short arms and bloody stumps for legs. That glimpse was enough to drive me insane.

Tommy was the timekeeper, gleefully clapping as the two danced in what had been our living room, his teeth stained with blood. The slice across his neck smiled too, the soft flesh still bleeding. Blood dripped from the wound like spittle, dotting the skin around it and spraying when Tommy laughed. And did he laugh. The sound was raspy, detached. But he forced it through, the pink of his muscles peaking through his ruined neck as he did it.

One of the demons held a knife. It cut itself in front of me, in front of its partner, and was rewarded with a twirl and dip, encouragement to do it again. From the wound spilled blood and a cloudy discharge, like the embryos found in raw eggs.

Ta ta dat da, da da da da.

The beat of the music was incessant, like a monk's chant, filling my head with wordless droning. Swing, just the way Tommy liked it. With each slice of the knife—shinning steel with a serrated edge like the jagged teeth of a shark—into the demon's leathery skin, Tommy's grin widened. And the other demon twirled and dipped…

Angie made it possible for him to come, to take up residence in my mind, my very soul. She cast him out of her and into me.

The chair would have been better, I am convinced. And I would have deserved every volt I got.

ANGIE

Angie. Angelique. Zaji. Constantine. Vanessa. Take your pick of those names and more. She used many.

I knew her as Angie, but over time, she told me about her other lives in London, Italy, and Africa. She told me about her time in the Caribbean on the island of St. Martin, recounting those days with such detail I could almost smell the turquoise salt water and feel the white sand of Orient Beach under my feet. She confided in me. In the beginning, I'm sure, it was out of a need to confess, a need to purge her spirit before she died. In the end, it was to help me survive. Angie could have left Raskin Correctional at any time, but chose not to. She wanted to die, had sought after death for years. Her only sorrow was in the sacrifice, her beloved whose blood she drank and smeared over her skin to sink in like so much lotion, the fate of her child left alone to face the world and the creatures that dwelled both on and below it. She regretted those things. The pain was sometimes so great, I feared she might withdraw completely. Her words were my roadmap, my textbook. I needed her to finish, needed her to tell me everything she knew. It was like I knew I would follow in her footsteps before the opportunity was laid before me. And so did she.

Marcel lost it when she found out her man was marrying another woman. The news came in a letter. In neat penmanship, Ralph told her that he would love her forever. He said that she would always have a place in his heart, but that he had to move on. He had to live for himself. He told her that he had met a woman that he intended to marry. The ceremony would take place the following week. By the time Marcel got the letter, it was three weeks late, so Ralph had already taken his vows and was a married man. Marcel's scream could be heard five cells over.

"How could he?" she yelled in her cell, her voice growing more shrill and out of control with every word. "After everything I did for him! Why couldn't he wait for me? Why couldn't he wait?"

Marcel's cries made me nauseous. It was as if her anger, her pain because Ralph didn't wait, made me realize my own mortality. It hit me hard. I felt my eyes watering as she screamed on, cursing him and back talking the guards who told her to simmer down. "Why can't he wait for me?" she kept asking. I remember laughing bitterly at the question, its irony piercing me like a sword. Wait? For eternity? We were condemned. Dead women. We were gone already. I felt hot tears on my cheek as my mind wrapped around the inevitability of it.

"Marcel, pipe down," one of the guards said. She was one of the nice ones. A skinny, brown-haired woman with a man's frame and acne-ridden skin, Officer Greenwood always tried to help us work through whatever was making us angry or sad. Most of the other guards just smacked us with their billy clubs or took us to solitary, never caring what the issue was. After all, we were just inmates. Who cared what was wrong with a dead woman anyway? But Officer Greenwood was different.

"Shut your mouth before I have to take you to solitary," Officer Greenwood cautioned. Marcel didn't pay her any attention. She kept yelling, screaming at the top of her lungs.

"That fucking bastard! Hard up motherfucker! After everything I gave him!"

"Marcel, at least the man told you himself and didn't pass the message on through one of your relatives. He didn't have to tell you at all. It's not like you can do anything about it," Officer Greenwood said, her voice even-toned and patient.

"Why? Why?" Marcel demanded. I could hear her bare feet slapping the floor as she moved closer to the cell bars. None of us wanted to hear the answer to the question Marcel asked, have it vocalized. Even Officer Greenwood hesitated.

"I'll tell you why," Officer Johnson said, the keys on her hip jangling as she made her way to Marcel's cell. She walked with a purpose past my cell, a look of enjoyment etched on her face. I could hear the shuffling of feet as she stepped in front Officer Greenwood to open the cell door.

"Because you ain't never getting' outta here, that's why," Officer Johnson continued. The squeak of the cell door opening sounded in the hallway. "You're a dead woman. Dead and gone already to the people on the outside. The only thing to wait for now is your body, all crispy fried." Officer Johnson laughed heartily. She enjoyed reminding us about our fate in the most inhumane ways, counting our days for us, smiling in the face of our despair.

"Come on Greenwood," Officer Johnson said, "let's take this bitch down to solitary and let her scream until her throat gets raw."

I heard two sets of feet trudging into Marcel's cell. It didn't sound like she resisted.

"Come on Marcel. We'll take you down to a private little room where you can scream to your heart's content," Officer Johnson said as they led Marcel out of her cell. Marcel didn't say anything, hadn't spoken at all since her cell was opened.

"You can't play with these bitches," Officer Johnson told Officer Greenwood as they walked down the hall toward the solitary unit. "They hem and haw about the same shit every day. You gotta shut them up, put some discipline on 'em. Then they'll learn to respect you." Officer Greenwood didn't say a word.

Officer Johnson patted herself on the back the whole walk down the corridor, spouting off about her methods when dealing with inmates, giving Officer Greenwood an education on how to handle us, like she was a rookie instead of having been on the job for three years. All I could do was shake my head. I could hear Marcel sniffling all the way down the hall. With Marcel gone, Angie and I only had each other to talk to. She was in a strange mood. A talkative one. Every day of the week that Marcel was gone, Angie told me one story after another about her home, where she'd been, adding more pieces to the puzzle of how she came to be in the cell next to me. I listened to her stories and found escape in them. She talked about faraway places, tropical and exotic. Places I was sure I would never see. I didn't believe all of the stories at first. Some of them sounded made up, like something cultivated by her imagination. But later I came to understand how true her words were. Every one of them.

"I'm over two hundred years old," Angie said the night Marcel was taken to solitary.

"What?" I must have spoken too loudly, because the night shift guard promptly told me to shut up or she'd come in my cell and shut me up. I barely heard the threat, my ears trained on the sound coming from Angie's cell. I was straining to hear her, needing her to explain what she said.

"You gonna get them on us if you don't quiet down." Angie's voice was unfathomably calm given the words she had spoken.
I could feel my mouth hanging open, but I couldn't bring myself to close it. I kept telling myself I didn't hear her right. She couldn't have said she was over two hundred years old. My grandfather was a hundred and ten when he died. His leathery skin laid on his brittle, frail bones, clinging to them, as though his body was devoid of natural fat. His voice was nothing more than a whisper in his last years, the faintest touch of bass toning the breath that forced his words out of his mouth. He sounded like an engine wearing down, overheating after a long drive. The woman in the cell next to mine didn't sound anything like that. Her voice sounded strong and spunky, more alive than Marcel's or mine did, more alive than anyone else's in that hellhole. Over two hundred years old? It just wasn't possible. No one could live that long, let alone be able to talk. I had never heard of anyone living longer than my grandfather, hadn't heard of anyone getting anywhere close to that age. It just wasn't possible! The body couldn't function that long, could it?
My mind couldn't wrap around Angie being any older than thirty, and even that was a stretch; she had a young girl's lilt in her voice, especially when she talked about the pleasures of life on the outside. Finally, I turned toward the wall that we shared. In a hushed tone I asked,
"Angie, why are you talking crazy?"
"I'm not," she said without the faintest hint of emotion. She was serious. "I'm about to tell you things I've never told anyone before, things I shouldn't utter aloud at all. But I'm going to. I want to let it out and you are the best person to tell. He's come to you already, I know. He sees your

soul as I do."

Her words hit me hard, leaving a coldness in the wake of the blast. My nightmares had increased over the past couple weeks. Voices calling out to me in the blackness of my dreams, Tommy standing in the shadows. There was someone else there as well, a new person whose face I had yet to see. He had come every once in a while in the beginning, but for the past couple of night's he came every time I closed my eyes. He said that he wanted to take me away from everything, to save me from my fate. He said that I'm not ready to die yet, I'm not supposed to. He told me that if I go with him he'll see to it that I never do. His words were spoken with the sweetest of voices, so compassionate and gentle, sensual at times. He seduced me with the reality he proposed. He touched me and his hands felt real on my skin, warm and patient like Tommy's had. And I want him to touch me. I accepted him every night. He went further and further each time, leaving me on the brink of orgasm. I woke up most mornings with my hand over my sex, my middle finger on my sweet spot with a plea on my lips. I hadn't told the girls about him. He was just a fantasy, a concoction of my imagination, which was getting more and more vivid with each passing day. When his visits started to trickle into my waking life, his voice caressing the air like a fanning feather, I accepted it, figuring that must be what it was like to lose your mind. I took solace in that. At least I'd be crazy by the time they put me out of my misery. At least then I might not care what happened.

To hear Angie speak about my visitor, the man in my mind who was going to make everything all right, frightened me. How could she know about him? Was he Death, visiting Angie in the dark of night too, taunting her like he did me? That idea shook me, made me feel as though I could fall over from the slightest breeze. I was starting to believe what he said about there being another way. I was about to succumb to him, to join him wherever he asked me to go. I had hoped that going with him would mean mental release. I fancied that the guards would find me sitting in my cell gazing out at some spot on the floor, silent and drooling, like a nutcase. I wanted the retreat, wanted the release. But now that someone else knew about him, I wondered if he was a godsend or a spawn of the devil.

"How do you know about him?" I had to ask, even though I dreaded the answer.

"I know because I see him when he comes to you. I know who he is. He may seem all satin and silk to you, with his promises of release, and of life eternal, but he is nothing but pure evil. *E Diablo mes* as we say in my native tongue. The Devil himself."

I shut my eyes when she said it. It couldn't be! Even though I had my doubts about him, this magical voice that spoke to me when I hurt, when I cried, I couldn't make myself believe that he was the Devil. I needed him to make it out of Raskin Correctional; I needed him to help me die. I wasn't willing to give up the fantasy of him. I wasn't ready to buy in to the idea that I wasn't crazy at all, and that I was just being toyed with by the devil. I needed him too much.

"I know you don't believe me," Angie sighed. "He's embedded himself in you, made you think he's real. Either that or you're crazy. Either prospect works in his favor. See, you need something to grab on to, just like everyone else in here, everyone in the world that has desires that go unfulfilled. We're easy targets. He gets into us whatever way he can, offering the thing that we want most. Sex, money, power, it's all the same to him. He works his way in and takes root, like a tick invading skin. We don't know it's happening until it's too late and he has burrowed all the way in and lodged himself there. That's how he gets us. Our souls are his for the taking then, and we're helpless to do anything about it."

I snickered and asked, "Why would the Devil need to harvest souls here? Haven't all of us already handed him our souls on a silver platter?" Angie's response stopped me dead in my tracks. "It's not your soul he wants," she said quietly.

Angie sighed before continuing, "Maybe what I tell you will help you fight him off, help you deny him what he wants. Maybe, in telling you everything, I can save my son."

I didn't have any idea how her telling me anything would help save her son, nor what she was trying to save him from, and at that moment, I didn't care. I just wanted to know how I got involved in this, why I was the one he chose to speak to.

"If you're right, why me? Why not Marcel or someone else in here? Why not you?"

I heard Angie sniffle before answering. "Marcel is weak, and he knows it. The demons tormenting her mind would never allow her to do his bidding were he to let her live. But you are different. He chose you because you are the strongest one, the only one who might be able to do what he wants. And you know things. Things I said that maybe I shouldn't have. You remember the things that Marcel has either forgotten she heard, or never heard in the first place. He wants to get the answers from you that he can't get from me."

Angie paused for a moment, gathering herself. I could hear her sheets rustling as she positioned herself on the bed. She said, finally,

"He has already gotten to me, which is why I must die."

In the Beginning

Angie filled my head with the story of her life for the rest of that day and into the night. I received my tray of food, but let the oddly dark soup cool and left the day-old bread to sit in its pool of brittle crumbs. Her words formed pictures in my mind like a movie in a theater. I could see everything she talked about, could almost feel and taste the air. I wondered, not for the first time, if she was planting those images in my head, much like the man in the shadows did during his nightly visits.

"My people migrated from Niger to Togo before I was born," Angie started. "A great number of them made the journey in 1574: my mother and father's family back four generations each, along with the Elders and their families. The children from my mother and father's families had been promised to each other at birth either in marriage or in servitude. So they stayed together, settling in the same village. Dahomey.

"The two families lived in Dahomey for centuries, living through the destruction of Forts Allada and Whydah, participating in the sale of their people into slavery, getting caught and sold into it themselves—."

"What?" I cut in. I couldn't believe what I was hearing. All of it sounded incredible. I could see people migrating in arid climate to find a place to call home, could see them taking pride in settling. I couldn't imagine those same people selling their own people into bondage. "Are you saying that your family sold other Black people into slavery? How could they do that?"

"Weapons," Angie replied dully. "That and the fact that no one knew what slavery would turn out to be. If it meant work, and being someone else's property, well, that was commonplace. No one could have known what slavery would become. "

Angie paused, her mind wandering. I sat in forced silence, waiting for her to continue.

"I was born in 1738, only two years after my parents were married. My childhood was normal. I loved life, respected my Elders, and dreamt of being a teacher. I noticed the boys in my village later than most—I was fifteen when they first started to catch my eye I was considered a late bloomer even then. I figured I didn't need to pay attention to them. I was promised to a boy from my father's family as soon as he came of age. In a year I would be a wife and would have to perform my wifely duties anyway, so I didn't see the point in wasting time on boys before I needed to. So I studied every book I could find instead, learning about African history and western culture. I read Shakespeare in English, something no other person in our village could do. I tutored the men who were preparing to move to Europe to find work. I was on my way to teach the old man Sule basic phrases in English for his trip to England when I met him.

"He showed himself to me on the path leading to Sule's house. It was late in the afternoon, the night's chill was starting to overtake the heat of noonday. My bare feet padded into the dirt, stirring up little clouds of dust that landed on my feet and legs. My eyes were trained on the pattern the clouds made against the robin's egg blue sky. The gnarled limbs of the treetops reached up like the fingers of the Elders, curled and wrinkled at the tips. I fancied that the limbs pointed at the Orisha that watched over our crops and us, swaying in the wind with them as though dancing.

"I almost bumped into him while I was looking at up at the trees. His footfalls were silent against the dirt road, his breathing muted. I didn't know he was there until he spoke.

"'Where you goin' girl?' He startled me. I took a step backwards, sucking in air as I did it. His voice was as smooth as silk, and his tone was a rich baritone, deep, but not rumbling. A smile crept over his lips at my reaction. His teeth were straight, and the whitest I'd ever seen. His features were sharp; high cheekbones, even brown skin, squared jaw covered with facial hair that was trimmed and detailed into a perfect goatee. His hair was soft and curly. His eyes were green like the color of moss. I cocked my head and stared closer at him. I had never seen a man like him before. I was very much attracted to him.

"'Do you speak English?' he asked, his face searching mine for understanding. I hadn't realized he was addressing me in any language other than Fon. The sound of his voice, his inflection and pitch, sounded like my native language. But alas, to hear him address me again, I knew that I had been mistaken. Something twitched within me before I answered. It felt like my stomach dropped ever so slightly. The feeling made me hesitate, but I ignored it. I wanted to talk to this man, this beautiful stranger.

"'I do,' I said, my voice thick and tentative. I cleared my throat and continued, 'I was on my way to tutor Sule on his English before I met you. I'm sorry I got in your way.'

"'No, it was my fault. I'm afraid I walk rather lightly and tend to sneak up on the unsuspecting.' His smile was radiant. I could feel myself melting in its wake.

"He had an accent, one that I couldn't place. It was flowery, seductive, mesmerizing. I felt unsteady on my feet.

"'I've never seen you here before,' I said, hoping that by speaking, by doing anything other than staring into his gorgeous eyes, I would be able to calm my racing heartbeat.

"'I'm not from here,' he said. I could almost feel his rich baritone inside me.

"'Where are you from?'

"'So many questions from a girl I don't know,' he said, playfully. He was older than me, but not by much; he was maybe eighteen or twenty years old. A man his age should have been married with a family, at least that was what we were taught in my culture. But he wasn't like my people. He was from a different place, cut from a different cloth. I felt ashamed being so drawn to this man who was more appealing to me than anyone in my village. His coyness, among other things, intrigued me.

"'My apologies, sir. I didn't mean to pry,' I said as I bowed my head slightly, diverting my eyes from his. I could be coy also.

"'By what name do they call you?' he asked.

"'My name?' I repeated with levity in my voice. I enjoyed having him ask the questions. A maturity I didn't know I possessed was starting to come out.

"'Yes. If I know your name I won't feel as though I am telling my secrets to a stranger.'

"'Your homeland is considered a secret, then?'

"'Among other things.' He didn't try to hide the laughter in his voice. 'So, what is it?'

I paused for a moment, letting the question linger in the air. His lips formed a boyish grin, indenting his cheeks with perfect dimples while he waited for me to answer. I enjoyed the feeling of control like I never thought I would. Somehow this man, this stranger, had brought womanly wiles out of me.

"'My name is Zaji,' I told him, and smiled to match his. 'Your turn. What is your name?'

"'Zaji.' My name rolled off his tongue and caressed his lips like fine wine. I felt myself stir as he uttered it once more. "Such a beautiful name for a beautiful woman."

"I could feel my cheeks flushing with embarrassment as he spoke, but I had no desire to turn away. The man before me was mesmerizing, invigorating in a way that I had never experienced before. I wanted to talk with him, to stand on the dirt road and listen to everything he had to say, for as long as he wanted to say it. I had the strangest feeling that he knew my intentions, could read them in my eyes like words written on the pages of a book.

"'Are you from here, Zaji?' The words melted in the air like ice into water on a hot summer day.

"'My village is just around the bend. A stone's throw.'

"'Perhaps my travels will take me near your village one day. I might see you when you least expect it.' His eyes twinkled brightly as the light of the sun bounced off of them, all but blinding me to his knowing stare.

"'Maybe it will.'

"He backed away from me then, putting distance that I didn't want between us. To separate from him was to lose this new girl who had been speaking through me, forming words with my lips and tongue that I had never dared to utter. I took a step toward him to bridge the gap.

"'Off to finish your errand?' I asked quite awkwardly, trying to keep the conversation going. Trying to keep him from leaving.

"'I don't recall mentioning one to you, but yes, I do have things to attend to.' He looked amused.

"I smiled sheepishly, the extent of my ploys to keep him there expended. 'Very well,' I almost whispered as I turned to walk away.

"'How did you know I had an errand today?' he asked suddenly, taking a step toward me. I turned to see a thoughtful look on his face. 'Do you have the gift of sight, Zaji? You must if you know the personal business of a man whom you've never met before.' A smile played at his lips. His luscious lips.

"'It doesn't take a clairvoyant to recognize a man with a mission in mind. Your deliberate step was all I needed.'

"He laughed under his breath before speaking again. I felt accomplished. Never before had I engaged in such free, unabashed banter with a man. I was flirting with him and he knew it. I was pretty good at it. And it felt right. I amazed myself with my sharp tongue. I could feel heat rising on the back of my neck as I hung on the silence, but the new woman that I portrayed myself to be didn't show it.

"'Well, maybe one day my deliberate steps will take me to your door,' he replied as he flashed a smile so brilliant, it almost stopped my heart.

"'Until then, beautiful Zaji,' he said as he slowly backed away from me, keeping eye contact all the while. He turned around at the fork in the road and walked out of sight. I turned away also, on the off chance that he might look back at me to see if I was watching after him. I didn't want to dispel my meticulously spun air of confidence by succumbing to that childish inclination. I entered Sule's house and proceeded with his lesson, but I didn't pay attention to his diction or pronunciation. My mind was completely occupied with the memory of the stranger's face.

"I didn't see the man again for weeks. I took the same route to Sule's house every time I tutored him. I even made extra trips in an attempt to bump into him. But we never met along the road, never bumped into each other by mistake. My heart ached to see him again.

"My prayers were answered one day when I was cleaning my family's clothes at the river. Sweat coated my body and my work clothes hung from me like rags. I had just finished the last of the clothes when I saw him standing by a tree. His stance was casual; he leaned against the tree like a man resting from a day's work. His eyes were trained on me with an intensity that was so strong, I almost felt them crawling over my skin. I looked back at him, trying to match his gaze, but found that my stare paled in comparison to his. It was disconcerting, his unwavering stare, but exciting also. This man was different than the men in my village. He was learned, a man of the world. You could tell that by the exotic lilt of his voice. He was attractive in ways that the men in my village could never be. And he seemed genuinely interested in me.

"I called out to him from the water, the bold girl he had awoken in our first meeting coming to the forefront again. 'Are you planning to stand there and stare at me all day?'

"His laughter was music to my ears.

"'A bit brazen for a young girl, aren't you?' he said as he walked toward me, his gait slow and steady. 'Most girls your age are shy and demure.'

"'You've met many young girls, I take it?' I hardly meant for that to slip out of my mouth. I didn't want to appear desperate or possessive. I didn't even know the man! I gathered mother's clothing, focusing my eyes on the task at hand rather than on his handsome face.

"'None as memorable,' he said, letting the phrase linger in the air. I looked up to smile at him and found that he stood closer to me than I thought. He looked down at me from across the laundry. His feet almost touched mine on either side of the tree stump I used as a table. I breathed deeply of him, his scent filling my nostrils, intoxicating me.

"'As?' I asked. I didn't know what else to say. I could smell my nervousness on my skin, the sharp sweetness of my naiveté.

"'What brings you here, to this watering hole of all places?' he asked, changing the subject.

"'Mother's laundry, of course.'

"'That's all?'

"'What else?' It was my turn to leave him hanging.

"'I knew, somehow, that we would see each other again,' he said.

"'Did you?' I picked up the laundry and started to walk. I knew he would follow. He hadn't stood by the tree watching me for however long just to let me get away. I was enjoying the game very much.

"'I felt it.' He touched my arm and the feel of his skin against mine stopped me in my tracks. I looked up again to face him and was met with his soft lips as he pressed them against mine. They puckered once, twice, lingering longer every time. He opened his mouth a little and I followed suit. He slid his tongue into my mouth tentatively and I touched mine to it, giving him the permission to explore. His arms raised and encircled me. His open palms caressed my shoulder blades as he kissed me deeper. I had never kissed that way before, had never been embraced by a man other than my father. I had seen young couples in the village kissing like we were, had even seen my parents doing it, but I had never experienced it myself. My mother told me that it would happen when it was time for me to take a husband. The girl inside me that wanted to find a husband on her own, without the help of her parents, protested. She wanted to kiss many boys before deciding to kiss one person forever. She wanted to kiss and do other things, things that only married women were supposed to do. Friends of mine who had done it sang its praises and I wanted to do it myself, but mother told me about all the terrible things that awaited girls who did it before they were married. She spoke of mutilations and stoning as consequences. I didn't know whether she was telling me tales to frighten me or not, and I didn't want to find out. So I put the notion of kissing, touching, and sex out of my mind until I was supposed to get married… until he changed everything.

"I accepted his touch like a flower accepts water. I drank him in, kissing him without regard, learning to do so by his experienced tongue. I could feel myself becoming aroused. I had felt it before while watching the young men work around their father's houses, clad in barely anything at all. During those times, my arousal was only visual; I liked what I saw. This time, with my beautiful stranger, I could feel my body rising to meet his, my loins throbbing to be touched. It was shocking, exciting, and unbearable all at the same time.

"When we pulled away from the kiss, I knew that I would sleep with him. His lips were still parted, his skin was flushed; he had enjoyed the kiss as well. We stood silent, looking at each other for a long time, before sitting down under the shade of an iroko tree. He traced the outline of my face with the tip of his finger, his touch raising goose bumps on my flesh. Propped up on his elbow, he gazed into my eyes, seeing my soul. I wanted him. I wanted the experience and I wanted him to be the one to give it to me. He was a passerby from a different land. He had seen more than I thought I would ever see. I thought I could experience some of the world through him. I was hungry for it.

"He rolled on top of me, pressing his hand into the growth at the base of the tree to keep his weight from bearing down on me. We kissed again, our tongues playing, circling each other in a sensual chase. My garment was pulled over my head with ease, and he paid attention to every facet of my body as I lay prone in the shade. He disrobed and I felt his toned body with my roving hands. He moved his kisses from my mouth to my neck, then to my breasts. I closed my eyes, squeezing my eyelids tightly against one another, blocking out the world. I wanted to feel every sensation without distraction. He teased me to the point where I thought I would boil over before he entered me. The flash of pain was superseded by the pleasure that encompassed my entire body, from top to bottom. I could feel moisture beneath me and knew it was the blood of my virginity, but I didn't care. I was in another world as he pressed into me, slowly at first, and then with force as I begged him to go harder, faster, deeper if he could. I used my hands to press his buttocks in, forcing his member further and further inside me. I was beside myself. I would never have imagined that I would be so forthright, so urgent. It was as though I needed him to penetrate me, needed him to bring me to climax. And he did. As I arched my back off the ground beneath me, enjoying the tingling sensation that overtook my body and mind, I felt the tiniest prick atop my breast. I opened my eyes to see his face buried in my bosom, his eyes shut in a quiet ecstasy. He burrowed his face deeper, the prick quickly becoming a pinch, the pressure building by the second. He seemed to enjoy himself as he nuzzled my breast, his member stiffening and his hips gyrating absently. I liked the way he looked when he did it. I liked the way it felt.

"When we were both spent and sweaty, we lay beneath the tree as lovers.

"'I've never done that before,' I said breathlessly. 'You were my first.'

"'I know,' he said, filling me with uncertainty at once. Was my inexperience that obvious? Did I perform poorly? I opened my mouth to speak, but he started before I could make a sound. 'I felt your tension in the beginning, but only then,' he said, trying to reassure me. 'It was wonderful, my beautiful Zaji.'

"I smiled and turned toward him, resting my head upon his chest. After what seemed like only a moment, he reminded me of Mother's laundry. He suggested that I go back home before someone began to worry.

"'I want to stay here. I want to make this moment last forever,' I whined. He chuckled and said,

"'There will be other times, my dear. We will meet again.'

"He dressed quickly, standing fully clothed before I had even reached for my garment. Worry stood in my eyes mingling with embarrassing tears as I watched him prepare to leave. Even though he said he enjoyed himself, I wondered. Doubt washed over me. Suddenly, all the confidence and satisfaction I'd enjoyed before disappeared. I felt like a fool. He leaned down, his face pressed close to mine, and said, with a knowing smile, 'I promise.'

"With a quick kiss on the lips, he was gone.

"I went home that evening spent, the sweetness he left inside me fading as the day progressed. I was withdrawn, lost in my own thoughts, savoring the memory of our time together, even as the soreness set in. My father didn't notice. He was always busy doing one thing or another with the Elders. The amount of time he spent at home was relegated to the evening hours, close to or past the time my sister and I went to sleep. Even when he was home when we were awake, he didn't have much to say to us. We were girls and it was my mother's duty to care for us, to entertain us. Had we been boys he would have been obligated to take more of an active role. Instead of spending time with us, Father would go outside and lay down in the yard. He would gaze up at the stars as if he meant to join them as they looked down over our village, our world. I longed to talk to him during those times. I wanted to ask him what he saw when he looked up at the sky, where the stars took him, what they showed him. I went outside to do it once, even though my sister protested, begging me to leave Father alone, to let him have his time to himself. Her words were more for me than for Father; his aloofness made Oni fear him. But I didn't.

The night was cool with a light wind. It blew my hair from my forehead and touched me with its cool hand. Father was ahead of me, lying on his back in the dirt that surrounded our home. He hummed a low tune, the beat seeming to rest on the air above his upturned mouth for a second before floating away. I took a step toward him, but he did not stir. I called him, keeping my voice as low as I could, but he did not answer.

"'To,' *(Father)* I repeated, but he still didn't answer. I stepped closer and saw that his eyes were open and a smile played at the corners of his mouth. He looked so calm, so at peace, that bothering him with my questions seemed inconsiderate, inappropriate somehow. I walked inside, leaving him to his night show. He was outside the night I met the stranger, as he always was, oblivious to what was going on inside and liking it that way.

"Mother, Oni, and I finished every night with girl talk. We shared the goings on in the village like gossipers on a housing bench in New York City. Mother shared her stories from the morning market, like the news that Yawo and Esi were having an affair, and that Abena's in-laws were making her leave the home she had shared with her late husband, Kwaku. That was no surprise. Everyone in the village thought that Abena had killed Kwaku in his sleep. Oni and I didn't have such exciting news to share, but we told Mother our stories anyway. We talked about our schoolwork and the boys we liked. She would always turn her eyes downward when we went on about the boys. She didn't like the arranged marriage custom of our culture any more than we did, but there was nothing she could do about it. She never insisted that we stop talking about boys, never dismissed it as foolish. Instead, she laughed with us, letting us share the moments we knew would be nothing more than fanciful memories in the near future.

"That night, though, I was quiet during our talk, offering a laugh or smile at their news, but not sharing any of my own. My mind was back at the river with my handsome stranger. I could see his face, pleasantly illuminated by the sunlight that trickled in through the leaves of the iroko tree. I could taste his saliva, his sweat, his desire. I could feel his hands on me again, caressing my skin as though it was fine silk. The conversation my mother and sister were having paled in comparison to my precious memory.

"It was then that I realized I didn't know his name. My face flushed as I thought of all that we shared and the emotions he roused within me. All of that with a man who was as nameless to me as a stranger on the streets of Rome. I began racking my brain, trying to recall every word he had ever said to me, his every utterance, hoping that it would bring forth his name. Nothing came. As the night drew to a close and my mother and sister retired for bed, I looked out of the window of our house at the very stars my father gazed upon, hoping that my stranger was looking at them too.

"That night I dreamt of him, my stranger. He came to me in a haze, his body shrouded by the folds of fog, obscured from my sight. The fog rolled over me, touching each crevice of my body with its coolness. My skin felt charged, invigorated as the fog engulfed it. I arched my back in anticipation as it covered me.

"He seemed to come from the fog, out of it, as though made by it. His features were filled in like blood aspirated in a hypodermic needle; the beautiful brown of his skin rolling in like a wave. I was mesmerized. He seemed to hover over me, close enough for me to see every feature of his gorgeous face, yet just far enough away to seem intangible.

"I could hear my breathing, steady and even as I slept, but it was different from the panting I felt rising in my chest. I was asleep, experiencing the most vivid dream I ever had. I could feel his touch, feel my pulse quicken, see him as though he was in front of me.

"I smiled at the lovely visage of my handsome stranger, dressed in the finest Western clothes. His eyes twinkled at me, imparting the secret that only he and I shared. I reached for him and he came closer, close enough to kiss. I felt a coolness on my lips that startled me. I opened my mouth and allowed his tongue to enter it, surprised by how real the kiss felt. *What a vivid dream*, the part of my mind that wanted to indulge in the fantasy chimed. The skeptical part, the part that had been on edge since the moment my path crossed with that of my stranger, warned me. *No dream is ever this real*, it admonished. *Something isn't right.* I ignored the little voice that nettled me, casting it aside in favor of the exquisite fantasy.

"He touched me with a patient hand, gently caressing my cheek, neck, and shoulders the way an experienced lover would touch a lifelong mate. My body reacted of its own volition, trembling and rising to his touch. His mouth closing over my breast was the first time I felt uneasy. His tongue, rougher than it had been before, darted around my nipple rapidly, the skin beneath it beginning to burn from the friction. I began to wonder what could make his tongue feel so abrasive, like a cat's kiss. But I forced the fear to dissipate as he gathered me into his embrace. I told myself to enjoy the ride. It was only a dream anyway.

"His arms felt like cushions around my body at first. His hands were ever-moving, roaming, exciting me in ways that I had never dreamed of. But then his touch grew firmer, more urgent. He started to squeeze me tighter than I wanted to be held, tighter than any human should be held. I shrieked in protest, but the sound was muted, nothing more than a faint squeak in the waking world. It didn't rouse my sister at all; it was the sort of sound that could be ignored in the night, like a furnace coming on or a house settling in its foundation. I pressed my hands to what should have been his shoulders, but found that I could reach right through him. I screamed in my dream, trying to wrench away from the man who, a moment before, had brought me such pleasure. But he held firm, not letting me move an inch. I was pinned beneath him.

"He took me by force, spreading my legs with none of the gentleness he had shown me earlier that day. He thrust himself inside me. It hurt like an open wound. His penis was hot like fire. It pressed into my unwilling vagina with the ferocity of a lion going for the kill. I was bleeding, I was sure of it; my mind waffling between believing I was embroiled in a dream and believing that what was happening was real. I thrashed my legs, trying to lift him off of me, but he was immoveable, as solid as a rock. He looked down at me, smiling as sweetly as he had by the river. I could feel the tears standing in my eyes as he continued to penetrate me, his smile somehow seeming cold and unfeeling. 'Kenklen do,' (*Please stop*) I begged in my native tongue, fear taking over my senses as completely as the dark shrouded our house in the night, but he continued, pounding harder with each stroke.

"He bit me as he would many times after that, puncturing my veins and drawing my blood into his expectant mouth. I screeched, pressing against him with newfound strength, trying to force him away from my neck. The fog that made up his body was rigid and as cold as ice. Once satiated, he lifted his head to look at me, his face contorting from the attractive stranger I had met on the road and had trusted with my body, to a horned beast whose murderous smile was ringed with blood. His body swelled grotesquely, like that of a mosquito, his tissue edematous, filled to capacity with my blood. He licked his lips with his bloody tongue, spreading the crimson wetness around like lipstick. He was larger than life, perched above me as plump as a man who has lived a existence of indulgence. He seemed to enjoy his girth, admiring himself as a man would a woman. His spectacle made me sick. I closed my eyes to him and turned my head, willing him away.

"His hand touched my chin gently at first; his touch felt like pin pricks on my skin. The sensitivity of the touch was disarming and part of me wanted to lean into it, but I wrenched my face away from his grasp. Whatever he was, he wasn't the man I thought him to be. When I didn't comply with his gentle nudging, he pulled my chin forcefully, turning my face to his. 'See me,' he hissed. I imagined a serpentine tongue jutting out of his mouth to lick the air. I cringed at the thought of looking the demon in the face again, but I knew I had to. Reluctantly, I opened my eyes.

"His body regained a normal state as I watched. Where his body stopped, his face continued, metamorphosizing, becoming featureless, fading from within and leaving a hazy countenance in its place. I blinked through my tears, trying to focus, to see the man who was violating me, but I couldn't make out anything discernable. The outline of his head was enough to make bile rise in my throat. He had horns on both sides of his head and the base of his chin flapped from his back and forth motion as he penetrated me, like fleshy ears on a bouncing boar. I screamed my disgust as loud as I could, but that only made him ride me harder and faster. 'Koño abo a fiernu!' (*Damn you to Hell!)* I said, hot tears streaming from my eyes. He seemed to focus more intensely on me then, looking at me from behind the haze that covered his face. He let out a ground-shaking laugh that chilled my heart.

"I passed out and didn't wake until the following morning. My sister had already gotten up and had joined my parents in the yard for morning work. I sat up, immediately feeling a sting from my abdomen down to my thighs. I felt as if I had been attacked by a wild animal, clenched in its jaws and flung to the ground like waste. My head ached as I pulled myself from the throes of sleep, trying to clear my mind for the day. I rose from the bed on shaky legs. Reluctantly, I turned toward my bed, afraid of what the covers might reveal. Blood stained the area where I slept.

"He came to me many times after that in the dead of night, under the cover of the fog, always ethereal—I didn't see him in human form again for centuries. Sometimes he chose to reveal himself, materializing before my eyes just before he entered me. Other times, he remained a shadow, nothingness. At first I resisted him, fighting him every time he entered my dreams to torture me. But I soon abandoned that, the effort was not worth the outcome. He wanted me and he was going to get me. I was there for his pleasure and nothing more… or so I thought. I hated myself for being so vulnerable, so easily duped by a lustful glance, the hint of adventure. I laughed and cried at my naiveté, the emotions intertwining, mixing, becoming one and the same with each breath. I had become the devil's concubine and I hated myself for it.

"One night, after one of his visits, I laughed bitterly at how little I knew about my nightly tormentor. I didn't know his name, where he was from, who his people were. Nothing. My laughter was so loud, so frenzied, I almost woke my sister. To fret over his name? What a sadistic joke. I knew his name well, even though it was never uttered aloud. Some part of me knew it the moment I met him, but never got the chance to warn the rest of me. He was the devil if he was anyone at all."

I hadn't realized that I hadn't taken a breath for a while until Angie paused. My lungs were burning and my lips were parched. I inhaled loudly through my nose and raked my dry tongue across my lips. The story Angie told was chimerical, unfathomable, though I wouldn't have called it such then. I would have called it craziness and how poignant that description would have been. I was sure Angie was talking absolute nonsense, babbling like the girls holed up in the psych ward. I wanted to dismiss her as such and let her ramblings put me to sleep, but something told me to be still and listen. Moreover, a voice in my mind, barely audible if at all, beseeched me to remember.

Even though I didn't want to believe her, Angie was serious. Her voice was stern, angry almost, when she spoke about her stranger. I saw him in my mind, imagined how he might have looked. I understood how he had enticed her. I had a sinking feeling inside me that I had been baited just as easily; the promises he made were so sweet.

"I died with his smiling face before my eyes," Angie started again. "He had come once more, taking the sex he desired without having to tame a struggling girl; I had grown weary of the fight. When he was done he leaned in to me, his incorporeal lips hovering just over my neck. His voice was light, as though carried by the air. It cooed to me like the sound of a sated lover on the brink of a deep sleep.

"'Thank you, my darling Zaji.'

"The words enraged me. Everything he had done to me was by force. Through no will of my own, I complied. Except that first time. Could that be what he was referring to? Could he be thanking me for allowing him access to use me as he saw fit? How dare he! I cursed myself for letting him use me, for the initial invitation I had uttered that warm day by the river.

"I lashed my angry tongue at him, ignoring the impending doom his presence conjured within me. 'How dare you speak thanks to me? You have taken everything I am, my very essence has been wasted and discarded at your leisure.'

"'But you have given me the ultimate gift. What I have wanted since the moment I met you,' he replied.

"I didn't know what he was talking about. The sound of his voice was driving me mad.

"'What are you speaking of?' I yelled.

"'You were chosen, almost from the moment of your birth. I knew you would be the one with whom I would share my world, the one who would bear me a child.'

"I started to believe that my parents had sold me to him, had given me away to get some worldly possession, some vain trinket. My mind blazed in anger at them for forsaking me, believing in the possibility wholeheartedly. He met my anger with a chilling smile.

"It was as though everything else in the world had disappeared in that moment. I couldn't hear any sound, not from my sister who slept in the same room as I did, not from the insects that ruled the night. I could only hear his voice, growing stronger with every word. Before my eyes he began to solidify, to flesh out, to become a living body. He almost looked as he did the day we met. His handsome face smiled at me in genuine happiness.

'A child?' I whispered. The mere thought of carrying his baby made my stomach turn. I cringed away from him, grimacing in disgust.
"He laughed at my reaction, taking pleasure in my sorrow. 'Our offspring would not be of this earth,' he said, his voice dripping with a velvety sweetness that, if overheard might have sounded appealing, but to me, was nothing more than poison from his rancid lips. He leaned closer to me, his nebulous features almost merging with mine. 'A child of that sort could not serve my purposes. You will bear the fruit of a mortal man and he will be a specimen capable of physical and intellectual domination. He will live forever as I do. As you will. He will walk the earth as a man and dwell in his domain beneath the sea as a prince. A fine dhampir. He will be flesh and blood as you were, and he will inhabit the mist, the fog, the very air as I do.

They will serve him as they serve me.'

"My mind was cluttered with images that I knew were not my own. He was invading me as he would in the centuries to come, manipulating my mind to see what he wanted to see, gaining free reign over it as he had enjoyed with my body. I uttered a protest, flung my arms weakly, futilely trying to resist.

"'Eo,' (*No*) I said, my voice nothing more than a whisper. I was more fatigued than I had ever been. I felt as though I had run miles in the hot sun, trying to escape an attacker, my legs pushing me forward as fast as they could. I was emotionally and physically spent.

"I blinked rapidly, trying to clear my mind, but the clutter of images remained: pictures of dead men whose blood flowed into the sea and of monkeys sinking their teeth into the supple flesh of a woman's breast. I felt nauseous; my head was spinning like a top. I shut my eyes to the room, trying to settle myself.

"It was then that he closed in on me, lifting me from the bed and biting my neck. The warmth of his breath against my skin was in contrast to the cold enamel of his teeth trespassing within me. He drank heartily, more so than usual, my life's blood exciting him to erection. I was helpless. The pain was excruciating. Suspended over the bed, I was unable to get a foothold on anything, unable to push him away. I could feel my extremities growing cold, first my fingers and toes, then my arms and legs. My bosom was the last to shed its warmth, and I pressed my numb hands to it desperately. My eyes were open when I died, staring at the being that had taken my life, as he sucked gleefully, ingesting every drop.

"Mother found my body the next morning. Oni had already risen and left the house for school before Mother entered our bedroom in search of me. I had been allowed a measure of freedom in the last year of my life, and Mother was trying to respect my privacy. When I hadn't responded to her calls, she entered the room and found me dead. I heard her screams, heard the pain in her voice as she cried over me, but I couldn't move. I willed myself to rise, to strike out at her for selling my soul, but I could not. Thank God. To reanimate before her would have surely killed her.

"I listened as she gasped for air, sobbing and gagging as though she were choking. Her sorrow was immense, the weight of it almost took her from the world I so coveted before she could see her daughter off. I started to change my mind. Maybe it wasn't her that sold me to him. Perhaps Father, then. He had always been so cold, so aloof with us. Was it beyond him to sell a daughter for the promise of wealth? *What is the good of two girls anyway,* a little voice in my head chimed in.

"I lay immobile, the heat of anger burning my insides, as my father leaned over my body. I wanted to spit in his face, but I couldn't pucker my lips. It was while I was struggling against the confines of rigor that I heard his impassioned cry.

"Father's outburst melted all the anger that welled within me, washed it away in one quick burst. He yelled until his lungs gave way to wheezing. I imagined that his mouth hung open, distorted in a painful grimace. And then I knew. It could not have been him. No man would cry in such pain over that which he cared nothing about.

"My mind reeled, trying desperately to clear itself of the poison that had been planted there by him, my lover, my killer. I knew then that I had to learn to control my thoughts, to keep them in place, or he would push them out and fill my head with his own ideals. I also knew that, the first chance I got, I would run.

"Mother dressed me for burial with a heavy heart. She had learned of my secrets while bathing my body. Father was confused, but didn't go against her when she requested that I be buried instead of burned. I was laid in the ground next to the wanderers who had been cut down by the beasts of the jungle, in the tradition of paupers. My sister argued with mother, accusing her of damning my soul because she placed me in the ground rather than burning my flesh. But Mother held firm to her decision. She kept me whole.

"I awoke, my body covered in a garment from each of my family members. Rings of gold adorned my fingers, a gift from the neighbors, and a shield was placed at my side. As I uncovered my head and rested my hand against the shield, I chuckled. No earthly guard could save me from what lay ahead."

Angie told me about her visit with her mother on the night she died, recounting the details as she had the day after waking up from the dream. She paused after that, her heart aching.

"I ran back to my grave after Mother went inside," Angie continued, sounding drained. "I got back into my grave, and covered myself with the dirt that had encased me. I pulled the garments over my face as they had been placed during my ceremony, stretching them tightly across my throat. I remained in the ground for decades after that night, trying to kill myself. I thought that if I deprived myself of food—what was surely the blood of humans, given the unnatural cravings that tortured me—I would rest forever. And I would be rid of him. Forever. It worked for a while. Though my hunger persisted, I was able to will myself to remain buried. It was the smell that finally made me rise from the grave. The putrid smell of the dead decaying all around me."

Angie was scaring me. All her talk about being dead and coming back to life sounded like a story out of a book, but somehow, I knew she wasn't lying, wasn't making up a tale to tell another jailbird, bullshitting to pass the time. Angie never went in for the posturing that happened in jail. Every time a new girl was locked up with us, she would try to impress us with stories about what she did on the outside. I always found it interesting to hear what the girls would come up with. They would tell the weaker girls how they ruled their block trying to put fear in them before they even got settled in. They would tell the rougher ones about how they beat someone on the outside up, or stole their money without remorse, without a care for what happened to them. The stories always sounded like lies, as though they were being made up on the spot. I would bet my time that most of them were, but there wasn't a sucker around who would take that bet. Angie never went in for that kind of stuff. If a girl started talking to her about what she had done on the outside, Angie would stop her in her tracks, and ask, "If you were so smart, so tough, how did you get caught?" The girls hated her for humiliating them like that, but never retaliated. I guess they felt the strangeness that surrounded Angie like I did—like I always had—and left her alone.

The story frightened me, but it wasn't just her words. It was the truth in them that had me shivering. She spoke about things that couldn't be real, but just might be. That she knew things that I had never told anyone proved she had some kind of gift. I curled into myself, hugging my knees to my chest, trying to stop myself from shaking. Angie was supernatural, not human. Dead and risen, by her account. Awakened. Even though Angie said her family practiced Voodoo, I kept the crucifix I had fashioned out of a dried palm leaf that the prison's Pastor gave me last Palm Sunday under the covers with me just the same.

"I rose from my earthen bed after decades of confinement needing to feed. The hunger was so great within me, I was blinded by it," Angie said, breaking the momentary silence. "The feeling was rivaled by a compulsion to return to my home, to gaze upon the faces of my family. It burned within me, equaling the desire to feed, at times, superseding it. Succumbing, I started out toward my father's home.

"Children played on the road that ran parallel to my home. Seeing them roused the desire to feed, painfully cramping my chest and stomach. I receded into the bush, putting distance between them and myself. I knew I had to eat. But I didn't want to act out my savagery on those innocents. I knew my thirst would be satisfied soon, but not with them. I stayed still long after their gleeful voices had passed, until I could no longer hear the blood rushing in their veins.

"The house was empty, unkempt. Wild weeds sprouted from patches of land; the brush seemed to have covered it with a grassy hand, leaving its mark. The façade looked worn, in need of work. My vision, better than it had ever been in life, cascaded over the barren home, devoid of the character it had possessed when I was alive. Devoid of life itself.

"I made my way to the window, bold in the midday light, not caring if I was spotted. I looked in through the window to view the interior. There was nothing inside. A thick layer of dust had settled on the stone floor where my sister and I played games. Grime coated the walls where my mother had recorded our measurements. The house was empty, as dead as

I was. My family was gone.

"I turned to face the road in front of my house, looking vainly for answers to unspoken questions. Had they moved? Were they dead? How long had I been gone? I sucked in deeply, saddened by the prospect of my family's death. Though my subconscious knew it was inevitable, that I would live to see them die, I had pushed the thought aside, not allowing it to take root. But then, standing in desolation, I came to realize that what I had feared most had come to fruition. Mother and Father had been in their early thirties when I died. Surely I had slept for ten or twenty years—the fatigue of decades of unrest was heavy indeed. My parents might have survived ten years after my death, but no more than that—the oldest person in our tribe had lived fifty years, and the second oldest had lived until forty-seven. I felt a tickle at my eyes in response to my grief. The sensation was different than the stinging of new-formed tears. I indulged the peculiarity, wanting to see what would come from it. A thick, dark red drop fell from my eyes and onto the dirt road. I was repulsed by it, and took a step backward.

"My parents were dead, I was sure, but what of my sister? Oni was younger than I. She should have been in her thirties, if my slumber had indeed been twenty years. She was probably married with children of her own to raise and nurture. My heart ached to see her, to touch her face, to meet my nieces and nephews. I took a westward step, smelling the air for a familiar scent. It was that action, that animalistic display that stopped me in my tracks. What an abomination! An anathema, a travesty of life. There I stood, a stilled heart in my chest, congealed blood in my veins. I was no longer a part of the living, yet I roamed the earth, not as a spirit, but as a physical being, as tangible as those whose blood runs warm. I couldn't go to my sister, couldn't introduce my heinous nature to her life. It would have been nothing less than cruel. I didn't even want to find her and spy, to catch glimpses of her life. She would be a beautiful woman, I imagined, married to a handsome man. Their children would be angels, Oni and her mate in miniature. I longed to see her, but I knew that I never would. I was dead to her. Things were as they should be. The dead should remain so.

IN THE BEGINNING

"A breeze lifted the hem of my skirt, making the tattered white dress circle my ankles. I looked down at the dance of swirling fabric, ripped and pitted, and laughed. What beast was I that could rise from the ground to stand decades after my death? What manner of creature was I that could withstand the rays of direct sunlight unshaded and open? Folklore said that an *asiman* could only walk the earth under the cover of night, yet I stood with the sun warming my face. Might I be some other monstrosity? A witch reincarnated? A wayward ghost?

"The laughter in my head was deep and rich—familiar. It brought back the memories I had tried to suppress. It reminded of me of what I was with unwavering clarity.

"I turned my head and saw that I didn't cast a shadow on the dirt road. It was as if the sunlight shone through me instead of on me, like I wasn't there. A bitter chuckle rose from my throat. My voice, dormant for so long, sounded ethereal until it worked into a rich alto I had not possessed in life. My soprano lilt was forever gone, had died with my body. Maybe that was for the best. To live the life of the undead, the parasite, the vampire, I needed to be cunning, seductive and beguiling. The juvenile pitch of my former voice would not do.

"As I stood on the street of my youth, another being driven by the quest for blood, I realized that my time there was over. I turned my back on my house, my family, and my former life forever."

From Dahomey to Raskin Correctional

"I left my village for good after feeding on an unsuspecting young warrior I caught while hunting," Angie continued.

"Dahomey," I repeated. The name had been echoing in my head since the first time she said it. It sounded like a place that I had heard of before, where the women were warriors and fought for their country. But I couldn't put my finger on its location.

"It was a part of Togo when I lived there, on the West Coast of Africa." I nodded my head, remembering that the place had been named by one of the Black power rebels that were forming underground groups in Harlem neighborhoods before I was arrested. 'They stole our people from West Africa: Ghana, Togo, Benin—yeah, they called that the Slave Coast,' they used to yell out to the small crowds that gathered at their monthly meetings. 'The White man snatched our people up and brought them here, to the U. S. of A.!'

"First I went to London." Angie said, cutting through my memory. She sighed as though her words were heavy. "I perfected my English to fit in and tried to hide myself away from the world. I fed—I had to. The blood is sustenance, like water and bread to you."

"How do you manage now?" I asked before realizing I had spoken. I wanted to take the words back, to snatch them from the air and cast them aside, sit on them if I had to. I wasn't sure I wanted to know the answer. I hadn't heard of any problems, hadn't heard rumors of any fights that Angie had been involved in where she could have taken an inmate's blood, but that didn't make me any less nervous about what she might say. My hands began to twitch, my upper lip started to quiver, nervous ticks taking hold of me the way they always did when I was afraid.

Silence.

I sat waiting, each breath I took sounding loud in the quiet cell. I wanted to know more. If blood was her food, how could she give it up? I was afraid to ask anything more. After it was apparent that she wasn't going to respond, I decided to leave it alone.

"I've suppressed the craving," she offered, sensing my need to know more.

"You can do that?" I asked a bit too quickly.

"No."

The suspense was killing me, but I didn't dare press her about it. I should have, but I didn't. Angie went back to the account of her life then, eager to change the subject and I felt a load lift from my shoulders when she did. My mind had wandered, contemplating the things she could be replacing the supply of human blood with: rats, bugs—we seemed to have a never ending supply of cockroaches and spiders—the blood from her own veins. I even went as far as to wonder if someone on the outside wasn't helping her. Supplying her with blood on a regular basis. Smuggling it in. Maybe one of the guards? Angie never had any visitors. None of us did, for that matter, so who else could it be? I envisioned Officer Greenwood sneaking in bags of blood from the banks, or bringing her corpses from the morgue. Maybe she fed Angie the unruly inmates from other cellblocks, the ones who wouldn't behave, even in the hole. Officer Greenwood would have to tape their mouths and bind their hands and legs so that they couldn't fight, couldn't resist. Or maybe Officer Greenwood let Angie drink from her own neck. If promised eternal life, who wouldn't?

"You have a vivid imagination Lucky," Angie said, stopping in the middle of an account of London in the early 1800s that had gone ignored. "Try to hold onto that. It will be your only escape in the years to come."

My mind stopped turning over the scenarios and fell blank, dumbstruck. Angie had known what I was thinking right then and there. That was different than knowing about a dream I may have had or what I might be feeling. Those things could be explained away, though loosely. Maybe she was intuitive, clairvoyant, empathetic, all to the nth degree. But how could she know my thoughts as I formulated them in my mind, reading them like words in a book? It was then that awe transcended fear and skepticism. It was then that I truly started to believe.

"After leaving London, I went to the island of St. Martin. I got there right after the French abolished slavery, but before the Dutch released their reins," Angie continued. "The island was struggling then. The people, left with machinery in need of repair as a pittance, harvested sugar as they had when they were enslaved. But sugar could be gotten for a much cheaper price elsewhere, and the island was embroiled in a depression.

"I worked arm and arm with people from my homeland who had been shipped over to St. Martin over the course of sixty-five years. They spoke a choppy language, one that, I didn't understand at first. While in London, I studied language and literature, indulging the interests I had as a living girl. I had never come upon a language that sounded similar to what the people of St. Martin spoke. Gradually though, I caught on, finding threads of Spanish and Portuguese intertwined with those of Dutch and Kreyol. I could even hear some of my native tongue interspersed with English. Papaimento, they called it. And I learned it in earnest.

"I shed my African name and adopted the name Vanessa. It flowed from the tongue sensually and made me stir the first time I heard it. It was my moniker for fifty years.

"I worked as all the women did, out in the fields until my hands bled. I had to be careful about reacting to the sudden pain of a cut on the tips of my fingers because I was afraid the women around me would see the frayed skin rejuvenate itself within seconds. I let the sun cook my skin, until tan turned to red, painful and sore, but by evening my natural tone would return as vibrant as it was when I was alive. For a time, I cried my self to sleep, cringing from the metallic smell of the tears that sprang from my eyes and stained my pillowcase.

"I fed. I had to. Starving myself would not bring death, only immense hunger, the likes of which I had never suffered before. I drank the blood of those who roamed the island, having to feed two or three times a week to satisfy my hunger.

"I took a lover after a year of living on the island. She was a girl of twenty-one with beautiful brown skin and short-cropped hair. Her eyes were wondrous; they looked out at the world with a light that was blinding. She was experienced in the ways of women where I was not. Though she was stunning, her perky breasts and shapely hips were not the only reason I chose her to bed. I couldn't risk being with a man and allowing the prophecy to come true.

"Colette would come over on rainy afternoons when the fields were drenched and the people retreated to their homes, battening down the hatches. My place was near the water, away from the townsfolk who regarded me as an outsider. Though they respected the work I did, they kept me at arms length. I was new to their island and they had to warm up to me. Colette was as much of an outsider as I was, at least as far as the elders of the island were concerned. She was unabashed about what she did. She would watch women on the beach as men did, whistling to them to get their attention. She sometimes ferried over to her girlfriend's house on Saba. She was available to the European guests' wives who boated over to the island after a week on the sea. The elders hated her behavior and shunned her for it. The young men and women were divided: some were angered, others were accepting. Some wanted to try it but didn't want anyone else to know. I, too, was intrigued, so as one outcast to another, I invited her to my home.

"There wasn't much I could share with her about my past. I couldn't tell her about my home—there were too many West Africans on the island, and she herself had Ghanaian blood. I couldn't run the risk of her asking too many questions, ones that I wouldn't be able to answer with anything other than taking her life. I told her about pockets of my life, whatever I could parse from the bloodletting.

"Carmen asked where I was from and I told her that I came from London. She asked why I left and I didn't have to lie. I recounted the story of my companion, a wealthy White man of moderate age with power and prestige among the elite. He had a history of traveling to Africa to cavort with the girls there, so he was naturally drawn to me. His wife was oblivious, and even if she had known, I would have been construed as nothing more than a tart, a blackamoor prostitute with no other means of making a living. That sort of thing was accepted in polite company, as long as a child was never produced. And I took measures to be sure that never happened.

"Having tried to mutilate my organs before leaving my homeland in an attempt to thwart the prophecy, I found that nothing I did proved long lasting. I removed my clitoris to abate my desires, but it grew back in the next moment. I sewed my vagina closed, leaving only the smallest hole for waste (which has since proven unnecessary), but a deep breath ripped the sutures and reopened it. My desire for the company of a man was immense, even after death. More so since. The hunger for blood and desire for sex were intertwined, one exacerbating the other, teasing it to a boiling point.

"My lover willingly filled the bill. He courted me swiftly, meeting me at a bazaar one evening, and lavishing flowers on me the next. I was not one to be treated as a common harlot, and he deduced that before I ever spoke a word. I drew out the courtship, allowing him to buy me gifts and give me money for the pleasure of my time. When I finally decided to sleep with him, he was so excited he prematurely ejaculated on the bedspread. I laughed and told him that the spread would be where all of his seed would fall from then on. And it did.

"My lover satisfied me. Robert was the first consistent lover I ever had, and I enjoyed the companionship he provided. He paid for all of my expenses, which became more considerable as time went one, and he put money aside for me for the proverbial rainy day. We romped between the bed sheets at the finest hotels, arriving under the cover of night so as not to be seen for the better part of ten years. Robert gave me precious gemstones to rival his wife's collection. After her death in the eighth year of our frolicking, he showered me two-fold. She had been barren, their union never producing any children, so his fortune was to be left to no one. Instead, he decided to give it to me, to spend it all on me while he was alive to see me enjoy it. And enjoy it I did.

"I studied in the presence of Job Ben Solomon, the scholarly African Prince kidnapped into slavery who was later freed and paraded among the British elite before his return to Gambia. I went to the theatre and dressed in the finest of garments. I dined well and danced the evenings away with Robert unabashedly on my arm. I bought property and first edition books, my penchant for reading still in tact. I lived.

"I left London after Robert died in our tenth year. I stayed just long enough to watch as his body was laid in the earth next to his wife's.

"The story was idyllic to Colette. She was mesmerized with the regality of London and wanted to know more, but I told her it was too painful to revisit. She seemed satisfied with that, nodding in a knowing way that betrayed her hidden pains. She never asked about London again."

I had questions I wanted to ask about London also, but I dared not. Where Colette was trying to be polite and not dredge up painful memories, I was afraid of the answers that might have been given. My mind conjured visions of bloodshed and carnage behind old buildings and beneath bridges. I didn't want to know if I was right. Angie cleared her throat and continued,

"Colette and I became friends as well as lovers. She taught me about my body, touching it in ways that I had not imagined possible. She showed me my true nature as a woman. I felt more sensual with her than I ever had before."

Angie paused, visions of powdery sand and warm, turquoise water filling her mind. She transferred those images to me. I could see her, a slender, medium-brown skinned woman with eyes that revealed her sensuality. Her cheeks were chiseled and her chin was strong. Her lips were full, proportioned to her face. They spread into a beautiful smile while I watched, curving up at the edges to reveal straight white teeth. Her hair was braided in an intricate design, the braids weaving around each other on her scalp and cascading down the center of her back. The sun kissed her cheek and shoulders.

She was naked, basking in the sunlight as she sat at the shore of the empty beach. The wind lifted her hair from her back to surround her head. She squinted against the sun and looked out at the water, allowing it to lap at her feet. She was radiant.

I couldn't help but look at her body. It was beautiful, sculpted like a statue. Her breasts were round with brown nipples, beautiful accents to her slender body. Her stomach was flat, toned to show the muscle beneath.

Her hips were full and curved such that they gave her body the sought after hourglass. Her thighs were muscular. Her feet were slim. All of the hair on her body was black, jet black.

I tried not to look at her body, tried to focus on her face, or the ocean and beach, but I couldn't help myself. Her public hair formed a perfect 'V' between her legs. It troubled me that I noticed that, but I did. It had been so long since I had been with a man that any stimulation would do. And this wasn't just any woman standing naked in my dreams. It was Angie, the woman whose sultry voice I heard talking to me from the other side of the wall, Angie, whose tongue caressed words in different languages, Angie, whom I had envied since I had been in jail for her sense of calm, her sense of being. Angie. I could feel myself pulsating as I enjoyed her body.

I could feel my temperature rising as I gazed at her, could feel myself throbbing as she uncrossed her legs to rest them both on the sand. I was embarrassed. Never before had I fancied women, but Angie was a vision against the white sand. She played the movie for me, made me smell the air and feel the sand underneath my feet. And I loved it.

I had never been anywhere that looked so beautiful with palm trees and turquoise water. The furthest I had ever traveled was down south to my mother's home in Georgia. The landscape, though different from what I knew in New York City, was nothing to write home about. Cotton fields and plantation houses on one part of town, dilapidated ramblers and overgrown lawns on another. Railroad tracks separated the town into poor and rich, which typically meant White and Black. The tracks even ran through the cemetery, separating the rows of tall marble monuments on the White side and the cement slab or rock adorned dirt graves of the Blacks. That was the one thing that stuck with me from my visits to the South. That cemetery. My grandmother's grave wasn't far from the tracks. Momma used to make fun, saying that grandma could sit up and wave at Missus on a clear night if she wanted to.

The tropical scenery that back dropped Angie's beautiful body was like nothing I had ever seen. I wanted to go there, to feel the wind upon my face. The more I yearned for it, the more Angie fed me until I was embroiled in the dream. Until it wasn't a dream at all.

I let my imagination wander and approached the water. I could see my bare feet, my unkempt toe nails looking back at me with gnarled faces. That didn't matter to me then. What mattered was that I could see my feet, could physically see them, the sun shining on them, the sand that clustered around my toes. I felt laughter rising in my throat as I took one, two, three steps toward the water's edge, determined to put my foot in, to see what the turquoise water felt like. When I reached the surf, I hesitated. I watched as the water caressed the beach and knew that I was at the crossroads.

If I could feel the water on my skin I was stepping over to another side, going to some realm where reality had no boundaries. I knew that to feel the water meant to lose my mind, the side that was rational, logical about life and the things in it. The side that knew what was real and what wasn't. All of that would go away the moment that water touched my skin. After watching the water draw closer and closer to me with every wave that broke, I realized that I didn't care. If touching the water was to give in to insanity, so be it. What else did I have to live for? If my body was supposed to die, why not let my mind have some fun before it goes?

A woman walked toward Angie as I dipped my foot into the warm water. Finding that my legs and arms were bare, free of the horrible prison outfit they made us wear I ran into the water, meeting the waves partway. I immersed myself in its warmth; the flow of the water sent chills down my spine as it soothed me. When I resurfaced, a laugh, pure and rich, emitted from my diaphragm. I was in heaven.

Angie and the woman embraced on the sand. I could see them from the water, but I had grown disinterested. The velvety touch of turquoise entranced me. I couldn't get enough of it.

The fact that I couldn't swim passed fleetingly in my mind. A trip to Orchard Beach at Pelham Bay Park had proven that years before when I was a young girl. My mother and I went to the beach with a couple of people from the neighborhood. The adults picnicked while the kids went swimming in the murky, dark-green water of the Long Island Sound. It was the new beach. The one that had been created a couple of years before

I was born. The water was supposed to be calmer there, easier to play around in since it was far away from the Atlantic. Somehow, I found a way to get sucked under anyway, strong current or not. One of the men from our block had to jump in and pull me out of the drink before I succumbed to it. I hadn't been in the water since then. But none of that mattered anymore. I was no longer afraid of the water, no longer cautious. As I floated on my back expertly, like I had been doing it for years, I mused that in this reality, anything was possible. Those who couldn't swim could, those who wouldn't smile would. Those who were imprisoned were set free. Angie and the woman were lying down on the beach, drinking wine and eating fruit. I could hear their voices on the air as they talked excitedly, laughing about something I couldn't quite make out. I smiled. It had been so long since I heard the sound of laughter, true laughter borne of happiness and contentment. It warmed me inside the way the sun did outside.

I opened my eyes to look at the sun, staring right at it, knowing that nothing would happen to me—I wouldn't burn my retinas or make myself dizzy. Reality and unreality didn't play by the same rules.

The sun was high in the sky, glowing brightly, warming my skin with its rays. Its glowing sides seeming to melt into the blue sky, shimmering there. It started to spread, the bright yellow bleeding into the blue, engulfing it. I watched as the sun became the sky, became the space, obliterating the beach, the sand, the water, leaving nothing but yellow, bright and pulsating. The brightness intensified, fading from yellow to white. The white flashed like a strobe to bring me back to the dark, dank cell at Raskin Correctional. I was sitting on my bed with my ear pressed to the wall as I had been before, as I had been the whole time. A profound sadness came over me at the loss of the dream, the loss of escape.

"The body of a young adult and the soul of an ancient," Angie said, breaking the silence. I felt my embarrassment rise hotly in my cheeks again. She knew I was looking at her, that I had admired, even wanted to touch her. I hoped she didn't say anything about it. I wanted to keep the image in my head to myself, untainted by exposure. "You were very beautiful," I decided to say, hoping that would be the last word on the subject.

"Things stay the same when you are like me. You will soon see. He will make you his in due time."

I let her words hang in the air, unsure of what to make of them. The fear I should have felt at that assertion didn't come. Instead, I was strangely numb. I looked at the corners of my room, searching for my visitor, so used to his presence after months of appearances. He wasn't there. At least, I couldn't see him. I had the feeling that he was there though, hiding himself in the darkness, taking the form of the night air. Watching. Listening. Waiting.

"How did you do that?" I asked, unable to stop the question from forming on my lips. "How did you bring me into your memory? Everything was so vivid. So real."

"You will possess the same gift and I beg you to use it to save my boy. Many things will come to you when you are reborn."

The desperation in her voice upset me on many levels. I suddenly felt a sense of unease creeping along my body like a spider.

"I spent several years with Colette," Angie continued. "She became older before my eyes, the ravages of time taking their toll. She grew suspicious of me as I remained the same. My skin did not wrinkle, my breasts did not sag. My hair kept its natural luster, never turning gray, never thinning out. Before my eyes, Colette grew into a middle-aged woman with toughened skin and infirmities.

"She questioned me, lightly at first, about how I was able to keep my girlish figure and features. I was able to deflect her at first, but then her questions grew stronger. She started to accuse me of being a witch, as the townsfolk had taken to doing. She told me that I had been seen skulking around in the shadow of night, killing people and drinking their blood. I didn't know whether she knew what she was saying or not, but at that point it didn't matter. Our differences were showing and people were talking. Something had to be done.

"I left the island on a ferry to Mayaguana. I stayed there for a couple of years. After finding more of the same treatment I had experienced in St.

Martin, I left and moved to New York. I hoped that the big city would make me anonymous"

Angie's voice sounded heavy when she talked about leaving the islands but brightened when she spoke of New York. "New York was truly alive in the thirties. Black people from the South had migrated North, finding jobs and housing in abundance. They worked as day laborers, chambermaids, shoe shiners, anything to put food on the table, and they lived five to a room in low rent neighborhoods to get by. They had cabarets in Black only nightclubs featuring talent from around the neighborhood. They had rent parties and fish frys. Life's worries were forgotten over the poker table, or in the club with the juke playing.

"The well-to-do Blacks lived in Harlem on the Gold Coast. I bought a row house there that had a brick front and hardwood floors on the inside. Oh, the parties I threw there! One of my neighbors was a hairdresser with a salon in Rockland County. He called the place Village People, since it was in the Village of Nyack. Jim was the only Black person to have a store on Nyack's Main Street. Everyone who had a car went over the bridge to get their hair done at his salon. Jim was our street's own success story.

"We were living it up. It was the best and the worst time to be Black in New York.

"It was there, twenty-five years after I had decided to make New York my home, that I met my true love. He was just a boy, so young and unfettered. He had elaborate dreams of painting and traveling in Europe where his work would be appreciated. I bought him canvases, more than he could ever fill. I bought paints and supplies, easels and lamps. I posed for him and he created incredible masterpieces. Never before had I seen myself through the eyes of another in such a form. Photographs paled in comparison to oil on canvas. His work was magnificent."

I could imagine the dreamy look Angie's face must have held. She sounded so euphoric.

"Is this the one—?" I stuttered. Angie never really talked about him, about what happened. She said she killed him for his blood and that was all. There was sadness in her voice whenever she spoke about him. I never probed, never wanted to push her over the edge. She had instilled a fear in me that was unfounded and irrational, at least that was what I thought before that day. Sitting on the other side of the wall from her, feeling the warmth of her body as though I had touched her skin, I was sure that my fear was appropriate. And prudent.

"The times had changed so drastically in the short time I had been living there," Angie said, ignoring my question. "Harlem went from a flourishing metropolis, a mecca of sorts for Southern Blacks in the North, to a rapidly declining slum; the bad part of town. Oppression reared its ugly head and batted its eyes at people of color. Blacks were being hosed, bitten by dogs, beaten with clubs. Hanged, in some cases further North. I was jaded and antsy, ready to make a move. I was thinking of California, seeing myself swimming in the Pacific. How I missed the water. New Yorkers weren't the water lovers that the people of St. Martin were and with good reason. Their pickings were slim. I missed it. And I hated what was going on in the streets, right in front of my eyes. I was preparing to leave when I met him." Angie recounted the day they met as though it happened the day before. They were both walking along 125th street. They paused to listen to a speaker at the corner of 125th and 5th Avenue—there was always someone taking post to talk about one topic or another. Often the theme was religion—"You better find God before it's too late!" "Struggle now but reap the benefits in Heaven!"—but that day the young Black man on the corner talked about empowerment and fighting against the oppression that had draped Black people everywhere like a cloak.

"Jonathan was such a fine young man," Angie sighed. "He was picture perfect with his unblemished skin and ripe young muscles. The crevices of his body are forever etched in my mind.

"I killed him like I had killed before, but not out of hunger or need. It was for protection. I couldn't tell him what I was just like I couldn't tell the others, but for him there was more danger in not knowing." Angie was crying. I heard her muted sobs and felt my own eyes sting as well. "Jonathan was more special to me than anyone else has ever been," she continued. "Maybe that's why I was caught unaware. His love disarmed me."

I couldn't take it any longer. I had to know about the baby, the reason she was telling me all of this. I had waited long enough.

"What about the baby? If you killed Jonathan and were arrested on the spot, where is the baby? Did you have it in here?"

Angie was quiet. I could hear her sniffle faintly. I began to wonder if I had been too forward, that old fear creeping up again. Finally, she answered in a voice that was without anger,

"He is out there somewhere. I left Jonathan for seven months without telling him where I was going. I intended to stay away, to move on to another town, another life. I had even taken another name. The people in Laurinburg, North Carolina knew me as Rebecca. I got a place with a sharecropping family. They agreed to take me in as long as I worked in the fields. My cut of the harvest profit was to be small, much less than what the rest of the sharecroppers were making, and that was hardly enough to live on as it was. But I didn't stay long enough to get my pay.

"I had my baby there, after a long day of working in the cotton fields under the blazing sun. The bed linens in my room were soaked through with blood, staining the floor beneath. I begged the women not to touch it, to leave me alone while I birthed my child, but they would hear nothing of it. Lucinda's death still haunts me. The raw tips of her fingers were exposed from a day of picking—she had put in extra time that day to meet the quota. Lucinda was contaminated with my blood when she wiped my thighs clean of it. She died a day after my son was born, seeming to just drop dead. I mourned her, even while I sat vigil by her grave thinking of ways to kill her should she rise from the dead. She and her family had opened their doors to me, had befriended me. Her death was a mistake.

"As soon as I was able, I left the sharecropper's home and North Carolina all together. I traveled to Florida with my child in my arms. I refused to let him suckle my breast, afraid that my milk would taint him further. His crying caused me more pain than I could ever have imagined.

"I left my son in the garden of a Black woman who had the kindest face I had ever seen. I waited to see her come out of her ramshackle house to find him there. Once she discovered my boy and the money I wrapped in his blanket, I left. I have not seen him since."

I could see the baby through my window into her mind. He was beautiful. She had wrapped his naked body in a baby blue blanket. His face was angelic, his smooth skin a paler version of what it would be later in life, almost paper thin. His little hands clasped the corners of the blanket.

"What did you name him?" I asked.

"I didn't. I left that up to the woman who would be his mother. I don't know his name." She sounded sorrowful. "It's better that way."

The image of the baby stuck in my mind. I felt an odd coolness within me as I languished over his features. The coolness spread throughout my body, filling the crevices, saturating them. I felt violated. I became afraid of its presence.

"See how easily he enters you?" Angie said from her cell. Her voice seemed to float in front of me. I blinked back bitter tears. "You must ward against him, deny him. If not, you will surely lose yourself. And my son. You are his only hope."

I concentrated harder than I ever had before. I shut windows and slammed doors, closing my mind off to him. I locked the image of the baby in a vault made especially for him and vowed that, no matter what, I wouldn't open that door for anyone. The coolness lingered for a while, ever probing, looking. After what seemed like forever, it dissipated and I allowed myself to take a breath.

Angie was silent.

I could feel her worry in the air. It was electric. I felt the weight of the task on my shoulders. It was heavy like the weight of two men. It crushed me.

"Why me?" I asked, my voice taking on an uncharacteristic whine. "Why not someone else? Anyone else?"

"Because he has chosen you, Lucky." Her voice was calm and still.

That was no consolation. I got angry. I beat my hands against my thin mattress. Muted thumps sounded from each blow.

"What if I say no?" I challenged, knowing that to deny service to either of them was to seal my fate. I would surely die, either by his hand or hers, with the State pulling a close third. I would be gone; my body would be as cold and rigid as stone. Lucky would cease to exist. I had been trying to sell myself on that when it was my life's inevitable end. I told myself that dead was better than caged any day. But now, facing the prospect of freedom against certain death—and painful, bloody death, I was sure—I was afraid. He would offer me life after death. All she wanted was protection for her son. A small pittance to pay for immortality.

"He will come to you with promises after I die," Angie said. "Accept them. Let him make you what I am, but only after you have trained your mind to hide your true thoughts, your true mission. If he sees what you are up to, he will kill you in the most painful of ways. You are disposable to him. He can always find another."

"But how will I find your son? How will I ever know who he is? He could be anywhere in the world."

"He is not far," Angie said, her voice low and gravelly. "I can feel him."

"But what does that have to do with me?" My mind was twisting and turning, fraught from the stress of Angie's request and tired from keeping my visitor at bay.

"You will know. As soon as you become what I am, you will be able to sense him as you will sense any other of our kind. He has my blood flowing through his veins. It is diluted by human blood, but it's still there. Find my things when you get out of here. My scent will be on them. I have left clothes, jewelry, and money in the world that will belong to you after my death. I have some of his father's things as well. I packed them away as keepsakes when I thought I would leave him forever. Get our scents and you will be able to find his."

Like a dog, I was supposed to go around sniffing people to find a man who didn't know he was being hunted. I laughed sarcastically and opened my mouth to tell Angie just how ridiculous I thought her little errand was, but the desperation in her voice stopped me.

"Lucky, please do this for me. Save my boy from a fate he doesn't deserve. Don't let my death be in vain."

With a sigh of resignation, I listened as Angie trained me. Over the next couple of days she tested my mind, trying to probe me for information, and each time accessing less and less. I was good at blocking my thoughts from view. I had been hiding them from myself for most of my life. Marcel was leery of our closeness. It was like we had become bosom buddies, inseparable in the time that she was in solitary. We were always friends, as much as we could have been in jail. But Angie and I talked more and more to each other and less and less to Marcel. There was so much I had to learn and we didn't have much time. Angie's date was only a week away.

When Marcel asked us what we were up to, Angie told her that I was trying to learn Papiamento. She said I had a cousin who lived in the Caribbean and I wanted to write to her in her native tongue. Marcel was only placated when she heard me speak.

Angie transplanted the words in my mind and I said them as though they were my own. "Halo Marcel! Mi coiusin ta fo'i Aruba," I yelled so that she could hear me clearly. I was as amazed to hear them spew from my mouth as Marcel was. She mumbled something about how stupid it was for me to learn something like that given the fact that we were all going to die soon anyway. Both Angie and I ignored her comment. She had become bitter since her stay in solitary. The weight of time ticking away was heavy on her.

On the day that Angie was killed, I received confirmation of my date. A mere two weeks after hers and one week after Marcel's. They took Angie to the Rest Room, where inmates were supposed to spend their last night. I never understood why they didn't just leave us where we were. Among friends. Among people who would actually miss us. Marcel shouted her goodbyes to Angie through the bars of her cell. Officer Greenwood allowed Angie a second in front of Marcel's cell, even though the route didn't pass her door. Marcel's voice was thick and mucousy as she said goodbye to her friend.

"Safe journey, Angie."

"Same to you Marcel," Angie said, her voice sounding strong. "You will be fine."

Marcel sniffled and grunted, "Yeah."

Angie and Officer Greenwood shuffled by my cell next. I stood and walked toward the bars that separated us. There was my friend, my mentor. I had never seen her with my own eyes before. She looked exactly as she had that day on the beach in St. Martin.

I opened my mouth to speak, but found that my voice had abandoned me. Tears welled in the corners of my eyes and I let them fall freely.

"It's all right," Angie said as Officer Greenwood started to walk her away. "Remember that."

I nodded my head in silence, unable to say a word.

We said our goodbyes in our mind, talking with more freedom than we ever could verbally. She wasn't frightened. Instead, she was determined. She wanted death, welcomed it.

"How could you do it? If you weren't in here, I mean. How could you kill yourself?" I asked her. It was something I might need to know down the road. "Watch a sunrise or go into a church?"

Angie's laughter cut into my mind like a sharp blade. "That's how Hollywood says you can kill a vampire, but it's not true. Did you ever notice me sleeping during the day? Ever hear the creaking of my coffin lid as I opened it?"

I started to feel silly.

"Fantasy for the masses," she finished.

"So how do you die?"

"My body must be burned. Organs, skin, bones, everything must be burned beyond functionality. Only then will I be released. Only then will my soul be able to rest."

"So why didn't you do it yourself? Take yourself out of your misery?"

Angie seemed to ruminate on the question. When she finally answered, I could hear the pain her words caused. "Because my son was out there alone. His children, me and soon you, and others like us, can't kill ourselves, Lucky. He owns us; we are bound to him. Our offspring, though bound to him, is not tethered as we are. Suicide only works if it is done before he gets to you, before he claims you as his." Angie sounded bitter. "He makes it seem so fantastic, living forever with eternal youth. But that couldn't be further from the truth. It's a curse, a vicious cycle. You must kill to stay alive, and in doing so, you send more souls to him. Your damnation is immediate upon the first drink you take to quench your hunger, and drink you will."

Angie's words echoed in my head, taking hold and lodging themselves there. For a person like Angie, who was only a girl when she was turned, life after death must have been horrible. She had been innocent, guiltless of any crime. Damnation seemed like never ending torture. For a person like me, damnation was part of the game.

"Be careful Lucky. Find my son. Protect him. Remember what I taught you and block him from your mind."

That was the last thing Angie said to me.

The next morning Officer Greenwood came to her post on my ward. She strolled in front of our cells in a daze. Her eyes seemed to gaze out in the distance at something none of us could see. On her third pass, I asked her, "You okay Officer Greenwood?" I probed her mind as I spoke, honing the skills that Angie had taught me. She turned to look at me, surprised at the unusual display of concern coming from an inmate. I could see it all. Her mind played the memory of Angie's last night like a movie on a screen.

Officer Greenwood worked Angie's execution along with two other guards that worked in different wards of the prison. They walked her down the last mile—the corridor between the Rest Room and the execution chamber—a half-hour before the scheduled time. Angie's face was serene. She didn't struggle against them, didn't speak out loud. She just walked in time with the guards down the long hallway, taking her last strides with dignity. Her calm demeanor unnerved Officer Greenwood.

They put Angie in the chair, securing the leg, waist, chest, and arm straps without incident. Angie's face remained stoic; her eyes stared ahead. Officer Greenwood secured the neck strap. Angie looked up at her, and with a soft smile, said,

"Thank you for your kindness Officer Greenwood. You have a good heart."

A tear formed in Officer Greenwood's eye. She coughed to try and conceal the rising emotion from her colleagues.

Another guard affixed the wet sponge to Angie's bald head—she had been shaved earlier that afternoon. The conductors and sponges were in place, the straps tightened in the usual manner. Everything was ready.

The warden read the summation of Angie's crime and asked her if she had anything she wanted to say before being put to death. Angie breathed deeply before speaking, taking in the metallic scent of the air, letting it fill her lungs one last time.

She spoke in her native tongue, her words indecipherable to everyone else in the room. But I understood them. She had taught me enough so that I would. "Elin kaka eyo yavo," she said in a voice that was crisp and clear. *Finally, this torment is over.*

The executioner flipped the switch on the warden's cue, waited the mandatory thirty seconds, and then turned off the juice. Angie still sat fresh, as though nothing had happened. He flipped it again, waiting longer before turning it off the second time, but Angie still appeared unaffected. The warden, doctor, and guards looked among each other in confusion. The chair had been checked the night before and it had been given an okay. There was no obstruction to the flow of electricity. There shouldn't have been a problem.

"What is it Bob?" the warden asked. "It's not working?"

"The juice is flowing fine, sir. I don't know what's wrong with the damned thing."

The warden looked at Angie and saw no damage. It was as if they had just gotten her out of the cell. He didn't want the publicity of a botched execution, not with the stats they had pulled the year before. Raskin Correctional was on top, number one out of all the prisons in New York for executions, and he didn't want this episode to put a blemish on their standing. He was thankful he had sent out few invitations to witness the execution. Only two members of the press had shown up, and they were from small, local newspapers. None of the victim's family was in attendance. No one knew if the condemned woman had any family whatsoever.

"Try it again, Bob," the warden said hurriedly, wanting to get the foul business of the execution behind him.

Bob flipped the switch a third time. Angie flicked her eyes over to the switch. Channeling everything she had ever learned about mind control and telepathic energy, she forced Bob's hand to up the amperage from six to eight, to ten, as far up as fifteen—until there was nothing more to give. Her body started to convulse in the chair, but she held her grip on him.

Bob screamed out, unable to take his hand off the lever.

"Lay off it, man!" the warden yelled when the smell of burning skin wafted into the air, making him gag. Angie's skin was beginning to singe.

"I can't!" Bob yelled back.

Angie's eyes burst into a milky white foam streaked with blood that dripped down her cheeks like tears. The soft skin of her hairline separated from her scalp and burned away, melting like candle wax. Saliva and blood ran out of her mouth and down her chin in torrents. Blood sprang up through her pores to bubble on her skin, warmed by the heat of her body as it cooled. Her body bucked from the current, straining against the straps that bound her to the chair. Her chin was pressed so tightly against the leather binding, the skin at her jaw line split. Her blood, heated to a boil, bubbled out of the wound and ran down her chin and neck to stain her prison uniform. Officer Greenwood ran over to Bob to try and yank his hand off the lever, but together neither of them could remove it. The other officer, a burly man of six feet tall and two hundred fifty pounds, fainted dead away.

Angie's skin disappeared in a cloud of ash. Her exposed muscle tissue and organs withered and caught fire. Her skull rocked atop the neck restraints before dropping onto her lap.

The executioner finally yanked his hand free with Officer Greenwood's help, just as Angie's head tumbled onto her thighs. The lever returned to the OFF position seemingly of its own volition, and the electricity stopped flowing. The warden sprayed Angie with the fire extinguisher, fighting the flames back until they succumbed to the carbon dioxide. They stood looking at the smoldering corpse in silence. Summoning his courage, the warden approached the chair, flanked by Officer Greenwood and Bob. Angie's body was reduced to a charred skeleton.

"What the hell happened here?" the warden asked no one in particular.

"Sir, I tried to get my hand off. I just couldn't," Bob said, turning away from the body.

"Bob's hand was stuck sir. It was like it had been glued on. I couldn't get it off either," Officer Greenwood offered, hoping it would help Bob's fate. The other guard rose from the floor noisily. The warden turned to face him and said, "It was an accident. A fluke, do you understand me? All that matters is that this inmate has been executed. We'll have the chair checked out tomorrow, just like we always do."

The guard shook his head silently, grateful that no one mentioned a big man like him passing out at the first sight of blood. If what the warden wanted him to do was keep his mouth shut about what happened, he would do it. He didn't see the whole thing anyway. He was laying on his back a good part of the time.

The doctor, who had been standing away from the commotion around the chair, pinned in place in shock, finally snapped out of it and walked over to the body. He positioned himself to place his stethoscope on Angie's chest, before realizing the ridiculousness of the gesture. The woman's head was in her lap. He thought if he had detected a pulse, he would lose his mind.

"You better call it, sir," the executioner said as he and Officer Greenwood prepared the body bag.

"Yes," the warden said, pulling his shoulders back and straightening his tie. The sooner he got back to business, the faster they could put the unfortunate episode behind them. "Time of death: 11:15 p.m., June 9, 1955." His eyes passed over what was left of Angie reluctantly. He hesitated before saying, finally, "Take her to the morgue. We've got two more to do tonight, and we're running behind schedule."

Officer Greenwood's eyes were vacant. I could hear the thought that resonated in her mind, *My God, what did we do? The flames… dear God, what did we do?* I wanted to tell her that it was okay, that Angie got what she wanted, but I didn't. I thought that if she heard me tinkering around in her head, talking to her from the inside, she might go crazy. So I asked her again, aloud,

"You okay?"

"Y-yeah," she stuttered. "I'm fine. I'm fine."

She turned and walked away, finishing her rounds. She went through the rest of the day in silence, opting out of shooting the shit with the other guards. Officer Greenwood quit that afternoon and never came back.

NEXT

They took Marcel next.

We had been talking all week. Marcel was more chatty than usual. She talked about Angie's home in Africa, she talked about her people in the South. She asked me if I believed in Heaven and Hell. I told her I didn't know and I meant that. All of the stuff that Angie had told me was starting to sound like a crazy woman's tale in my head. It had been a week since her death, and nothing happened. No visits from the shadow man, no promises. Only her name echoed in my head, and for all I knew, I was putting it there like some kind of self-punishment. I stopped believing in Angie and the stuff she fed me. It was all a crock. I was scheduled to die and the state planned on carrying out the sentence. In two week's time I would follow Angie's and Marcel's footsteps to the electric chair, come hell or high water. There wouldn't be any intervention from a shadow man offering the gift of eternal life. There would only be death, cold and hard.

"Well, what do you think happens when we die? What happens to our souls?" Marcel's voice pleaded for a response she could make heads or tails of. She needed something to hold on to. She only had a day before her time was up.

"What's a soul anyway, Marcel?" I responded callously.

"It's the essence of who you are." She sounded taken aback by the question.

"Don't give me that Catholic School mumbo jumbo! A soul is nothing. The whole idea of it is made up. The only reason people talk about a soul is so they can feel like some part of them exists after their body is gone. They can't deal with the fact that dead is dead."

"Lucky, the Bible says—."

"I don't care what the Bible says, Marcel! How could there be a God? Would he have let us do what we did to get in here? Would he let us die in the fucking electric chair? Or is he just turning his back on us?"

"Lucky, don't talk like that. God cares about you and me as much as He cares about the people on the outside."

"Right." I was bitter. Angie had filled my head with a bunch of lies and I bought into them hook, line, and sinker. But nothing happened. Death was staring me right in the face, and all I could do was look back at it.

Marcel was quiet for a while. Finally she said, "You better get right with God, Lucky. Before it's too late."

I snickered and said, "Or what? My *soul* will go to Hell?" I laughed heartily and it felt good. "In case you haven't noticed Marcel, *this* is Hell. What worse can the devil do to me?" I laughed again, turning away from the wall. I didn't want to hear anymore of Marcel's religious garbage. She'd be dead in a day and I would be in a week. Maybe I'd see her when I to the other side. We could work next to each other on the chain gang.

"You don't want to find out Lucky. Believe that," Marcel said, but I ignored her.

"Let me worry about mine, and you worry about yours," I said, my voice harsher than it needed to be. "I don't need God anymore than he needs me."

That night, after they took Marcel from her cell to spend her last night on earth in the Rest Room, I wasn't so sure.

The silence was deafening. I had gotten used to the sound of Angie's movements on the other side of the wall and the faint whimpering I could hear from Marcel's cell at night. I had gotten used to being part of a group. Being friends with Angie and Marcel made me feel whole again, like a person, not a caged animal. With them gone, life went back to what it had been my first night there. The blinders were pulled away from my eyes and I squinted in the harsh light reality shined.

I felt like a fool who was about to die.

I cried myself to sleep most nights. The guards left me alone. They probably saw their share of tears coming from the women in their cellblock. I never understood how they got used to it, the self pity, the despair. How could they listen to a person crying their heart out night after night, until, finally, they walked to their death? I listened to their thoughts in the beginning, until it became more than I could handle. I learned more than I wanted to know about the nightshift guard who took leave just before my execution, Officer Pembrose. Our crying wasn't the only thing that occupied his thoughts. In his mind I saw women's faces twisted in fear, their bodies scantily clad, their breasts bared. Arms reached out to encircle the women's necks, choking them. Officer Pembrose would chuckle at that thought, the memory tickling him more than he showed outwardly. The thing that bothered me most, that scared me worst, was when he determined who would be his next conquest. It was a face that I recognized among the staff of the prison.

I stopped using the gift after that. There was no value in it. I was going to die and all those mind tricks Angie had shown me were useless. She was just trying to amuse herself in her last days, I told myself. She wasn't some vampire, some tortured soul who had traveled the world. She didn't have a son out there somewhere, and even if she did, he wasn't being hunted down by the devil. Angie was just a troubled woman who had been facing death in a matter of days. It got to her. She was trying to get her mind off the inevitable and I was the idiot who got sucked into her elaborate fairytale.

It was two nights before I was supposed to leave my cell for good and spend the night in the waiting room. My last visiting day had come and gone without company. No letters came professing love or sorrow at my impending fate. There was nothing. It was as if I had never existed outside the walls of Raskin Correctional. Like I had been forgotten the moment I left.

The guards asked me if I wanted anyone on the list to witness my execution. I laughed bitterly. The faces of many on the outside who would like to see me dead filled my mind. I would have too many to list, so I said no instead.

I curled up on my bed that night, my eyes painfully dry, devoid of tears by then. I wrapped my arms around myself, trying to keep warm. The summer heat covered the building like a warm, wet rag, but I couldn't seem to stop shivering. The touch of my hands on my skin felt foreign, like tiny needles.

And then I saw him.

He pulled away from the shadows, shedding them like a person would shed an overcoat. "Lucky." My name rolled off his tongue like fresh water over pebbles.

"I didn't expect to see you again." I thought I had spoken the words aloud, but I didn't hear them bounce off the walls. I looked over at the guards' desk. Officer Nutley, the new guy on the night shift, didn't lift his head. My shadow man spoke to me in my mind and I had responded in kind. At first I didn't believe it. I even spoke aloud to show my defiance.

"Ain't nobody here anyway. Just some old shadows playing with my mind. Stupid," I said and sucked my teeth. Officer Nutley put down his book; the spine banged against the table.

"What's going on in there Miss?" he called out looking over at me. I turned to look at him. He was so fresh, so wet behind the ears. He still called women like us Miss. All of them did at first, except the truly mean ones. They tried to treat us with a little dignity. But that got old quickly enough. After about a month or so on the job, they'd resort to girl or gal, even broad sometimes. They hardly ever used our first names. Addressing us like that was too close to respect, too humane. Officer Nutley would loose his politeness as the green faded, just like all the rest of them. I read him then, testing my skills to see if I could still do it. Officer Nutley's mind was a jumble of phrases, all of them angry. *Why did I have to take this piece of shit job? I'm gonna fuck around and get myself killed in here. Look at that crazy bitch. In there talking to herself. I hope she doesn't try to play that insane act with me. That shit'll never work.'* I laughed out loud at his thoughts, amazed that I could still read them. I thought the skills Angie taught me were gone, thought I had pushed them away, but they were still there, as sharp as a tack.

"Did you hear me? What's all the racket in there?" He looked as if he was about to stand.

"Nothing. Sorry," I said quickly, stifling my laughter and settling down. With a smile I watched Officer Nutley settle and turn back to his book.

"Did you think I would abandon you? Leave you at a time like this?" My shadow man was closer now, almost close enough to kiss.

"I didn't know. I don't believe in this stuff anyway."

"Don't you?" God, he was seductive. "How can you tell me you don't believe when I can touch you and you can feel it?" He touched my face, traced my jaw line, and let his fingers run down my neck. His hand was flushed with warmth. I wanted him to touch my breast, my stomach, my sex. It had been so long since I had been touched by someone and I wanted it. Needed it. "Don't you believe I am here for you?"

"This is crazy. I must be crazy." I shook my head. To the passerby I would have looked like I had lost my mind, like I had crumbled under the stress of impending death. I sat straight up in bed, my eyes closed, my back arched, my head cocked to the side. My lips moved, mouthing the words I spoke to my visitor in my mind. Yes, I decided. I am crazy.

"No, Lucerne. You are chosen. You are more important to me than you realize."

My eyes snapped open to look at him again, his caramel skin seeming as smooth as velvet in the dim light. "Why?" I asked.

"Don't you deserve it? Should you die here in this prison at the hands of those who want nothing more than your blood? Should you have to die at all?"

I didn't want to die. I was terrified of it. And he knew it.

"I can make it so you'll never feel the pain of suffering and death again. I can make this life end and a new one start. I can and will do this for you, Lucky. If you will be with me."

He touched me again, his hand lingering on my neck and then my collarbone. I could feel my nipples perking up in anticipation of his caress.

"But why? Why me?" Something in my mind couldn't—wouldn't—just let go. I remembered what Angie said about hiding my thoughts from him and I did so. I felt confident that he couldn't see the secrets Angie had shared. If he had, he probably would have killed me. So I held firm, hoping he wouldn't yank the offer away altogether.

"Because, my dear. I love you."

NEXT

The words filled my head and enfolded me like a silk robe. I melted. His hand traced the shape of my breast, teasing me to a moan before finally cupping it, closing his warmth around it. He leaned in to me then, kissing my lips softly at first, then purposefully. I gave in, knowing that his presence wasn't real, that he was in my head. But it didn't matter. His touch, his kiss all felt like those of a flesh and blood man. I welcomed it.

Officer Nutley fumbled the keys as he raced to my cell. He saw me gasping for air, my arms outstretched, reaching for something unseen just beyond my grasp. He would tell the review board that the sounds I made were like moans of desire. He would say he ignored them because he thought I might have been pleasuring myself. Officer Nutley would hang his head when he told them that he stayed where he was and let me continue so I could have my privacy. Given that I was going to be executed in two days, he thought he could at least do that for me.

My lover, the shadow man, Angie's Promise Keeper, squeezed the life out of me. He constricted my heart and drank the air from my lungs like fine wine. The pain of death was offset by the invigorating transfusion of life from my ressurector. Officer Nutley and another guard on the floor tried to resuscitate me, but I pushed away their attempts at saving my life, allowing myself to sink deeper and deeper into death's warm embrace. His kisses on my neck were so intoxicating, I barely felt the pressure of his teeth as they bore into my flesh. My lover drew me to him, holding me tight even as the guards pressed and prodded my body. I couldn't help but wonder why they were trying so hard. They were planning to kill me in a matter of days. I was doing them a favor.

When I lay down in mortal death, I knew that I would awaken the next nightfall to immortal life.

A New Day Through Bloody Eyes

I woke up in a body bag in the morgue in the basement of the prison hours later. The coroner wasn't scheduled to come in until the next morning, so the guards put my body in a bag and left it in a body tray in the cooler. The death of an inmate was hardly the kind of thing to rush out of bed for. I awoke to a blackness so impenetrable, I thought it might eat me whole. I pressed against the vinyl bag that surrounded me in a panic, scratching at it like a cat. Through the teeth of the zipper I could see a light. Even though the space that lay beyond the bag was dark, it was less concentrated. The hue wasn't as deep as the blackness I was confined in. I worked the zipper down enough so that I could press my finger through the separation. I unzipped the bag and found myself inside the refrigeration unit.

Then I heard his voice. It cut through the silence like a knife through melted butter. It was the voice of my lover, velvet and sweet in its caress. "Lucerne," he called ever so sweetly, like a mother waking a child from a nap. His voice was so faint, I almost didn't hear it. "Lucerne, my darling. It's time."

I had always detested my name, had favored Lucky, but to hear it pass so eloquently over his lips sent shivers down my spine.

"But I can't. It's too dark," I said, afraid of what the sound of my voice must mean. I knew I had died, knew it the moment it happened. I heard the slowing beat of my heart in my head, could feel the life being pulled from me. That I could hear him talking and could reply in kind meant that I must have truly come back to life. Just like Angie said I would.

"Come out Lucerne, and see the world with fresh eyes." His rich baritone echoed off the walls of the cooler like the beat of a drum, rattling my teeth and springing me into action. I was alive. I was free.

The door unlatched easily. It had been shut by a guard so eager to leave the morgue that he didn't make sure the door had locked. Stepping out of the refrigeration unit, I could see what had the guard in such a hurry. Three dead bodies lay uncovered on autopsy tables. I stared at them, one with its head and right leg shaved, the smooth skin scarred with three-degree burns, another with the sickly appearance cancer gives in the advanced stages, the last with no outward signs of illness, but dead just the same. I couldn't contain the smile that crept across my lips, or the laugh that rushed through my body and out of my mouth. I was alive! There I stood, disrobed but otherwise the same as I had been hours before, alive after death. The air had never smelled sweeter than it did at that moment, the medicinal scent of the morgue mingled with singed flesh notwithstanding. I had to stop myself from dancing into the night.

I left the morgue cautiously, unsure if there would be a guard at the door. When I entered the hallway and saw that there wasn't one, I almost laughed out loud. Why would the morgue need a guard? All of the prisoners inside were dead. At least, they should be.

I snuck out of the cavernous basement deftly, escaping in the disguise of a mortuary assistant. The night guards sitting in the booth out front didn't cast me a second glance, not even as I looked around the unfamiliar room searching for the exit. And what if they had? There wasn't anything they could do to me. I was dead already.

But alive! So very alive. I could feel the cool breeze on my face. It caressed my skin like a lover, teasing sensations from me that I had long since forgotten. I felt my stride, wide and graceful, for the first time in a long while. I felt each step as the heel of my foot rolled through the arch, as my hips leaned in and flowed, juggling my weight. No longer did the chains that tied my legs together, allowing only the smallest breadth for short, stumbling steps encumber me. For good measure, I took two gigantic leaps in the air, covering more ground than I had been able to the whole time I'd been incarcerated. And it felt good.

The midnight sun was the most precious thing I had ever beheld in my life. It's hard describe the joy I felt. I was free. Gone were the days when I lamented about my life and the fate that awaited me in the bowels of the prison. Gone were the days of wondering what the electric current issued by the chair would feel like flowing through my body, wondering if I would be able to taste the burn on my lips, or smell my skin as it cooked. Never would I have to worry about dying and being left to fend for myself in the afterlife, seeing Tommy at every turn. I had faced death and it wasn't as bad as I thought it would be. The pain was like a cramp in my heart, one that choked the muscle in its grip as strong as a vice, forcing it to slow, and then finally, to stop. And then there was nothing. No angels floating over my body, calling my soul out, no hellfire burning at my back. I didn't see my ancestors, relatives who might have come to meet me at the gates of Heaven or Hell. Not even Angie came to welcome me. The stillness of death was all encompassing.

But I survived.

I made the rounds that night. After donning new clothes I had skimmed from a department store—old habits die hard— I went back into the old neighborhood. The drinkers were out on the stoop as they always were; a brown paper bag concealed their cheap wine from view. A game of craps was being played beneath the stairs. The clacking of dice against the wall sounded loud to my ultra-sensitive ears. I could hear them bickering about the weight of the dice, could hear the crinkling of the bills being exchanged between sweaty hands. Hell, I could hear the shooter's excited breathing, and I had to have been 20 feet away. I was learning new things about myself, finding out about new talents that had been reborn with me. And I liked it.

The hunger I had woken up with was superseded by my awe. I pushed the urge to feed aside and marveled at my eyesight, magnified like never before. My sense of smell had been enhanced as well. I sampled the stale smelling breath of the winos on the stoop and could tell what they hid in their bags. I could smell the garbage through the bags and cans left to be collected at the end of the street. I could smell the winos blood from where I stood, although I didn't know that was what tantalized me.

 I heard voices I recognized and thought about going up to them and saying hello. I knew all of them: Jerry and Carl from the 5th floor, Candace from the 2nd. I heard Martin and Willie's voices from behind the stairs. They would all be surprised to see me. They probably thought I was already dead. Everyone knew what I had done. To them I was gone, history. Forgotten. I thought about walking over just to shake them up. And I almost did, but something inside me told me not to. I wasn't supposed to be there. I was supposed to be in prison, dead in a matter of days. Seeing me would freak them out, for sure—I could imagine Candace's shriek and Carl's cussing. They'd be scared that night, but later they'd tell someone about it. Maybe not the cops, but someone around the neighborhood. I didn't need to call attention to myself, so I decided to stay away. I didn't need the temptation either. I rode uptown on the bus, boarding with the money I found in a jacket left at the morgue. I got off a block away from the apartment building Tommy and I lived in. As I strolled toward it, I marveled at how unchanged everything looked. The building looked the same as it did when Tommy and I called it home. I didn't know what I expected it to look like—it hadn't been that long since I had laid my eyes on it, but it troubled me that the place didn't look any different. It gave me the feeling that nothing had happened, when so much had.

I peered up at our 5th floor apartment, my eyes trained on the window that sat in what used to be our living room.

Someone else lived there. I could see the light from their television set bouncing off the lime green colored wall, black and white flickers of movement in an otherwise dark room. I could see the new occupant as he shifted in his seat, settling into a well worn easy chair. He was about forty years old with a scruffy, overgrown beard and nappy, grown out hair. I didn't see the silhouette of another person sitting near him, didn't see movement in any of the other windows. I didn't know then that he would be my first taste. All I knew was that I had to get into that apartment again.

I made my way up to the apartment quickly, taking the stairs two at a time, enjoying the flexing of my muscles. I knocked once. I was excited. And hungry. The man came to the door wearing only his boxer shorts and undershirt. With a hand in the elastic waistband of his pants and the other on the door, he asked,

"Who are you?"

As he looked me up and down a sly, dirty smile ran across his lips. He was disgusting. At that moment he ceased to be a man, flesh and blood. He became nothing more than a meal and I felt no pity for him.

I pushed him into the apartment with newfound strength. He stumbled backward and regained his footing, squaring off with me. That made me all the more angry.

"You crazy bitch! Who the fuck do you think you are?" he spat. His words rang of bravado, but I knew better. His mind shrieked in fear, *What the fuck is going on? What the hell does she want?'* He was right to be afraid of me. I was a little afraid of myself too.

 I said nothing as I stepped towards him. He held his ground, though his mind told him to run out of the house and call the police. "You better get the fuck outta here if you know what's good for you!" He tried to sound angry but my serious demeanor unnerved him, made him jittery. I took another step forward and he flinched reflexively. I couldn't help but laugh out loud.

He swung at me, throwing the punch with everything he had. I caught his hand in mid air, surprising myself. My strength and agility had increased as well. Not bad for a woman who just stepped out of the morgue.

His scream made me realize how tightly I was holding his hand. The bones had broken under the pressure and were poking through his skin. His body sank to the floor as sweat and tears wet his face.

"Go ahead," he panted, "take whatever you want. Just let me go, please." The smell of his blood wafted up to my nose like sweet perfume. I brought his ruined hand closer to take in more of its scent. The man moaned and whimpered, but I no longer heard him. The blood had become the only thing important to me.

"Please, just let me go. I have money in the bedroom. You can have all of it." I looked at him, stared right into his eyes. He pleaded with me with his words, but pleaded to God in his mind. 'Please God, get me out of this. Make her let me go. Please! I'll do anything.' My lips parted in a wicked grin.

"God isn't listening," I whispered as my teeth elongated into fangs. Feeling them drop from my gums was like taking the first bite of a favorite meal;

it was exquisite.

I plunged my teeth into his throat harder than I needed to, breaking the skin jaggedly and spilling a lot of blood. I drank frantically, lapping up the drops with fervor. I was famished and that crude man served to satisfy my appetite.

Later though, after my hunger had been sated, I was disgusted. I looked upon the man, my prey, my meal, and cried until my eyes ached. It wasn't because I had killed someone. I had done that before. It was because of the reason I killed. I took a man twice my size down to drink his blood. To drink from his neck as a baby does from its mother's breast. To feed. I was a beast, no longer human. I could barely stand to be in my own skin.

I awoke the next morning to find the man's body lying at my feet. I had fallen asleep through my tears and left the body there to fester. I stood and began the arduous task of moving him, disposing of his remains. He was stiff, rigor mortis having set in overnight. His face still held the look of unmitigated terror at the sight of my fangs, at the knowledge that his life was over.

I grieved for him. No person should have to die that way, too terrified to know whether to fight or flee, having urine and feces running down their legs in dueling trails as though racing each other to see which could reach the base of the ankle first. Predicting death and allowing the damned to take a peek at it before enclosing it around them is a strange form of torture indeed.

I grieved for myself, for what I had become. I wondered if death might have been the better choice of the two.

I couldn't stay at the apartment Tommy and I shared for long, not after what I had done. Soon the police would come looking for the wretched man who had served as my first meal in the afterlife. Someone at his job or perhaps a neighbor would miss him, would realize that he was gone. I was afraid of what I might do if I felt like I had to protect myself. I left the place I had once called home that night. I had grown attached to it again and leaving was like ripping off a bit of skin from my forearm.

I rebelled. I heard him calling for me, but I turned my back, closing off my mind the way Angie had taught me. I was angry with him for dangling such forbidden fruit in front of me. I was angry at Angie for not forcing me away from it. I was angry at myself for not having enough integrity to turn it down. I wallowed in this self-pity for a number of years.

I wandered the streets, making acquaintances with the winos and bums that littered the sidewalks after dark. They didn't accept me easily; it wasn't every day that someone who didn't need to stayed on the streets all night. Sometimes I brought food with me and gave it to them, sometimes wine. I listened to their stories, encouraged their paranoia. When my hunger was unbearable, I chose the healthiest of the lot to feed upon, sometimes after days of waiting. It took me a long time to become accustomed to the hunt. Even now, after all these years, it still doesn't sit well with me.

I tried to kill myself, to end it all rather than to feed. I went into a greasy spoon's restroom and sliced my throat. I held my neck over the sink, expecting to bleed out, but nothing came. Instead, I watched in horror through the grimy mirror as my skin merged and reformed, sealing the gash within seconds. I stole a gun and shot myself with it, in the chest and then the head, when the latter didn't work. My body rejected the bullets, pushing them out, and filling the holes they made with fresh, rejuvenated tissue. Asphyxiation, jumping, drowning, none of it worked. I was invincible and I hated myself for it.

I spent ten years on the streets with the vagabonds and outcasts of society. I couldn't bear what I had become. Living on the streets with people who didn't ask questions, allowed me to wallow in self-pity in virtual obscurity. Until he found me.

One night a drunk girl they called Susie cried out in her sleep, affecting a masculine voice that was both velvety and gritty at the same time. She had just joined our lot, having only been in the alley I shared with three other homeless men for a few days. She didn't know any of us; she had kept to herself even more than I had. But that night she spoke to me in clear, precise words,

"I see you, Lucky."

A New Day Through Bloody Eyes

The announcement broke through the night, lifting me out of the slumber I was falling into, startling me. I looked around for the owner of the voice, expecting to see a man, tall and muscular, standing in front of me. Instead, I saw Susie sitting up in her bed of rags and cardboard, facing me. Her eyes were shut yet her face was squared to mine. I stared in silence, not believing that she uttered the words. She spoke again in a voice that was not her own.

"Did you think you could hide from me?"

"What?" I heard myself ask before I realized it. The voice stirred old feelings of lust in me that I hadn't felt the likes of in years. They also brought to light another emotion, one I wasn't ready to deal with: fear. He had found me.

A wry smile spread across Susie's cracked lips, revealing her blackened teeth and inflamed gums.

"You are mine, Lucky. You belong to me."

A chill raced along my spine as laughter to frighten the angel of death himself erupted from Susie's mouth.

Susie's laughter rumbled the covers around her, shook the crate in which she slept. Her body shook with it, to the point of convulsing, jerking in frightening bursts. Then, suddenly, she stilled. Her mouth retained the hideous smile as her body sat rigidly straight, facing me still.

She sat that way for what seemed like hours. I inched closer to her, to see if she was breathing. A horrible snap had sounded while she convulsed, and her neck appeared to be discoloring. She didn't move as I got closer, didn't flinch at all.

I made my way into her box, careful not to touch her. The box depressed and cracked with the added weight. When I was close enough so that I was sure she could hear me, I whispered,

"Susie?"

Her eyes opened upon hearing her name, the irises as white as those of a blind man. The voice she had affected before had grown deeper, more urgent. She growled,

"Come!"

As though her limbs, head, and torso had been attached to a puppeteer's cords, ones that had suddenly been severed, the tension in her body dissipated and she fell backward. The thump of her head hitting the concrete was sickening.

The next morning the bums in our little alleyway found Susie dead. They left her body there to be picked up by the cops whenever they got around to it and packed up, never to return. They didn't want the hassle of answering questions and having to go to the police station. They didn't know what happened anyway, and wouldn't tell if they did, so they left. A couple of them looked for me on the streets after that, wondering if I would come for them next. I hadn't killed Susie, but they didn't have any way of knowing that. All they knew was that when they went to sleep I was there, in my heap of clothes and garbage. When they woke up, I was gone and Susie was dead.

WE MEET AGAIN

I came off the streets that morning and cleaned myself up. I bought
some clothing, styled the hair I had allowed to grow long, and put on
some makeup. Then I walked into the bank where Angie had deposited
her money. I did everything the way she told me to and was able to gain
access to the money she had accumulated over the years. Over the course
of a month, I set up my life. I bought a house in Rockland County, a half
hour outside of Manhattan. I invested in property around the county after
setting aside an amount that could sustain me for a decade. I decided that
it was time to stop running from him. It was time that I dealt with my lot.
And if was to do that, I wanted to have everything in place. Displeasing
him with my appearance, my station in life after 10 years, was not an
option. I had displeased him enough already, I was sure.

My new home was beautiful. It was a contemporary with a pool out back,
gated grounds, and a long driveway. I had never seen anything like it, let
alone lived in such lavish luxury. I enjoyed Angie's money.

He came to me in the library one evening, a year or so after the day he
spoke through Susie in the alley. The maid had already left for the evening
and the house was silent. I had taken to reading books in the study to
wile away in the hours before the hunt. I had never been much of a fan
of literature, but Baldwin and Wright were turning me into one. I was
engrossed in a novel when he spoke from the corner of the room. I
jumped, caught off guard. I chastised myself for letting my guard down
so completely again, for letting myself relax. I hadn't felt him probing my
mind, didn't know he was near. That I could be so oblivious frightened me.

"Lucky." His voice was as smooth and sensual as it had been the first time
I heard it. I fought against the urge to press myself against his body and let
him have me.

An inviting smile spread across my lips even as my mind protested. I
couldn't allow him to come into my life again, to control me as he had

before. Things were different now. I had come into my own. I was beginning to accept what I had become, knowing that I would be this way forever. Having him in the equation again meant it was time for me to repay him, time for me to do his bidding. I wasn't ready to play the game yet.

He walked toward my chair. I found myself lifting my chin to meet his face. I cursed my nipples for hardening as he approached, my labia for tingling. Damn him for having such an effect on me.

"You've been a naughty girl, hiding from me like that. Where have you been, my precious flower? I have been looking for you."

My back arched as he spoke, his words caressing my spine like a feather. The mixture of arousal and fear was intoxicating. Still, I said nothing.

"Not even a hello for me? The one who gave you everything you have? Made you everything you are?" He grabbed a chair and sat in front of me, crossing his legs such that the toe of his shoe touched my calf. I felt goose bumps spring up along my leg as though his bare skin rubbed against me instead of the sole of his wingtips.

"Angie's money paid for all of this. I don't recall you contributing a dime." My speech had already started to change from that of an uneducated twenty year old who didn't care about anything, to a worldly woman who had been exposed to the finer things in life. Angie's money had allowed me many outlets, travel and an appreciation for the arts among them. I was different than I had been in my first life. The Lucky he had met in that god forsaken jail cell died years before.

"Such a sharp tongue for a beautiful woman."

This was part of the game. He knew it and so did I.

"Hello, my secret visitor," I said in a tone of pleased acquiescence. My desire betrayed me at every turn.

"I think we are well past those pleasantries now, don't you think?"

I nodded, my tongue longing to dart between my lips and run over them slowly while he watched.

"Then what should I call you?" I asked.

"Father, perhaps, though that might seem a little naughty considering the things you think of when you see me." My face flushed. "Savior, Ressurector, Lover, or soon to be." His pause was torturous. "Even Tommy might do nicely."

My face felt as though it had been slapped, stinging as his lips formed the name of my past lover. The implications his voicing it aroused were many and they flooded my head, blocking rational thought. I knew he was watching the chaos in my mind and enjoying every second of it. I recovered and said,

"Satan might be more fitting."

"So it might," he conceded as his eyes roamed my body and caressed my soul. "The blood has done much for your disposition," he said, his voice thick with satisfaction. "No longer are you the cold-blooded killer begging for her life from within the confines of a dreary prison cell. You've turned into quite the lady, I see." A silence as thick as the humidity of a summer's day in New York City hung between us. It seemed like hours before he spoke again.

"Now that that's out of the way, we can get on with the rest of your life," he said, a sense of completion in his voice.

"The rest of my life?" I questioned. I had a feeling where the conversation was leading but I wanted to drag it out a bit. I wasn't ready for what he was going to ask, wasn't ready to follow through on my promise.

"Yes. What did you think? That I made you so you could loaf around in the lap of luxury for eternity? What, pray tell, would cause me to do something like that?"

"Your feelings for me, of course. You told me yourself that you loved me. I remember it well. It was right before I took my last breath."

Looking at him was like staring into the eyes of my wildest fantasy. His appearance had changed since last we met, surely just to accommodate my burgeoning tastes. His style of dress was more suited for the men that I chose to spend time with—dress slacks and shoes, Oxford pinpoint shirt with an open collar—as opposed to the guy with ill-fitting jeans and scoop neck shirt he wore when he came to me in my cell. His complexion was brownish-red, like that of a Native American and his hair was straight and slicked away from his face. Interesting the modifications he made to approach me this time around. His ability to be a chameleon frightened me. He could be anyone anywhere, at anytime.

"That's what you needed to hear," he said, cockiness coating his voice. "I could have told you anything then and you would have believed it."

"Is that what you did? So you don't love me after all?"

"But I do, my dear Lucky. I love you as one of my own. But it's time for you to show me how much you love me."

"I never claimed as much."

His brow furrowed and I began to fear that maybe I had gone too far. I fidgeted in my seat, hoping he didn't notice, but knowing he did.

"Really? Even after everything I've given you?" he said, his voice elevated, his calm demeanor rattled. "No more pain. No more suffering. I've given you life after yours would surely have been over. You walk the streets of New York with blood on your tongue and satisfaction in your gut when you should be rotting in the earth. Your soul runs free when it could be serving me in Hell."

"Won't it still?" I said sarcastically.

He stood and I stood with him. The fire in his eyes was enough to make me want to retreat, but I stood firm. He leaned in closer to me, so close that I could smell his anger. No breath escaped his lips.

"You will not disrespect me," he growled.

The backs of my legs pressed against the chair and I sat down. He towered over me, looming like a giant. I looked up at him, unable to mask the fear in my eyes at first. Something moved under his skin, the surface of his face seeming to writhe in tandem with it. I shut my eyes, hoping to blink the image away, afraid of what might reveal itself if I continued to look defiantly on. I wasn't being smart. I was provoking him, agitating the one who was capable of snuffing the life out of me. I decided to back off a bit, to hear what he had to say. I needed to get myself out of this situation before I ended up dead.

I flashed a nervous smile, trying to portray confidence in the presence of evil. I wasn't sure if it worked.

After a moment, he backed away, returning to his seat. Folding his left leg over his right, he said,

"I hope you understand that. You are here to do my bidding and nothing else. You are at my disposal, available to me whenever I want you. I let you have that time alone so you could learn about yourself and develop, but there was never, not one moment, that I didn't know where you were and what you were doing. I've always known you Lucky." His eyes bored into me like red hot pokers. "Don't think for one minute that you have any choice, any free will, in this life. I leave that notion to the one you ignored in your first life. I have no need for such nonsense."

I nodded again, willing myself to relax.

"Now, if you're quite finished, I'd like to get to the reason for my visit." His voice returned to the calm cadence he displayed before. I was more relieved than I let on.

"You mean it wasn't to see my smiling face?"

"I shall see that and more before this night is over, my dear, but before we move on to more... pleasant things," his eyes ravished me in an instant, "there is something I need to talk with you about."

"I'm all ears," I said, settling into the chair.

"Hopefully not, but that I will find out for myself later." I flushed hot again as his eyes cascaded over my body. Damn him.

"I have a little task for you to complete. After you are done I promise, you will not be needed for anything...strenuous. I need you to listen to me, Lucky. Listen to me like you've never listened to anyone before."

"Okay," I said, my insides twisting in knots. I hoped he couldn't see how hard I was concentrating on blocking his advances into my mind.

"It's a simple thing really," he continued, his well-manicured hand caressing his knee absently. "I've lost something that belongs to me and I want it back." He paused, glancing at a space above my head. "It's been far too long."

A strange emotion ran across his face, one that was both nostalgic and enraged at the same time. "All you have to do is find it for me."

"That doesn't sound too hard," I offered nervously, just to have something to say.

"My dear, it will be the hardest thing you've ever done." He shifted in his seat, his eyes piercing me, probing. A light film of sweat sprung from the pores at my hairline. I fought the urge to wipe it away.

"It isn't a thing that is missing, actually. It's a person. And you have to find him for me."

"Why me? Why not one of your other… people?" I challenged him. I needed to know why he thought I was so important. I wanted to feel him probe me for answers one more time to confirm what Angie had always told me. I needed him to show me that I was just a pawn, and had always been one.

"Because I trust you Lucky. You are the only one I would trust with such a delicate matter."

"But you don't even know me."

His laugh was genuine. "I know you inside and out." His mind dug in the crevices of my own like cold fingers, overturning rocks that had long been buried. I shivered, feeling the corners of my eyes squint. My face, however, remained calm and still.

"You will do this for me because I asked you to," he said, his voice confident.

"Yes, I will," I said because I had to. "Who is it?"

"A dear friend, though he doesn't know it yet. A relative of sorts. I need you to find him and bring him to me. He is to be delivered to me unharmed."

I felt sick. Angie had been right the whole time. Her son was in great danger, always had been. The weight of responsibility pushed me deeper into my seat, threatened to crush my spine all together.

"What is his name? Do you have a picture I can look at?"

"My dear, if it was that easy, do you think I would have needed you to do it? No, finding this boy, this man, will be all the more difficult because I don't know anything about him. Except that he belongs to me."

He went on to recount the story of a nameless girl whom he had changed into whatever abomination I am. That girl bore a son from a coupling with a human. He pontificated about how that boy's blood was that of ethereal royalty, tainted only by the human host. He said that the girl dumped the baby somewhere and killed herself before he could find out the child's whereabouts. How interesting it was to hear him talking about Angie as if she was of no significance, just some girl who could be cast aside. Death was too good for her, he said in closure.

"I want you to find him and bring him to me," he said, venom lacing his words. "That's all. Then, you will be free to do what you will."

"Forever?" I couldn't hide the giddiness in my voice.

"Forever is a relative term, is it not?"

Before I realized it, we were in bed. His hands, so many of them, roamed my body. Squeezing, pinching, rubbing, slapping. Feeding. I shrieked when I saw one of those hands, its palm unlined and smooth, the center of it containing a protrusion made of bone, almost like a fang. My blood dripped from it as I watched. His hands provided pleasure and pain at the same time; satin caresses over sharpened teeth. It took everything I had not to scream out loud.

He drank from me in hungry gulps, his tongue slithering up and down my neck as though tasting of a divine delicacy. And I enjoyed it. Dear God, I enjoyed it. Though I had experienced the touch of a man since being reborn, none had been as sensual, as all encompassing as him. He pleasured me from the faintest of touches, bringing me to orgasm even before removing his clothes. When he entered me, I was blind with passion, blind with fear. Never before had I experienced such raw emotion, never had I behaved like an animal in heat.

His hand coiled around my neck, tightening and loosening in rhythm with his thrusts. I reached my hands up to slap his back but found nothing to beat against. He was there, but not physically so; the body that stimulated me was no longer apparent to the eye. He was between worlds as we copulated, his passion exceeding the ability to be contained in one. I called out for mercy as his body sliced into me, pressing, thrusting further, as to come out of my back. And then he was still.

His physical form returned, as though its disappearance was nothing more than a trick of the light. Sweat glistened on the skin of his body du jour, much to my delight. I leaned in to lick the saltiness from his chest, circling my tongue around his nipples. Sweat had always been a sweet elixir to me, even before my rebirth. The sensation was intensified in my current state. I could no more stop myself from doing it than I could stop myself from feeding.

He smiled at me, his lips parting to reveal what at first appeared to be pointed fangs in a mouth blackened by rot and death. I blinked the visage away as his horrible countenance burned into my mind. As I watched, the visage changed to that of an attractive smile, all white teeth and pink gums. It was then that I panicked.

Had I betrayed Angie in that brief moment of passion? Had I allowed him access to my mind as well as my body?

I fell into myself, probing the crevices of my mind to see if they had been tapped. I ran through all of my secrets, all of the things I had blocked away from view. I couldn't tell. I decided to try to see what he knew by entering him.

His eyes widened at the breech, surprised that he was being violated. His back arched as clothing that had been cast aside during our lovemaking migrated back to him and covered his nakedness. His body tensed as I dug deeper, willing myself past the horrific barriers he set in place at every turn. There was nothing about Angie or her son aside from a longing that made my heart turn cold.

I didn't realize he was gone until I heard him speak, his voice emanating from inside me rather than in the room. I opened eyes that I hadn't realized were closed to find the room empty.

"A naughty little wench you have become indeed, Lucky. What exactly were you looking for?" I let his questions drop without an answer, feeling none that I would have given would be sufficient.

"Angelique taught you well. Surely, though, you must know where your loyalties lie. Do this for me and you will not have to worry about anything ever again. Disobey me and you shall suffer more than any immortal has ever been made to. You'll beg for death before we're half through.

Do you understand?"

To emphasize his point, he gripped my arm with a cold hand. The sensation of twisting, of pulling backward and my palm being forced toward my head engulfed me and drove me to my knees. I grabbed at my arm. It was inflamed and hot to the touch, but in tact. A panting breath escaped my lips.

"Do you understand?" he repeated, his tone more urgent.

"Yes, I understand," I whispered aloud.

"Good," he said as he released his grip. I remained on my knees, looking at the floor. I didn't think I could stand it if I saw him standing in front of me.

He didn't say anything more and after a while, I sensed that he had left. The only reminder that he had ever been there was the trail of blood that stained the inside of my thighs.

Finding William

It was a race. I had to find Angie's son before he did. I wasn't sure if he had found anything when he probed me, even though my search of his mind showed no indication that he had. I thought that if he had learned what I knew, he would have killed me for sure. He wouldn't tolerate any harboring of secrets from those among his number. If had seen what I was hiding, he would have tortured me and killed me, making sure that it was particularly painful. I knew that just as well as I knew what I had to do. I had to find Angie's son. I had to protect him. I was his only hope.

I set out with nothing to go on except his mother's scent. The things she had kept of his father's didn't contain a strong enough scent to use. They showed his talent, however. His paintings of Angie were breathtaking. Angie's scent was similar to my own, since our father in death was the same. I walked the streets, picking up the scents of people who passed by unaware that they were being scanned, being searched and sorted through. I went to gathering places like libraries and parks, went to social clubs and plays (I found that I enjoyed Broadway very much and took trophies from there with more frequency than I care to mention), subway stations and arenas. I rubbed shoulders with the city's elite and the unseen few. One of them recognized me and smiled through years of dirt and grime. It warmed me the way a smile from a teacher would when I was a girl. It was the first time in my immortal life that I felt emotion. It was the first time that I felt anything at all for the people around me except a desire to taste their blood.

I searched cemeteries looking for Angie's son who would have been in his early twenties by then, almost hoping to find him there. The air was ripe with the smell of decay, of dying roses and fattening larvae. Mourners wept for their loved ones buried in the ground beneath their feet. The smell of their tears tantalized me. So salty and warm; I could feel the pain inside them; the suffering was incredibly exquisite.

On Hart Island I smelled the musk of the day patrolman's body and the smell of sex still heavy on him and his clothes. The seawater did little to cover the stench of decay from the unclaimed bodies, the sweet death of flowers and shrubbery missing in the burial place of the forgotten.

I met the day patrolman on my way off the island. He was surprised to find me there, looking in on him as he molested the fresh body of a prostitute who had died in an alley in Brooklyn. He was so startled he jumped, knocking the corpse to the floor, the sound of it hitting the dirty tiles like a doughy thud. He turned, his erect penis pointing at me like much like a finger might. His voice was loud.

"What are you doing here? How did you get on the island?"

"Did I disturb you?" I asked, sarcasm dripping from my words. "It's clear that you are accustomed to being… alone."

"You bitch, I oughta take you in her place!" His stomach heaved, bouncing up and down as he jabbed a stubby finger at me. He was almost comical, his member shaking and gyrating as it withered, his chest puffed out, and his face reddened from embarrassment and anger. As amusing as he was, he had made a threat against me. And that would not be tolerated. Ever.

"Oh really? Not afraid I'll put up a fight?" I enjoyed angering him.

"You crack head bitch! What? Did you come all this way looking for your momma? Or maybe your pimp? I'll teach you to go sneaking up on people. You'll wish you had never ferried over here."

He was a burly man, about 5'10" with a pot belly that stuck out over his pants, swollen like a pregnant woman's stomach. His skin was pale and covered with dark, straight hair. His nose was crooked, he was missing several teeth, his balding head was dotted with perspiration. The stench emanating from him was stronger now, sex mixed with the sour smell of dried sweat and dirt. He was repulsive. But his women didn't seem to care. That's probably why he chose them. None of them could protest.

He lunged at me, but stumbled at the start; his pants were still down around his calves. In the moment's hesitation, I gripped his throat and tightened my fingers around his meaty neck. His eyes opened wide as I continued to squeeze tighter and tighter. He squeaked sounds of protest, of pleas, but I kept the pressure.

"What was that you were going to do to me?"

He squeaked more urgently.

"You were going to take me instead of the dead girl? Make me wish I had never ferried over to the island? I bet you thought you were going to make me cry, make me beg to be let go. Well who's begging now?"

He couldn't respond. I had already crushed his larynx and restricted his breathing passage. He was barely coherent enough to hear me speaking. I let go of him, allowing his body to drop to the floor. His eyes were dilated and glassed over. He had stopped breathing a minute or so before I released him. Though my stomach rumbled in hunger, I did not feed upon him. The thought of sinking my teeth into his grimy flesh made me ill. I turned to leave the room when I caught sight of the girl he had violated. She had been pretty at one time, before she let drugs and street life take over. She had been beaten to death; the bruises on her face were harsh in the gray afternoon light. He had opened her eyes so she could watch him when he defiled her. I shut them once more after closing her legs.

I sniffed the air in search of Angie's son, traveling out of New York and through New Jersey, Delaware, and Maryland. I made my way down to Florida and trekked through Louisiana and Texas on my way to California. I thought I found him in Los Angeles, but instead, met another of my kind prowling the streets in search of his next meal. He looked at me, smelling the sweet scent of my blood that was so similar to his own. His eyes softened as they roamed my body. A smile tickled the corner of his lips as he walked over to me, crossing the busy street with haste. He sensed that I wanted to slip away, to leave before being noticed. I turned away from him, averting my eyes, knowing that it didn't matter. What had drawn him was more than a glance in his direction from a woman he might have deemed pretty. What summoned him was the call of the blood, the tangy lure of the forbidden.

"Might you dine with me this evening? I suspect our tastes are quite similar." His smile was one of confidence. It betrayed secrets only he and I could know. To anyone watching, we looked like two people coming from

152

a long day of work, meeting up in the crowd as millions of others did. But underneath the clothes and adornments of the times lay the passions of ten men and the hunger of dozens more.

His hand was hot upon my arm. His eyes, crystal blue and piercing, stared into me, beseeching me to join him, to spend the night with him. A life of solitude is all those like us have to look forward to. Hardly the romantic account portrayed in popular literature. I was not immune to that reality, not by a long shot. Beneath his desire—of which there was much, since copulation rarely got the chance to find completion between the living and the undead—was the pleading of a lost soul for companionship, for comfort.

I felt it to, but could not relent.

"On our next meeting," I told him, meaning every word. "We will eat to our heart's content. Together."

His smile faltered only a little, and with a nod so slight I wasn't sure if I had seen it at all, he turned and left. The sigh that escaped my lips was genuine.

I searched the States and the Caribbean, following the route that modern Blacks seemed to take. Vacations at state beaches were being replaced by trysts to the Bahamas and the Netherland Antilles. I followed, wondering if maybe he had decided to cash in on the growing infatuation of the islands by opening a tiki bar on the beach. No such luck.

After fifteen years of looking all over the country, I finally caught his scent in Washington DC.

And at the most inopportune time.

I was at a nightclub dancing to the rhythmic beat of reggae, a style of music I had grown quite fond of after visiting the island of Jamaica. I rolled my hips, winding smooth figure eights to the hypnotic music. The movement felt silky, smooth like a tongue over glossy lips. I couldn't help but touch myself as I danced, running my hands down my sides, cupping my breasts, tracing the outline of my buttocks. The music was alive and I danced to it as though indulging for sustenance itself.

Sometimes I let myself have a little fun.

My hair tickled the middle of my back as I moved. I wore a tight fitting top that accentuated my breasts and the shape of my waist. I knew men and women alike were enamored with me that night. I felt their impassioned stares as I gyrated and swayed. It fueled me as much as the music did, made me want to continue with my show.

I couldn't deny that I wanted some of them too; the tall, handsome man in the corner who spoke with an accent from the Caribbean; the Spanish guy with jet black curls that danced along his shoulders at the bar; the brunette dancing with the muscular Black guy who stared at me with the most beautiful green eyes. There were many who caught my eye that night, but only one whom I was determined to make my own.

I watched her watching me from the far side of the bar. She was tentative, nervous, afraid to look at me face to face. I smiled at her, knowing the flutters it would cause in her stomach. I was teasing her and enjoying it. I accentuated every movement for her, the roll of my hips, the fingers that outlined the soft of my breast and the base of my neck; I wanted her to see me. To want me. I knew that I would have her just as I'd had every other one I selected. But it was what I wanted from her that was the question. I enjoyed making up my mind.

She got up and moved closer to the dance floor. Closer to me. Her view was unobstructed from where she sat; I could smell her burgeoning lust. She was about to approach me, to join me on the dance floor and succumb her will—I could feel it—when I noticed him. I broke eye contact with her and whipped my head around, searching for the owner of that scent, the musky sweetness of sweat, adrenaline, and testosterone that covered what was inherently there. Breaking away from the girl, this Gillian whose name I heard echo in my soul, whose voice called to me from inside, was almost painful, but I had to find him. I was too close to be concerned with the lust of my loins or the hunger in my stomach.

I walked toward the scent, following it like a trail. I walked between couples dancing pelvis to pelvis, grinding each other as the reggae beat permeated their minds, making them think only about their bodies rubbing against each other, making them want more. Sweaty hands cupped my buttocks as I walked, but I ignored them. He was close, just there, beyond the throng of dancers feeling each other up.

The scent was growing stronger.

A woman trying to be sexy enough to take the man in front of her home locked eyes with me. I looked back at her, trying to decide whether or not she would be worth returning for after finding Angie's son. She frowned at me; a gesture no doubt meant to mean, 'Get away from him. This one's mine.' She moved her body closer to the man instinctively, rubbing her perky breasts across his arm and chest. He leaned in to her, enjoying the unexpected aggression. I almost couldn't suppress my laughter.

It was him.

To stand behind him and smell Angie's scent again, full and pungent, washed me with emotion. I was filled with longing for my old friend, with feelings of protection for her son, with fear that I might be acting as a magnifying glass for my savior and nemesis.

And then he turned to me.

The song moved to an even slower grind and everyone on the dance floor bent their knees and opened their hips for a deeper, more meaningful thrust into their partner. The girl, whose attempts to claim Angie's son were amateurish at best, lifted her leg to coil it around his calf. He, in turn, caught her thigh and lifted it higher, placing it close to his waist. His hand caressed her shapely calf. He turned his head to look at it, showing me his profile.

He was exquisite.

He possessed a runner's build with tight muscles in his arms and legs, and flattering definition in his chest and shoulders. His hair was cut short on top and even shorter in the back; a perfect fade. His eyes were caramel brown. His nose was angular, his lips full and inviting. I couldn't take my eyes off of him. I walked around them to get a better look, mingling with the crowd just enough to be seen if someone was looking for me.

He glanced down at the girl's leg, licking his lips as he did. He pressed himself closer to her, daring to cup her buttocks with his free hand. I could smell his desire and it aroused me.

As he released her leg and pulled her waist closer to him, his eyes fell upon me. It was as if time stood still. The music was silenced, the dancers around us stilled. There was only he and I.

I offered the coy smile that I had learned over the years and I could almost hear his heart stop beating. His mouth, still slack from the smile it held before, tried to reciprocate, but didn't quite make it. A half smile, boyish in its charm, emerged on his lips. It was the sexiest thing I had ever seen.

The sounds of the club returned and my peripheral vision once again picked up the dancers swaying to the reggae beat. I smoothed my clothes, a nervous tick that I hadn't done since before I was reborn. I felt silly, girlish like I never had. I was eager and nervous at the same time.

He too returned to normal, dancing with the girl in his arms, though with less interest than before. He traded places with her, turning her such that her back faced me. I felt self-conscious the first couple of seconds that we looked at each other. I couldn't believe the effect he was having on me.

A man crossed the path of our gaze, blocking our view momentarily. His scent masked Angie's son's for what seemed like hours and I felt my body reaching out, yearning for its return. My mind reeled in that nanosecond of time. What was this feeling, this magnetic urge I was having? That he was handsome was not enough to make me swoon—I'd had lookers in my day. There was something else about him, something so basic even he didn't know he emitted it. It called to me, this pheromonal lure, tantalizing me, pulling me closer to him. I needed to have him, to hold him, kiss him, feel him. Duty and ethics abandoned—he would be mine.

And I would be his.

The man passed and cleared my view again. But Angie's son and the girl had receded deeper into the crowd of writhing dancers, her attempt to whisk him off to a secluded corner and sample the goods, no doubt. I scanned the floor and saw them making their way through the mass of people. His eyes were still trained on me.

I took a step toward the bar and sat next to the girl who had been watching me all night. A different side of me, the side who was a woman enticing a man, not a vampire on a seek and destroy mission, settled into the seat with marked confidence. I'd make him come to me. I had no doubt that he would. The girl from earlier that night would do well as a diversion while I passed time.

I engaged in small talk with the girl—

"What's in your drink?" I asked.

"Soda."

"Can I get you something stronger?"

—Come-ons I'd used before. She was eager, but struggled with demons of lust and confusion that toiled within her. If what I wanted was the company of a woman and a hearty meal thereafter, she would serve as an excellent choice. But it wasn't enough anymore. Even though that was my entire reason for being in the club, I no longer wanted it. The unblemished skin on her pale neck almost glowed in the strobe light, sending promises of satisfaction to all of my senses, but still I turned away. The one I wanted was near and nothing, not even the sweetest diversion, would stand in my way.

He emerged from the crowd without the girl after twenty minutes. I could sense him staring at me as I talked to Gillian, who had fallen in love with me in spite of herself; both of their eyes bored holes into me with their intensity. The attention was stimulating. I ate it up.

I watched as he walked over, his stride perfect and slow. He was nervous and so was I, even as I enticed my new admirer. I couldn't shake the feeling of butterflies in my stomach.

"I'm sorry to interrupt, but I need to talk to you," he interjected as Gillian spoke nervously, her lips hovering just above her glass. I smiled at the intensity of his voice, a touch of the suave even in his vulnerability. Whatever it was, it worked. But then again, anything would have.

"It's no interruption," I said, finding my voice and making it rich and calm, sexy around the edges. "I've been waiting to talk to you for longer than you could ever know."

I let the smile that snuck up on me creep across my lips and he reciprocated in kind. Gillian cleared her throat and took a sip of her warming soda. Her vulnerability was appetizing.

I wrote my name and number on a piece of paper and pressed it into her hand before standing, matching looks with Angie's son all the while. She opened the napkin as I let my hand linger on her shoulder, fingering her collarbone with my pinky. I cast one last glance at Gillian. Her face was so beautiful, so elegant with golden-brown hair framing her radiantly toffee-toned face. Yes, Gillian and I would meet again. I would make sure of that. Angie's son reached for my hand tentatively, his warm fingers encircling my own. His touch gave me a sense of familiarity, like I had touched him before. Like I was supposed to touch him. I smiled at his back like a schoolgirl while his shoulders bobbed and ducked through the crowd, clearing a path. I bit my bottom lip and followed him, walking in his footsteps as we made our way to the less crowded hallway.

The dim light couldn't shade his features from me, though I wondered what I must look like to him. His mortal eyes didn't adjust to the light as easily as mine did. It was that thought alone that made a shiver race down my spine. We weren't the same. He was alive; blood flowed through his veins in earnest. He needed sleep, food and water, needed sustenance in a way that I hadn't in years and never would again. He would never feel the need to hunt as I did, never drink of blood with relish to rival any physical stimuli. He would never understand what I am, I couldn't expect him to. He was alive and I was dead. Dead. And nothing, not desire, not will, not all encompassing need would change that. But as I stared into his eyes I realized that none of that mattered to me.

"I wanted to talk to you the moment I saw you, but I had… company," he started, unable to hide the sincerity in his face. I probed him then, just to be sure. I wasn't checking to see if he was Angie's son; I was positive of that. He had her scent. His lineage was undeniable. What I wanted to know was if he felt what I felt. Was he falling for me the way I was falling for him? I knew it was wrong, but I did it anyway. I gave in to the temptation to know. I wasn't able to probe into Tommy's mind to see his thoughts, his intentions. I had to go into love blindly like everyone else. But why suffer that pain again? Especially now? If he was to be a man who cared for nothing more than satisfaction, I would tell him what he needed to know and be on my merry way. I wouldn't open my mind and let him be found, but I would do nothing more to help him either. I would have satisfied Angie's last wish to the extent that I could have been expected to, and I would be able to go on with my life. But if he was feeling what I was, and was interested in love, then I would give myself to him.

I couldn't believe what I was thinking. The possible consequences filled my head in gory detail.

So I looked.

My body was covered in warmth, even as my mouth filled with the bitterness of my own blood.

"I know," I said, projecting a sense of calm that was false at its root. "I wanted to talk to you too. I thought that girl was going to take you out of here before I got the chance."

"Her?" He turned to face the door she must have gone out of when he let her down. "She didn't have a chance. Not after I saw you."

I smiled as I tested him, trying to detect a lie. There was none. "Why me?"

"I-I don't know. I thought at first that it was your eyes. They seemed to see right through me, but it's not just that. I can't put my finger on it because it's not just one thing. It's everything about you. You're fascinating."

I chuckled at his sincerity out of both embarrassment and flattery. He meant what he said, and, God help me, I believed him.

"What's your name?" he asked, breaking the silence that had grown between us.

"Jacqueline." I don't know why I gave him a different name. Maybe it was because I didn't feel like myself standing with him at that nightclub. I didn't feel like Lucky, the girl from the streets who knew more than her share about hard knocks. I wasn't that girl anymore, Lucky who got locked up for killing her boyfriend and his bitch in a rundown apartment in the middle of Manhattan, Lucky who damned near went crazy sitting in a cell, talking to her only friend in the world through a crack in the wall, Lucky who died in a cold cell only to awaken inside a body bag. That girl was gone and had been for years. I had changed. I had smoothed out my rough edges even as my teeth sharpened.

Why should I keep the name of someone who ceased to exist?

I was Jacqueline. Forever.

"Jacqueline," he said, lifting his head slightly and letting it roll off his tongue. "I feel like I've heard that name in my dreams."

For the first time in decades, I blushed.

"My name is Will. William really, but everyone calls me Will. Does anyone ever call you Jackie?"

The name sounded beautiful coming from his mouth. "You can."

He smiled and averted his eyes.

And so it began.

I found the man I had been searching for for fifteen years in a sweaty dance club full of lustful people pawing over their partners. The Devil wanted me to hand him over to do with as he decided. Angie's last wish was for me to protect her child. All I wanted to do was love him.

OF BLISS AND BLOOD

I rented an apartment in northwest DC so I would have a place in the area.
It was near Howard University and I enjoyed the sounds of the college
students when they played their music, congregated in the park, and milled
in the parking lot of the fast food joint on the corner. It was an exhilarating
time for them, being away from home for the first time, meeting people
from places they had only seen on the map in Geography class. Their
excited chatter and raging hormones sparked a hunger in me like I had
never felt, and I dined on some of the most beautiful of the lot.

Will came to visit me often, finding that he didn't want to stay away
anymore than I wanted him to. We were so compatible: we had read the
same books, had seen the same movies. He had an interest in early century
New York. I knew the history all too well. Sometimes I slipped, giving
away too much, telling him things that I would have only known had I lived
during that time and seen the places and the people with my own eyes.
Will questioned me to find out more, enamored with the stories I told, but
I found ways to get off the subject. He asked me how I knew so much
about the period. To him, I was a twenty-six year old woman who never
talked about studies and education, politics or religion. Our conversations
centered around the arts and literature, music and movies. Whether or not
I had attended college never came up. It was of no importance. So when
he asked how I could recount the Black migration from South to North in
such vivid detail, he could almost feel the ache of the trek in his own feet,
I shrugged and told him I heard about it from an aunt who made the move
herself, thumbing and cramming together with sweaty workers on buses
with no air-conditioning. When he asked how I could describe 5th Avenue
on a Sunday afternoon in such detail that he could smell the L'Air Du
Temps lingering lightly on the air as the ladies passed by, I laughed and told
him that I always wanted to write a book. He believed me. I didn't mention
that I had been on the sidewalk watching the parade up and down the

avenue, wanting to have what they had. I didn't mention that he could feel, taste, and smell the things I talked about because he had his mother's curse. I couldn't. He thought I was interesting and fun. Each time we talked about the old days I felt a twinge of nostalgia.

We spent hours together, walking the streets of DC and sightseeing at the monuments. He had moved to the city to attend the very college from which I had picked my last victims, Howard University. After graduating, he decided to stay in the city. He took a job at one of the startup companies that had set up business in Washington DC, bought a condo near the White House, and settled into his new town. He dated, but hadn't gotten into anything serious since the beginning of college. He often told me that he stayed single because he was waiting to meet me. The memory of his voice speaking those words haunts me still.

I hadn't mentioned anything to him about Angie or about who he was, not in all the weeks we had been together. I didn't know how to broach it, didn't know if I wanted to. Telling him what he was meant telling him what I am, and I didn't want to do that, not yet. I was having more fun than I had since being reborn. No. I was having more fun than I had ever had in my life. More than I ever thought I could. I didn't want it to end. I know that sounds selfish, but it's true. I wanted to see where we could take our little romance. I wanted to see how far we could go. He was safe as long as he was with me, I told myself. As long as I kept my mind blocked, he couldn't be found. I made myself believe that if I was with him I could protect him. It sounded good in my head. I hoped it was true.

We talked about everything, wiling evenings away to talk of times past. The hunger that filled me on those nights when I wasn't able to feed was all encompassing, but I suppressed the pain. I only hoped he couldn't see the hunger in my eyes.

He told me about his life, about how he grew up poor and worked his way through college. He didn't dwell much on his childhood. I was only able to get him to talk about his mother once.

"She took me in the day she found me in her garden. She always called me her little beet because that's where I was when she found me, in the beets.

My real mother left me there hoping she would take me in. I guess she picked the right lady," he said, emotion thickening his voice.

"Did you ever find your real mother?" I already knew the answer. Even now I'm not sure why I asked the question.

"No. Nobody had any idea who it might be either. Momma never saw anyone hanging around the house that day and there wasn't a pregnant girl in town that turned up missing. Nothing. It's as if she vanished into thin air."

The silence that fell between us was thick. My silence was one of nervous anxiety. I wanted to know more, wanted to ask him if he felt anything strange from time to time, if he ever felt different from everyone else. I could see the differences in him. His similarity to my kind was uncanny. His penchant for rare meat, his incredible strength—he once shouldered an oak bookcase while I decided where it should go in the room—they mirrored my own. I wondered if he'd ever noticed that he was different, or if he had ever had thoughts he didn't understand, if he ever wanted to do something that wasn't considered normal. I wanted to ask him those questions, but I didn't know how. I wasn't even sure that I should.

"My Dad always pointed out the differences between me and them too," he said, breaking the silence and broaching the subject that was tossing around in my head. I began to wonder if he could sense what I was thinking. "I guess that's why we didn't have a good relationship."

"What do you mean?"

"He would always talk about the way I acted. Some of the things I did." I let a look of confusion hang on my face. I wanted him to continue but I didn't want to press him.

He shifted in his seat. "The way I like my food, my sleep patterns. My parents were early birds but I liked to sleep late. Nothing major, just things that were different."

There was more. It was written all over his face.

Finally, he continued, "When I was a kid I did something that I couldn't explain. None of us could. And he never let me live it down."

"What did you do?" My voice sounded louder than it should have.

He hesitated, obviously uncomfortable. He was dredging up memories that he didn't want to revisit.

"There was this woman in town that everyone said was a vampire—."

"A vampire?" I had to act surprised. To behave any other way would have made him suspicious.

"I know it sounds crazy, but we lived in a small town in Florida. People make up some strange shit in the backwoods." Our laughter sounded unnatural. Mine was filled with urgency, his with trepidation.

"So anyway, this woman dies. My sister was born the same night. There was a terrible storm too, winds blowing things around in the yard, trees falling, power lines down. The midwife didn't make it to the house in time, so my dad had to deliver Carol. I watched from the doorway in the beginning, scared to death of what was happening." He paused, remembering the sound of his mother's screams. Though I tried not to probe him, it was as if the images called out to my mind, pulling them toward his to see her haggard face.

"Sweat fell off my Dad's face like running water. He barked orders to us kids—

'Boil some water!'

'Get me some towels!'

'Get a rag for your mother's head!'

"—and we did whatever he wanted as fast as we could. It was when I brought the towels over to Dad and saw my mother spread open and bleeding that I became fixated. I dropped the towel to the floor and stared at her, my arms limp by my sides."

He stared at me as I searched for the right reaction. I ended up with a combination of disgust and interest. He seemed satisfied with it and continued,

"There was blood everywhere. On the sides of her legs, on her stomach. Her, you know, her—."

I smiled as he tripped over the word.

"I know what you mean," I said.

He smiled shyly. "Her- it was indiscernible. Maybe it was because at that age, I didn't know exactly what I was looking at, but I just remember blood in big clots. I asked Dad if it was supposed to look like that and he shooed me out of the room to get more towels. I didn't move when he told me to. I was enthralled by the blood. The... vagina itself was nothing to me, I couldn't have cared less about it. It was the blood, its rich hue, how it saturated the fibers of the towel so completely." He paused for a minute and looked away. He was embarrassed.

"I know this is grossing you out."

"What? The blood or the fact that you saw your mother's..."

"Don't say it!" His laughter was full bodied. "I just don't want you to think I'm some kind of freak or something."

"You haven't said anything freaky yet. So you saw your sister being born. What's freaky about that?"

"I haven't told you the freaky part yet." His eyes clouded over. The change was almost imperceptible, but there nonetheless.

"Oooooh," I moaned like a Halloween ghost, trying to keep the situation light. I didn't want him to stop. "Tell me."

With a sigh, he started, "After a couple of seconds filled with my mother's grunting and groaning, Dad pushed me, jarring me from my stare. 'Get some more towels, boy! You dropped these all over the floor!' he said. I snapped out of it toward the end of the sentence and left the room for more towels. But I couldn't get the image of the blood out of my mind.

"I came back to the room and tried to hold the towels under momma to catch the blood. Dad pulled me back, yelling something about me getting out of the room before the baby comes. He shoved the towels under momma and continued working on her. I left the room and joined my brothers and sisters. They were excited about the baby coming. I was trying to figure out how to get the dirty towels out of the room when all was said and done.

"Dad let us come in to see momma and Carol, saying we could only stay for a minute. He cleaned up while we oohed and aahed over the baby, dumping the water and throwing the bloody rags into the garbage. I went over to help dad, acting like a good son who wanted his weary father to sit down and get some rest. He bought it. I collected all the bloody rags and put them in the garbage, fighting the urge to bring a towel to my nose." He paused painfully. "I know that must sound sick."

He looked at me for a reaction and I gave him one. I frowned up my nose and stuck out my tongue. Then smiling at him, I nodded ever so slightly. He continued,

"I snuck out of the house with one of the rags tucked under my shirt. I didn't know where I was going until I got there. I had never been there before and didn't know the way, but somehow I ended up at Ms. Wrightwood's door. The vampire.

"She was a voluptuous woman with big breasts, ample hips, and a relatively small waist. She liked men, all kinds of men. She was White with pale skin and red hair. She had green eyes and full lips which she covered with red lipstick. We used to think the women spread the rumor about her being a vampire to try and keep their men and boys away from her. She had been known to cavort with many of the men who lived in town. Only my mother had told me that there was some truth to the rumor that she drank blood. I had always stayed away from her like I was told to. Until that night.

"I knocked on the door but no one came. I was thoroughly drenched by that time, so staying outside a while longer didn't matter. I walked around to her bedroom window and rapped on the glass. I could see her laying on the bed, her breasts exposed in the candlelight. It was the first time I had ever laid eyes on breasts that didn't belong to my mother and I felt myself stir. The nipples were pink instead of brown and the skin was so pale. I decided I would touch them if she let me. Somehow I knew she would.

"I knocked again, but she still didn't move. The window was cracked so I dug my fingers underneath and pushed it up just wide enough for me to crawl in. Her room was warm and inviting compared to the cold wind and rain outside. Candles were lit all over the room and their glow made strange shadows on the wall. I thought for a moment that I saw a man kneeling over her on the bed, staring down at her face as though he was going to kiss her, but when I blinked the image was gone. I walked toward her determined to get a better look at the breasts that pointed upward like the peaks of mountains. Finally, I was standing next to her bed and I could see the details of her areolas. And I liked it what I saw.

"I called out to her, softly so that I wouldn't wake her if she was asleep. I liked the idea of being in the room with her, looking at her body without her knowing. She didn't answer. I called out to her again to no response. Her head was turned to the side, her hair draped over her cheek such that I couldn't see her eyes. She hadn't moved since I had been in the room; I registered that fact in my mind absently. I called to her once more, this time asking if I might touch her. She said nothing. So I did.

"Her skin was cool under my hot hand. I only left it there for a moment, too afraid to do anything more than touch the soft flesh of her bosom where it met her ribcage. I was sure she would stir then, smack me, and tell me to get out. She wouldn't threaten to tell my parents, I knew. She never talked to any of the women and the men would never admit to dealing with her. I steeled myself for the slap, but it never came. She didn't move at all. I called to her again, alarmed now. I shook her arm lightly at first, then harder until her hair fell away from her face. Her eyes and mouth were open.

"I yanked my hand away, terrified. I had never seen a dead body before, wasn't sure that I was seeing one then either. To me, dead bodies were supposed to be stiff and cold, dressed in clothes you never saw them wearing when they were alive and stuffed into boxes. They weren't supposed to be half naked and soft, desirable. The thought that I had just touched a dead body made me sick.

"After I caught my breath, I leaned over her to see if she was breathing, moving, doing anything that resembled life. Nothing. My eyes filled with tears as I told her how sorry I was for touching her, how I'd never done anything like that before, how bad I felt. I thought she deserved my tears. Nobody else in town would cry over her. But I did, then and later.

"I put my hand on her chin and turned her face toward me. Her lifeless stare was almost more than I could take, but I looked anyway. Then I did it. It was like someone else had planted the thought in my mind. I pulled the rag saturated with my mother's blood out from under my shirt and pressed it to her lips. I didn't understand what I was doing, not even when I ringed the rag out, dripping blood into her open mouth. But somehow I knew I was doing what I was supposed to do. I was doing what the voice in my head wanted me to."

"Oh my God Will," I said, before I could catch myself. I couldn't believe the intensity of his urges, even as a child. I was also afraid of what it could mean.

"That's how Dad found me, sitting there holding a bloody rag over a dead woman's face. One of my brothers told Dad he saw me going out that way and Ms. Wrightwood's house was the first one to hit in that direction. Dad broke down the door after I didn't respond to his calls from the window. He stood in the doorway of the room looking at me with Ms. Wrightwood. He called to me once, twice maybe, but I didn't respond. I didn't even look in his direction. He picked me up, making sure he had the towel, and we left the house. He took me home, but left shortly after. I heard later that Ms. Wrightwood's house had burned down. No one seemed torn up over it. The police didn't even investigate the cause. Everyone assumed she was dead and let it go at that. Her body was never found."

"What happened to it?"

"My dad buried it after it burned in the fire. I don't know how I know that, but I do. He left the house after taking me home and set the place on fire. He waited until the house had burned to the ground, which wasn't long for a clapboard junker like hers, took what was left of her body out, and buried it somewhere. He thought I had something to do with her death, that maybe I had already sown my wild oats with her and had become jealous of her other men. It must have looked that way to him when he walked in, but it wasn't true. I hadn't sewn my oats with her or anyone by then. Hell, I had just turned thirteen! Dad never could figure out why I had the rag with momma's blood on it. Neither could I.

"Dad only brought up what happened when he was good and mad, and even then he never went too far into it. It was between us. He didn't want to hear the answers to the questions in his head, and I didn't want to answer them, so we didn't talk about it."

I was speechless. The blood was strong in him. Its influence was frightening.

"I told you it was weird. But it was a long time ago."

"Yeah," I said, trying to recover.

"My dad could never let it go completely. After a while, it became an issue for us, especially after mom died. He would go into it a little more, talking about how nasty I was to mess with such an old woman. I wondered if he had fooled around with her himself the way he spoke so bitterly about her. But I never asked. I just deflected his venom and shortened my visits. After he died I went back home to settle the house. When I was getting ready to leave, I cast an eye around the land that had been in my family for generations, the land that I was abandoned on, that my siblings were born on, that both my parents had died on. On that bright, sunny day I saw something off in the distance, at the very edge of the property. It looked like a man staring back at me. He was in shadows, draped in darkness as though cloaked in black from head to toe. I stared at him, willing his features to come into view, but as soon as I blinked he was gone. I left that day and haven't been back since."

Eager to end the conversation, Will hugged me close to him and said, "But that was a long time ago."

*

Will and I saw each other for weeks before having sex. I was afraid to. My previous encounters had always ended in a meal for me, and in death for my date. The sex itself was satisfying, but I always wanted more. The satisfaction of my body roused a need to feed that I hadn't been able to control. I was afraid that I wouldn't be able to stop myself. I felt the urge to sample him creeping up when we kissed, warming me like smooth cognac going down. His kisses were tantalizing; he aroused me with the slightest of touches. I felt out of control, as though some being, some uninhibited thing, took over, and all it wanted was more of him, more of his touch, his kiss, his skin upon mine. I always held back, always kept myself from the edge.

I didn't want him to turn out like all the others. I wanted him to live.

That night though, when he kissed me, I let myself go. We were sitting on the sofa of my small apartment, watching television and eating take-out. It was a rainy night and the sound of the rain hitting the concrete below my fifth floor balcony was soothing. None of the usual laughing and talking sounded from the sidewalk that night because of it. My street was a busy thoroughfare, mostly used by boys driving their cars around in circles while they cruised for girls. I enjoyed the sounds of the city, always had. That was one of the reasons I almost lost my mind in jail. The silence alone was enough to drive the sanest of people mad. On evenings, in late August and early September especially—the beginning of first semester—I stood on the balcony and watched the young girls sway and switch their perfect behinds for salivating suitors. I listened to the catcalls, the promises of what one could do if given a chance, the rejections and curses that soon followed. Often times I picked my meal from there, my perch above the busy street. I'd see a girl with a plump behind and ample bosom and begin to taste her as she sashayed further and further away. Or the guy standing with his foot propped up on the fence behind him, the waist of his pants hanging just low enough to reveal the patterned elastic band of his boxer shorts. He was posing for the women, but trying not to look like he was. He threw on his macho aura like an overcoat and mugged at the girls with a lascivious snarl because that's what he thought they liked. I liked it. Very much so, in fact. I frequently chose that type to satisfy my needs.

But this night was quiet. The rain drove everyone inside. Will rented a horror movie from Europe by some director I had never heard of. It was a low budget job about a woman who kept seeing dead bodies reanimate in her daydreams. It was cheap, it was corny, it was perfect. We drew closer and closer as the movie played, sitting next to each other at first and ending up in each others arms by the end. Will's arm draped my shoulders and his hand caressed my hair. I knew he was staring at me, watching me as I watched the movie. He did that sometimes, watched me when he thought I was asleep or unaware. It didn't make me uncomfortable as it might have before, when I didn't know anything about being in love. In love. My God, even now I can barely believe it happened.

Will peppered my neck with little kisses, nudging me so that I'd turn toward him. He caressed my shoulders, springing goosebumps on my flesh. I turned to him and looked into his eyes. He was so handsome, so sincere; a beautiful man indeed. I smiled to myself as I thought of my brief glimpse at his mother's face. How she would love to see how her son turned out, a man of integrity and intelligence. The smile died on my lips as I thought of the disappointment she would no doubt feel knowing I had not done what I promised. But I was doing it, I rationalized. Being with him was protection enough.

Will kissed me with such sensitivity, such feeling, I couldn't help but give in. I let myself go for the first time, kissing him back deeply, intensely. I let myself react, do all the things I wanted to, things I hadn't done in a long time. While he kissed me, I remembered my last living orgasm, by my own hands in my cell at the prison: As I pleasured myself I dreamed of my visitor, that handsome man that stepped out of the shadows from time to time to talk to me, to please my senses. That memory filled me with sadness and loss for more than just the life I surrendered. I was determined to replace that memory.

The hunger surged, but I forced it back, succumbing instead to the tingling of my flesh beneath his sure hands. He wanted me. His touches were gentle but urgent; his hands were powerful but soft. I gave in. I let him kiss my neck, trail his lips to my breast, flick his tongue down to my navel. I let him taste of me and he did so with zeal. I kissed him also, lapping at his skin, enjoying the taste of his sweat. We enjoyed each other first on the floor of my simple apartment and then again on my bed. When he entered me the chill of death fled, anxiously replaced with his heat. It was like nothing I had ever experienced. I loved it and hated it at the same time. His lovemaking was strong, much more so than any mortal man I had ever been with. Intense. I imagined that the women he had been with before had been intimidated by his approach; his rhythm was so exacting, so consistent. He reminded me of lovers I had taken that were like myself, night dwellers and lost souls searching for someone else to relate to. Those couplings had been lackluster, both of us pounding away to prove who was the tougher, the stronger, the lonelier. Those couplings always left me unsatisfied.

And hungry.

The desire to feed was great. As he pressed his body close to mine, gyrating his hips, pleasing my body with his own, I fought to suppress my hunger. His neck was so close. I could hear the blood rushing through his veins. I bit my lip until it bled and sucked from there, hoping to quell the desire to bite into his veins. It worked to satisfy the ferocious twisting in my gut, but not the animal desire. Sweat from his brow dripped onto my upturned face as my canines grew. I arched my back reflexively, my body welcoming the idea of blood instinctively. I lifted my head from the bed and leaned into his vulnerable neck. The smell of him was intoxicating and I swooned at the prospect of sampling his delectable blood. His moans of desire broke my spell, though, and tears welled in my eyes. I buried my head in his chest and cried about what I almost did. I almost drank the lifeblood of the man whom I was sure I was in love with. The man I had tracked down to protect. My tears were tinny as they ran from my eyes to my mouth, as red as the blood that I coveted so. Will climaxed as I wiped my tears from his chest and my face. Fighting the incorrigible urge to lick my fingers clean of the blood, I wiped it on my dark comforter that dangled off the bed and onto the floor. Will, his eyes clenched shut, never noticed.

He buried his head in my bosom, kissed me there, and then rolled over and settled in for the night, falling asleep almost as soon as his head hit the pillow. I met midnight with thoughts of our lovemaking on my mind, and a warning on my heart. *Don't fall too deep,* a little voice in my head warned. *You are there to protect him, not to love him. He can never know what you are.* I knew I was sent to protect him, that I had been searching for years to find him and warn him against the dangers that lurked in the dark. I knew that I messed things up by getting involved with him. It would be all the more awkward telling him what to watch out for this way. I didn't want him to find out what I was. I was too afraid he would reject me, cast me out like some freak. Like the freak that I was. I chastised myself for even caring what he might think. After all, that wasn't what I was there to care about. My job was simple: Find Will and warn him. Period. I had overstepped my bounds in a big way.

As I watched him sleep, I realized that everything that was rolling around in my head, all the concerns about how he might regard me, or how he would take the warning, were inconsequential. I had done the one thing that, had I avoided it, would have saved me from of the concerns that dominated my mind. I fell for him. Hard.

Time to Give the Devil his Due

I'm pregnant.

I woke up with that sentiment in my mind and knew immediately that it was true. Will and I had been together for more than six months and had enjoyed each other with reckless abandon. I wasn't thinking about what could happen. I was just having a good time.

The morning was hazy, as though a veil had been thrown over the sun. Will slept quietly on the other side of the bed, unaware that I had gotten up. I went out and met with a bag lady that, from the confines of her cardboard bedroom, never saw me coming. It had been a while since I preyed on that segment of society, one that I had called family for a number of years. I did it only out of necessity. Having not fed in weeks, my hunger threatened to make me turn on my love, and I couldn't let that happen.

When I returned to the apartment to find Will still sleeping, I began noticing the changes in the room. The air was thicker than it had been before I left, stifling like a humid summer afternoon. The haze, visible before, seemed almost palpable then.

We weren't alone.

It didn't take long for me to see him standing over Will as he slept. I lurched toward him, my hands outstretched.

He merely laughed.

"And what would you do? Claw at me with your nails? Try to rip my flesh from my bones as you pull me away from your beloved? Do you think it would work, my dear?"

"Get away from him!" I hissed.

His laughter filled the room.

"Relax, dear one," he said condescendingly. "You shouldn't let yourself get so riled up. You are with child, after all."

Hearing him speak the words I knew to be true made me sick to my stomach. I was pregnant. How could it be? I was dead, reanimated by the devil's blood. How could my womb produce a living child? I knew then the anguish Angie must have felt when she realized that she was with child. I wanted to punish myself for allowing it to happen. How could I bring forth a child who would be part vampire and part human? I had to fix it somehow. I had to change things. For good.

But could I?

Will kept sleeping as the devil looked over him with unnatural relish.

"You speak lies," I said, not believing the words myself.

He leveled his eyes at me. "You know that I speak the truth. Your hunger was indomitable this morning. I'm sure that the child enjoyed his meal."

Instinctively, my hands raised to my stomach. I felt a light pressing against my touch.

Imagination. It had to be, I told myself. I tried to make myself believe that he was just playing games, baiting me. And why not? Our days were over, Will's and mine. He had found us. He intended to keep his promise, I was sure of that. I had misled him, and I would be punished for my deception. There was no avoiding it. As for Will, God only knew what he had in store for him.

I would have preferred suffering some indescribable death than to have what happened occur.

"Surprised?" he said breaking the silence that seemed to last for hours. "Don't tell me you didn't know."

Though I wanted to refute him, I couldn't. I knew the moment I awoke that morning that something was very different.

He leaned in to me, keeping a hand over Will's sleeping body as he did it. The stretch was exaggerated, almost cartoonish, reminding me of a Stretch Armstrong doll. For effect, he allowed his skin to crack and bleed, dripping bright drops of crimson on the white sheets Will and I shared. I felt sick.

"Didn't expect to see me, did you? You thought you could find Angie's boy and hide him from me forever. Didn't you?"

I was speechless. There was no point in denying anything. It was over.

"But you never could hide from me, Lucky. You were never quite good enough to shut me out completely. I always knew you." A lecherous smile spread over his face before his lips broke into gaping wounds oozing blood and pus. "I've always been right by your side."

He turned his attention back to Will. His body retracted itself, sizing back to its original form—he wore the skin of an Asian man with a solid jaw and a widow's peak that day. He leaned over Will and looked at him, as though trying to decide where to take his first bite.

"Leave him alone!" I shrieked, taking a step closer to the being that sent fear through my body in torrents.

"Lucky Green, protector of the mortals. Or do you prefer Jackie? Either way, my dear, your loyalty is misplaced."

"What could you possibly want from him?" I asked desperately. "He doesn't even know what he is. He can't do anything for you. But I can. If I am with child, like you say I am, I am worth much more."

"On that point you are correct," he said, turning to face me once more.

"Then take me."

"I already have you," he said in a voice that didn't quite sound human. It reverberated against the walls, echoing, buzzing like a million bees.

"What then?" I couldn't hide the fear in my voice.

"He is a promise that I intend to keep."

Before I could move, before I could take another breath, he was on top of Will. His teeth penetrated the soft of his neck jaggedly and blood spurted toward the ceiling like a fountain. Will's eyes flapped open as blood poured from him, spurting with each beat of his heart. I ran over to him with the intention of beating the Devil off of him, but he disappeared just when I reached Will; the image of his smiling, bloody mouth was reflected in Will's eyes.

I tried to plug the wound with my fingers, but he was bleeding out rapidly. He stared up at me as he died, his face holding a question that I couldn't answer. He died in my arms quietly, his body as relaxed as it was earlier that morning when the hazy sun lit the room.

The Promise Keeper's laughter in my head and the blood on my hands were the only things out of place.

I SEE YOU

I couldn't get rid of it.

Nothing I tried worked.

I fed very little, yet my stomach grew fatter, rounder. My tears dried on my skin only to be covered over by a fresh batch. Will was gone. And I was carrying his child.

A child that was three-quarters immortal.

I delivered faster than I expected, the baby coming at seven months rather than nine. I bore the child in a hotel room in Atlanta, already on the road that would lead to the drop off point. I could no more raise the child than Angie could raise Will.

So I didn't.

Mirroring Angie's footsteps, I left my child, hungry for milk, on the steps of a house in Louisiana. The woman who opened the door was one that I had been watching for days. She was the churchgoing sort who tutored children in her home on weeknights. She was in her late thirties, unmarried, and didn't have children of her own. She opened the door and was surprised to see my son on her steps. She picked him up and, after casting a glance to her left and her right, took him inside.

That was the last time I saw my son... until today.

I was in the park watching kids play Frisbee and old men play chess, but I was especially interested in the woman reading a fashion magazine. She was alone and vulnerable. And I was hungry. I was thinking of the right way to lure her when I smelled the scent that was undeniably my own. I hadn't smelled it since the day I left my child in Louisiana. It caught me off guard and I turned my head from side to side, looking for the only one who could share the same scent. And that was when I saw you looking right back at me.

I was so surprised to see you; you're as handsome as I thought you would be. I stood to talk with you, but you walked away with a hotdog in your hand and a newspaper folded under your arm. I saw you walk into a building, back to an office where work was piled up on your desk. I probed you then, to see how you were. I'm sorry, I know I was intruding, but I needed to know.

I wanted so badly to talk to you, to tell you who I was. Did you see me? I thought you had. I felt your eyes on me. But maybe I was wrong. Maybe I just wanted it to be that way.

Something in your eyes, in the way your face looked, makes me think otherwise, though.

Even though I couldn't talk to you then, I have to make something clear to you now. You are a part of me. That means you will crave the blood. It's inevitable. I can only apologize for it.

Have you felt the urge already? My heart aches at the thought, but I know it will be as much a reality for you as it is for me. Be careful, son. The world is a different place now; it is much harder to be as we are in this day and age than when I was reborn.

I know you're reading this and thinking I'm just some crazy woman with a vivid imagination. I can understand why you would. But it's true. All of it. You have to believe me. Your life depends on it.

Now that I've seen you, I can't stay. I run the risk of revealing your location to him and I won't do that. To see your face has made everything I have been through worth it. Always know that Brian. I love you. But to have shown you would have been to ruin you, and I wanted you to have a chance.

Take what you read here to heart—all of the journals, the side notes, the stories I told, let them seep into you. Don't let one page of this worn out leather book fall out or disappear from your sight. When you're done reading, burn it in the fire until you're sure it's gone. You don't know how to block yourself from him. I'm not even sure that blocking him is possible anymore, if it ever was. He'll see the ink on the pages through your eyes like he was holding the book in his own hands.

There is only one way to escape him, only one way to hide. Because he didn't make you, your soul is untouchable if you die before he reaches you. If he kills you, he owns you. He'll control your soul and he'll use it as he sees fit. But if you die by your own hand, your soul will roam free, unclaimed. It can move from body to body, hiding within them, a silent partner to the original soul inhabiting the host. The young are particularly accepting; their souls are just learning how to live. They won't put up as much of a fight as an adult would. You could run forever that way, as long as you leave the host before The Promise Keeper comes for you. To be murdered would set you free from his servitude forever, but it would have to be random, a mistake. The reality of what must happen in order to escape his grasp is the same no matter what option you exercise. You must die before he claims you. In you he sees world diminiation, a fulfillment of a prophecy made before any of us were born. He needs you to win the war he has waged – you are the seed he has been sowing for an eternity. You are the promise he means to keep.

I can't help you anymore. I've done all I can do. I wonder if doing this much has jeopardized you more than doing nothing would have. I will lay my pen down tonight and never pick it up again. The flames will consume me and everything in my home. It shall certainly be a grand affair, one that will be for me and me alone. Don't come looking for me. There will be nothing left to find. It is what I must do to keep you safe.

I'll take with me the secret of your identity. But he knows you exist, knows you are out there, ripe for the picking. I know now that it was you he was talking about all along, not Angie's son—your father. It was you whom he saw through decades of murk, through the viscous membrane of the womb. I wish I had seen it earlier, for you would never have been conceived.

You haven't had any children, so the obligation ends with you. That makes him more eager to claim you. To die is more merciful than to live as his servant, his walking dead.

Mind me, now. Don't let him find you, Brian. There is no one left to protect you.

EPILOGUE

Brian sighed as he finished the journal. He had intended only to read a couple of pages of the manuscript before going up to bed. His girlfriend was waiting for him, no doubt in one of the kinky outfits he enjoyed. He had one in mind—a crotchless number that pinned her breasts down in the most uncomfortable looking way and drew her waist in with a corset. Yes, that would be a nice sight to see. It didn't really matter what she had on though, as long as she was still flowing heavy. Monica knew Brian's fetish well and made it a point to come over on the first day of her cycle—her heaviest—so he could taste her. He often told her she was the best thing he had ever tasted in his life. Whatever floats your boat, she thought. As long as she got off, she didn't care what he did.

He loved that about her.

Brian's face contorted as he read the last sentence. What had, at first, struck him as fantasy, an elaborate tale spun by an eccentric, some writer's unpublished manuscript, or the rantings of a madwoman (maybe one in the same), now rang with a measure of truth. It wasn't anything he could put his finger on, but something about the diary seemed familiar, like a story he had heard before, like the words to a song echoing in the catacombs of his memory. He could feel her fear and taste her tears. What was worse was that he could almost feel her presence.

The journal, an odd leather-bound book that had seen better days, was delivered to Brian's office and left to sit on his desk for two days while he dug himself out from under end of the semester paperwork. He was intrigued and thumbed it open, automatically feeling transported into some surreal realm. The first couple of sentences were innocent enough; it seemed to be a woman's journal about her life in prison and beyond. *Okay*, he remembered thinking, *why not?* He had been known to read and critique student manuscripts, so why not give this one a go? The fact that there was no name on the piece and no return address added to the strange air surrounding it. He was interested and he needed something good to read over the break anyway.

Some of the things the woman had written about were hitting close to home and that troubled Brian. The account of Harlem in the thirties and forties was one that he had studied extensively during his undergraduate career, the language choice—he had been studying the languages of African people throughout his college career, and had written his thesis on the subject two years before. Fon, though rarely found in written form, had become one of his favorites. Even the idea of vampirism intrigued him. During his travels in Haiti, Brian had stumbled upon the phenomenon that local villagers in Malona attributed to bloodsuckers and their minions. People were attacked in the fields while they worked, bitten with needle-like teeth on their arms and legs, their blood consumed by their attackers. A man, called *loogaroo*, or vampire, by the locals, was found dead. He had been killed, stabbed through the heart with a pointed stake hit with such force that it drove through his body and pierced the ground. Fact or fiction, the people in the village believed that vampires were alive. They had the scars to prove it.

Brian wasn't sure what to make of the journal. He had learned long ago never to dismiss things as nonsense; he knew there were things in the world that couldn't be explained, and others that sounded implausible when described. But real life vampires and devils? Prophecies and fulfillments? It sounded like something out of the movies. And something else, that Brian dared not consider.

The woman's solution for evading The Promise Keeper struck a cord in Brian that made his skin clammy with perspiration. A dream from his past bubbled at the surface of his memory, becoming clearer by the second. The dream, the nightmare, had always seemed more real than it should have, like it was more than a random manifestation of the thoughts floating around in his head. Every time Brian awoke from it, he felt as though he had been shown something he needed to remember. And he did remember, though none of it made sense. Until now.

He was standing on a roadway, yet he couldn't feel the asphalt beneath his feet. The day was sunny and warm, hot even; he could feel the heat of the sun on his skin. Something was different, he knew that even when he was asleep, but the memory coming back to him provided a view from a different vantage point, as though he were standing off to the side, in the grassy patch of land that bordered the road, perhaps, watching the action from afar. A woman stood on the highway, in her last trimester of pregnancy. A car crash stood behind her, what was left of two vehicles twisted in a mangled heap on the roadway. A man stood opposite her, his profile shimmering in the summer heat.

The woman looked frightened. Some part of Brian's mind wondered if she had been a passenger in one of the cars in the accident and if so, how she had managed to get away unscathed. The man's countenance was enough to draw his attention from rational logic to the unbelievable before him. The man stood drenched in shadows that were impossible in the noonday sun. His face was hidden, but Brian could see his head. It was elongated and slender. Where hair would normally crest stood two pointed protrusions, like horns, on either side of his head. His chin was split into two fleshy sides forming points similar to those on his head at their ends. They moved independently of each other, coiling like worms. A gray cloud, like smoke, blurred the man's facial features from view, but Brian could see his eyes through the haze. They were red, the color overtaking all of the white while Brian watched, as though bloodied by broken capillaries.

Brian remembered the woman asking the man who he was. The laugh that emitted from him was rich; a guttural baritone that seemed to rumble the very earth. The man spoke, but Brian couldn't remember what he said. Until the man addressed him.

"Wise choice, Brian, to hide yourself in the woman. Her blood is on your hands," he said. Brian's vantage point did not change—he was still looking at the scene from afar. He had the strange feeling he was being watched, even though neither the man nor the woman faced him. It was when her hand fluttered to her stomach in fear—in protection—that his heart sank. "Did you think you could hide from me forever?"

The man was talking through the woman to Brian, the baby inside her.

EPILOGUE

The ominous eyes glowered at the woman through the haze. She stared back at the creature before her; the mixture of confusion and fear that rose from her sweat was so toxic, its acidity was noticeable in the air. The man's dead-eyed stare made Brian's knees feel weak.

"Who are you?" the woman asked again, her voice barely above a whisper. "Who is Brian?" Brian could see the flicker of hope glinting in her eyes. Maybe it was all a mistake. The man obviously had the wrong person—he kept referring to a person named Brian, and there was no such person around. Her voice was low but steady. She thought she just might get out of the situation she was in. She would wake up and be on the road to her mother-in-law's house, happily riding along without a care in the world as she had minutes before. Her husband wouldn't be lying dead in their SUV and she wouldn't be standing before what had to be the Devil. *God, please let this be a mistake,* Brian could hear her utter within herself, a silent plea from a mother for her child.

The being seemed to readjust then, to look at her more intensely than he had before, as though seeing her for the first time. The force of his stare weakened her knees.

"Ignorance is bliss, child. Rejoice in it now, for it is a luxury you will soon cease to know."

Her breath caught in her throat as he continued, "You are mine, Brian. By right. She can't help you anymore."

The man's inordinately long and skeletal fingers unfolded from his palm and splayed against the air. The woman's screams deafened Brian as the creature's hand ruptured her amniotic sac and tore through the protective spongy tissue, ripping the child within which Brian's soul hid out of her body.

Brian got up from the armchair where he had read the entire diary. He stretched, closing his eyes and leaning into it. The dream disturbed him more than it ever had before. His outstretched arms seemed to cut into thick air, as if they had connected with a pillow. He opened his balled fist and extended his fingers, each of them slicing the air individually, feeling electric. In his other hand he held the journal tightly, afraid to put it down.

His mind tossed and turned with the contents of the diary. He imagined he could hear the voice of the woman who wrote it, the voice of a woman who claimed to be his mother.

Everyone knew that he was adopted, that fact had never been a secret. Someone could be playing a trick on him. Maybe someone who knew of his eccentric side, the side that he never let roam free by the light of day, some of his fetishes too extreme even for him to face in the harsh light. Brian wondered as he stood with his eyes shut listening to the electric hum that sounded beneath the silence. He thought remotely about his little vixen waiting for him on the bed upstairs, of her scrumptious blood waiting to be tasted, but he made no motion to join her.

She must have been tortured, Brian thought, knowing this would be his fate, but being helpless to prevent it. His mind abandoned thoughts of conspiracy almost without him realizing it, opting instead to ponder the idea of the woman and the story being real. It fit after all, didn't it? He, above any one else, knew full well what his fetishes implied. She must have pined for him, Brian went on, allowing his mind to give the woman a voice, to give her body and soul. He imagined that she might have felt the hunger that coursed through his body, never sated, as though it plagued her own. He could almost see her tears of pain streaking her face a bright crimson as she cried for him. Dying wouldn't have been a release, he surmised. It would have only been punishment.

Assuming it was true.

Brian opened his eyes and the sight made his shoulders snap forward, his stretch abandoned. The room was covered in a haze, metallic and surreal, surrounded by impenetrable darkness. He focused at the center, forcing himself to look, to see what was there, knowing inherently that something was.

You are mine, Brian.

Brian didn't know if he heard the words or if they were whispered in his mind. It no longer mattered. He knew that the man in his dream, if he dared to even call it that any longer, was The Promise Keeper talked about in the journal. But how could that be?

EPILOGUE

How could a stranger have written about his life, about a past that he never knew? How had she found him?

Brian was a rational man. He only believed in things he could see, touch, smell, and taste. He enjoyed a good story like anyone else, but he wasn't the kind to come away from it afraid that something was lurking in the shadows. Even as he reaffirmed those thoughts in his head, he found himself casting a cursory glance around the room. Though his mind protested, he knew that what the woman—his mother—spoke was true. Every word of it.

God help him.

Brian let his mind linger over the details of his grandmother, a woman he had never known, cut down in her prime and turned into a creature of the night, a monster to be feared, hated. Yet, she loved him. He thought of his mother, doomed to suffer the same fate. His mind went over the text again and again, unable to grasp the magnitude of what his family had done for him. His mother loved him so much that she sent him away to be raised without a memory of her, without an inkling of his origin. And then she took her life to protect him, just as his grandmother had. Love for the two women washed over him in torrents, threatening to bring him to his knees with its intensity. He felt lightheaded and bewildered by the newfound information, the knowledge of who he truly was. Though his mother never wanted him to know it, he was a half-breed. An impossible product of the living and the dead.

He knew it was all true.

Brian wanted to call out into the darkness, but his throat was dry. He tried to take a step away from the advancing cloud, fearing that he might be sucked into it, obliterated by its cover. He heard a voice whispering to him, beckoning with such urgency as to rattle his eardrums. It was the same voice that had reassured him throughout his life, the one that told him the journal wasn't a hoax, that it was the very bible in which he should believe: the one voice he trusted.

Burn the diary!

Brian looked at the diary in his sweaty hands, his knuckles turned white from the tightness of his grip. He doubted that he could make it to the kitchen to set the book on fire before what hid behind the veil of gray revealed itself. Painful clarity descended upon Brian. He realized then that this was his day of reckoning, the day when the sins of his ancestors would come to roost upon him. The revolver he took out of his desk drawer felt hot in his hand.

Brian pleaded with God that the dream—the fate he had been warned about all his life—would remain a fantasy and not turn into reality as he raised the gun. In that world, he couldn't run. He would be trapped in the confines of a stranger's womb, waiting for the icy hands of the Promise Keeper to wrench him free. In that world, no matter what Brian did, the Promise Keeper would claim him as his own, as a father does his son. Brian's mind raced and his heart thumped in his chest as he made out an outline, a man's silhouette against the silvery backdrop of the haze, the form writhing like maggots upon dead flesh.

Herndon, Virginia
Sterling, Virginia
December 2, 2002 – October 3, 2003

The devil comes in many sizes and colors
a smile
a look
a word
an utterance
Shape shifting through time
Riding on the wind
Harvesting the earth for souls
Reclaiming his kin

The Devil's Due by elle wood

ABOUT THE AUTHOR

L. Marie Wood is an award-winning psychological horror author and screenwriter. She won the Golden Stake Award for her novel *The Promise Keeper* and Best Horror and Best Afrofuturism/Horror/Sci-Fi screenplay awards at several film festivals.

An Active member of the HWA, Wood's short fiction has been published in *Slay: Stories of the Vampire Noire* and the Bram Stoker Finalist anthology, *Sycorax's Daughters*.

Learn more about her at www.lmariewood.com or join the discussion on Twitter at @LMarieWood1 or on Facebook at www.facebook.com/LMarieWood.

Also from
L. Marie Wood and
Cedar Grove Publishing

You thought you were dead. Waking up and looking all around you, you realize all you learned about The Afterlife was a fantasy. You don't know where you are, but you do know it's not a pleasant or suitable place. You need to run. Hard and fast.

Eventually, you meet others doomed to live in this terrifying Realm with you. Here are gathered the newly dead from all over the universe. A formidable race of giant beasts hunts them. The likes of which have never been seen by those in the living world. This place is like nothing you ever learned about in life--*neither Heaven nor Hell, neither Purgatory nor Sheol.*

You encounter clusters of people huddled together for safety. You're a lone wolf--*they don't trust you, nor you them. Perhaps with good reason.*

Patrick is key to the future of The Realm. He must right old wrongs and fight against all the terrors it has in store. He must fight to save his family and, most importantly, all of his descendants. His revelations will impact the living world, as well as what comes next.
Patrick is the future of humanity.
Can he succeed?

ISBN 13: 978-1-941958-95-7/eBook ISBN 978-1-941958-05-6 /
Kindle: 978-1-941958-04-9

ALSO FROM
L. MARIE WOOD AND
CEDAR GROVE PUBLISHING

A 2018 Bram Stoker Award Finalist! Thought-provoking, powerful, and revealing, this anthology is composed of 28 dark stories and 14 poems written by African-American women writers. The tales of what scares, threatens, and shocks them will enlighten and entertain readers. The works delve into demons and shape-shifters from "How to Speak to the Bogeyman" and "Tree of the Forest Seven Bells Turns the World Round Midnight" to far future offerings such as "The Malady of Need". These pieces cover vampires, ghosts, and

mermaids, as well as the unexpected price paid by women struggling for freedom and validation in the past.

Contributors include: Tiffany Austin, Tracey Baptiste, Regina N. Bradley, Patricia E. Canterbury, Crystal Connor, Joy M. Copeland, Amber Doe, Tish Jackson, Valjeanne Jeffers, Tenea D. Johnson, R. J. Joseph, A. D. Koboah Nicole Givens Kurtz, Kai Leakes, A. J. Locke, Carole McDonnell, Dana T. McKnight, LH Moore, L. Penelope, Zin E. Rocklyn, Eden Royce, Kiini Ibura Salaam, Andrea Vocab Sanderson, Nicole D. Sconiers, Cherene Sherrard, RaShell R. Smith-Spears, Sheree Renée Thomas, Lori Titus, Tanesha Nicole Tyler, Deborah Elizabeth Whaley, L. Marie Wood, K. Ceres Wright.

ISBN 13: 978-1-941958-44-5/eBook: ISBN 978-1-941958-45-2/Kindle: ISBN: 978-1-941958-51-3

THE REALM: CACAPHONY

Toddlers and playdates and white picket fences. Afternoons in the park, steak on the grill - all in the perfect neighborhood. Gabby was living a life that many people could only wish for and she was over it. It wasn't that she disliked her world - it wasn't that at all...she loved her family and the life that she and her husband had made.She just wanted more - more action, more stimulation, more excitement. Gabby was bored.

But while she spent her days washing sand out of hair and making PB&J sandwiches, a battle was going on in The Realm, a cosmic tug of war over the most inimitable of prizes: Gabby's very soul

STAY UP TO DATE ON THE LATEST RELEASES
FROM CEDAR GROVE PUBLISHING

JOIN OUR MAILING LIST AT:

CEDARGROVEBOOKS.COM

CPSIA information can be obtained
at www.ICGtesting.com
Printed in the USA
BVHW041917130521
607293BV00020B/345